DEVIL IN THE DETAIL

When the body of a young woman is discovered hanging upside down from a tree, the village reverberates with whispers of tarot, occult practices and pagan rituals. The mystery deepens when the autopsy reveals that the body had already been dead for a year before being put on gruesome display. Amidst ritual slaughter, outbreaks of fire, and a convincing clairvoyant, can Superintendent Mike Yeadings and his Thames Valley team, in the absence of DS Rosemary Zyczynski, lay the mystery, and the dangling victim, to rest?

*Clare Curzon titles available from
Severn House Large Print*

Flawed Light

DEVIL IN THE DETAIL

A Superintendent Mike Yeadings Mystery

Clare Curzon

Severn House Large Print
London & New York

This first large print edition published 2011
in Great Britain and the USA by
SEVERN HOUSE PUBLISHERS LTD of
9-15 High Street, Sutton, Surrey, SM1 1DF.
First world regular print edition published 2010 by
Severn House Publishers Ltd., London and New York.

British Library Cataloguing in Publication Data

Curzon, Clare.
    Devil in the detail.
    1. Yeadings, Mike (Fictitious character)--Fiction.
    2. Police--England--Thames Valley--Fiction. 3. Murder--
    Investigation--Fiction. 4. Detective and mystery stories.
    5. Large type books.
    I. Title
    823.9'14-dc22

    ISBN-13: 978-0-7278-7929-5

Severn House Publishers support The Forest Stewardship Council
[FSC], the leading international forest certification organisation. All
our titles that are printed on Greenpeace-approved FSC-certified paper
carry the FSC logo.

Printed and bound in Great Britain by the
MPG Books Group, Bodmin, Cornwall.

One

Angus Mott slid his key out of the lock and pushed the door open. 'Paula?'

No reply. No domestic noises. No baking smells. She was out.

As he went upstairs, there was still silence except for the soft scuff of his shoes on the new carpet. She'd been right about the plum colour, although he'd had his doubts until it was actually laid.

In the study he picked the required memory stick off the desk. Funny, he thought he'd left everything running when summoned by DI Salmon's urgent phone call. He must have shut down from habit, going straight out for an early check on the new crime scene; and he was glad he had because this promised to be the weirdest one ever.

It would mean overnight at the nick, so he scribbled a note for Paula; decided on a quick shower and shave while the SOCO team completed their preliminaries.

The bathroom door opened on to a fog of

5

scented steam. He saw the girl, her eyes closed, her torso half-covered in bubbles, before she was aware of him. A headset was clamped over a side-slipping topknot of dark brown hair as she shrugged and pouted to music from an iPod dangling outside the bath.

Angus reached down and removed the connection. There was a startled gasp, a squeal, a mighty splash as she attempted to rise and then fell back in the water.

'Who the devil are you?' he ground out. 'Get yourself dressed and see me outside.'

By then he'd guessed who she'd be. Paula had been interviewing women for help in the house. He'd run into one of the applicants, a formidably tight-lipped matron, when he'd arrived home three or four days back. This apparently successful one was a quite different matter.

She emerged wrapped in a pink bath sheet of Paula's, with her hair falling over her shoulders, one thick tress obscuring her left eye and half her face.

Peekaboo had never worked with Angus, and especially now when he felt under unwelcome pressure to make some kind of apology for his own intrusion. Instead, he snapped into the mode of deserved outrage. 'Where are your clothes?'

'In one of the rooms. She told me to make myself at home. How was I to know you would walk in on me?'

Perhaps she had a point there. 'You can go and put them on. I'll wait.' He turned his back, clamped his hands on the gallery rail and stared down into the hall. The cloakroom door was ajar and he made out the shape of the bulky maroon-coloured pram inside. As Paula was out, she must have taken the baby along in her car, abandoning their customary push in the park.

The girl appeared to have disappeared into the main bedroom. Further enraged, he followed in time to see her throw the covers roughly back over the nest she'd made in his and Paula's bed. Shoes, underclothes, jeans and a striped sweater lay on the floor nearby.

It hadn't been a bad day until then, but now it became insufferable. Accustomed to confronting violent criminals and cons of every degree and persuasion, he could not trust himself to deal with this presumptuous young woman. He must leave that to Paula, since she'd had the folly to employ her.

'Look,' he said grimly. 'I've no time to waste now. Explain to my wife what happened when she gets back.' He started for the stairs, turned back on one heel. 'What's your name?'

'Giselle,' she said, smiling beguilingly.

'For God's sake, Giselle *what*?'

'Gardner.'

He was none the wiser. Presumably Paula would only be away for a short while. Could he trust the girl to be left alone here in the

7

meantime?

'Did my wife lend you a key?'

'Yes.' The girl picked up a blue plastic purse from the pile of clothes, letting the towelling slip to her hips as she bent to retrieve it. 'Here.'

He took the back door key from her hand and pretended blindness to the rest of her. 'You won't need this again.'

As he went downstairs he could feel her eyes still on him. Something warned him she was smiling.

'It's all right,' she called down, as if to put everything right. 'Paula told me you were a copper and could be a bit stiff.'

Head tilted, she watched as he slammed the front door after himself. He's really quite dishy, she thought, and younger than expected. He wasn't likely to make a fuss once he'd had time to cool down.

She liked a man with a bit of a temper. And then it struck her: how heated would he get if he knew his wife was out to lunch with a boyfriend? She had taken the phone call for Paula who was busy with the baby, and the man had given her his name: Oliver Goodman. Then, when Paula spoke with him she'd been over the moon at the invitation; couldn't get tarted up and out of the house fast enough.

A promising situation. If she played it right, offering to stay stumm about that little connection could bring all sorts of benefits from the lady-wife.

By the time Angus returned to the crime scene the duty police surgeon, a desiccated woman with bottle-blonde hair, had been replaced by Professor Littlejohn. 'This has a whiff of the unusual,' he greeted Angus. 'Thought I'd get in at the start.'

Before anyone less competent made a pig's ear of the preliminaries, Angus registered the professor's ulterior message. DI Salmon appeared to have everything in hand, a generous area secured with bollards and tape, a clear path indicated for entrance, all present clothed in white coveralls and overshoes, except for the DI, who was standing offside, and himself as investigating officer.

'Who's been informed?' he asked Salmon.

'The Super, both sergeants. But DS Beaumont's due two further days' leave. Zyczynski's on her way back from Sulhamstead as we speak.'

'Good.' It had fallen to Z to fill a lecturer's slot at the Thames Valley Police College – a two-day assignment Salmon had been hoping to fill and was far from pleased to have been passed over. Not that being pleased ever featured high on the man's agenda. Angus had vetoed him for the job from the first. Salmon's sour attitude to the lower ranks was a distinct turn-off, whereas Rosemary Zyczynski would have had the trainee constables eager for more. When she walked into the room they'd stand bolt upright, pulling their bellies in.

Steve Faraday, civilian Scenes of Crime Officer, who was standing under the oak tree, waved a clipboard and started towards the two CID men.

'What progress?' Angus asked.

'The rope's not uncommon, nor the knot – a regular running noose. We're hoping for some useful traces from the tree bark. The most interesting thing is the regular circle of scorch marks, seven in all, in the surrounding grass. There are indications that something like spiked candleholders were driven into the ground and later removed. We've taken samples of guttered droppings. They're beeswax, with a curious, pungent smell. Not the sort that you'd buy for scenting the house. Nor quite the religious sort either. More exotic.'

'So was this was some perverted sort of ritual?'

'Yeah, it could be. Otherwise why hang the body the way it was – upside down, by one leg? As you can see, it's a young female. The Prof gives an age between twenty-five and thirty-five.'

'Tarot,' Angus muttered under his breath. But on the fortune-telling card the reversed, hanged figure was definitely male. And *seven* candles? Wasn't seven commonly associated with good luck? In witchcraft he would have expected five: some connection with pentacles and all that mumbo-jumbo. So were these weirdo

10

trimmings set up by someone with only vague notions of occult rites and intended to confuse the investigation of a straightforward murder? Instead of the usual efforts to conceal the body, this was pure flaunting of the act. A killer with in-yer-face instincts, the presentation taking some time and effort, perhaps requiring more than a lone perpetrator.

A closed van lurched over the grass in their direction, stopped and waited for Littlejohn to walk close, pass under the tape and give instructions about the handling of the body. He wasn't taking any chances, asking for the hands, head and feet to be separately bagged.

Angus left them to it. He would see the victim's features at close range soon enough at the post-mortem. 'When...?' he started to ask the pathologist.

'You're not expecting precise time-of-death right now?' Littlejohn complained.

'When ... will you be examining her?' Angus completed.

'Ah. That's different. Tomorrow morning, certainly. Earliest I can make is ten thirty. If I know your boss, he'll want to be in on this as well. Have you informed him?'

'He's at Kidlington on another case. I left a message at home for him. Nan will pass it on.'

'Be sure he gets it. Tell him I'll expect a slap-up dinner after this one's cleared up.'

When we've completed all the donkey work, bagged the villain, and with hindsight every-

11

thing looks to have been so simple, Angus considered. But when would that be, with three current cases barely tackled and another needing extra paperwork to get it past CPS and into court? It was a helluva time to have Beaumont off on leave.

And what's hanging Z up? he asked himself. She should have been here half an hour back.

Detective Sergeant Rosemary Zyczynski, delayed in a single-lane traffic tailback on the M4, sighed when the uniform constable rapped on her passenger window. She rolled it down. 'Officer?'

'Thought it was you, miss. Seen you in court. Like me to get you through sharpish?'

'That'd please my boss. Thanks.' He was a young over-hopeful, she thought, as he waved her up on the sloping bank above the hard shoulder choked with emergency vehicles. As she moved off, the following car closed up behind. Ahead, a muddied roadworks lorry drew out loaded with cones and gear for emergency traffic lights. Impasse for the moment.

She changed into reverse and held down the clutch, waiting for the driver behind to draw back. He'd made a wider sweep off the road and appeared tilted at a risky angle above her. Now he seemed to be struggling with his gearbox. Without warning the old banger surged forward, sliding down. Z felt a shuddering crunch and was showered with shattered glass

12

from the rear windows. Then the car over-turned on a broadside roll until lodging with orchestrated metallic shrieks that meant *expense! expense! expense!* against the driving cab of the roadworks lorry. Hanging from her seat belt, one shoulder crushed against the door and her legs caught under the steering column, Z tried to wipe sweat from her forehead. Her hand came away crimson. She blinked through a trickle of blood and saw the hapless constable's left leg hanging over her shattered windscreen. It was twitching alarmingly. 'Ring Ang—' she told herself foggily, but was unconscious before she could complete his name.

DI Salmon was livid. He'd too much on his plate already, and this unpalatable business with the hanging woman in Bells Wood promised to add extra complications. He'd a Home Office pathologist to deal with on this new case and he'd had contact enough with Professor Littlejohn to know that it wouldn't be an easy ride. The man was a stickler for detail and, being a prompt provider of information himself, would expect instant interaction and voluminous progress-reporting in return. Normally the extra paperwork could be passed on to one of the sergeants, but Beaumont was on leave and the other – a woman (which was further cause for complaint) – was skiving off after her ego trip down at the police college. He would like to blame DCI Angus Mott for that bit of favouritism, but he had to admit it had been his boss, Superintendent Yeadings himself, who had selected her. You would think that with his experience he'd have preferred to put forward someone capable of keeping a class of flighty young trainees in order while under instruction.

Yeadings could be a severe disciplinarian himself when occasion demanded, but was regrettably paternal with his nuclear Serious Crimes Team. Having pushed young Mott's promotion into the rank Salmon had provisionally held during the younger man's Bosnian adventure, the Boss had since overlooked several of the DCI's unorthodox moves, allowing in excuse that experiences gained during his interventional service in Kosovo had 'widened his horizons in a useful way'.

This Salmon found unacceptable, as being a failure of continuity in duty, and he smarted at no longer having the rank to override Mott's eccentricities.

He looked across to where the DCI was talking with Littlejohn. Something the grizzled old pathologist had said must have been humorous. Angus was grinning like an ape, then abruptly turned away to reach for his mobile phone.

Salmon watched his expression change to one of concern. More bad news. Not a second body so soon after this one, surely? Ever the pessimist, he started to walk across, expecting to learn the worst.

He heard the message with mixed reactions. It concerned the woman sergeant. The stupid girl had got herself injured in an RTC.

Road Traffic Collisions were no concern of Mike Yeadings, but he had been informed immediately the identification was made.

The M4 motorway, already clogged by restricted lanes under repair, was now further embarrassed by the attempted arrival of two emergency ambulances.

Unconscious, Z was transported by trolley to where space was found to turn one vehicle. Bleeding freely from temple and neck, she left a crimson trail on the senior paramedic's tunic which he attempted to replace before further dealing with his patient.

DI Zyczynski's eyes fluttered open on the image of a large, muscular black man stripped to minimal psychedelic shorts.

'Mm,' he growled in a melodious bass-baritone, 'I guessed that would bring you round. No, don't try sitting up. You gotta have some patching done first.'

'The traffic officer...?' she demanded.

'Being treated on the spot.'

Which meant it was touch-and-go, she thought, remembering the fresh-faced kid who'd offered to find her a way past the traffic snarl. Not a good move by either of them. If he pulled through he'd likely be up on a disciplinary charge. Maybe herself too. Lack of judgement all round.

She watched her rescuer button his fresh tunic. Her head was pounding and the ambulance sides seemed to waver like a canvas beach screen in a force-five wind. She closed her eyes. There was a lumpy gauze pad between her cheek and the low pillow, but it was too much trouble to try pulling it away.

'Stay with me, lady.' The bass-baritone came at her from a long distance. A polystyrene beaker was pressed against her lips and she struggled to swallow. It was something bitter and fizzy, vaguely familiar. She wondered, floating off into fog, whether he was a prize-fighter or a singer like that famous Paul Robeson she'd heard records of as a child.

And then she was a child again, way back before anything bad had happened: at home, toasting crumpets on the long brass fork, at an open log fire. The flames made her cheeks burn, and in the next room her mother was softly singing as she set the supper table. So Mum hadn't been killed after all. What she'd been told was all a mistake, that car crash. They were waiting now for Dad to get back from work.

'Don't be so bloody pessimistic,' Mott snarled at the long-faced Salmon.

'She's resilient,' Yeadings insisted, 'with youth on her side. Has anyone informed Max?

16

No? Well, I'll go see him.'

Salmon stared after him as he stomped out. The incident couldn't have happened at a worse time, and now Superintendent Yeadings had removed himself from the plan of action, leaving only himself and young Mott to finalize three old cases and take on this unholy business with the hanged woman. You couldn't count young DC Silver. He was good only for the computer stuff.

Someone else must be found to supplement the core team, as well as the usual round-up of uniform men for the initial scene searching. He considered the local CID on offer and scornfully decided there was no single man up to the standard he expected.

Two

Mike Yeadings had a higher opinion of the local talent. Two uniform constables he'd had an eye on for some time, Payne and Enderby, were dispatched home to return in plain clothes as Acting DCs. He was still a DS short with the loss of Rosemary Zyczynski. Priority was granted to the early days of a murder investigation, guaranteeing him at least forty, up to a possible seventy, lower and medium ranks for fingertip searching in the vicinity of the crime scene, house-to-house inquiries and sifting of rubbish disposal as the relevant scene would be rapidly extended to populated areas. A small lake toward the edge of the woodland beyond the isolated oak tree would require a team of divers, and a pair of dog handlers were already there, vital before the corporate scent of policeman could override all else.

Bells Wood itself, covering roughly ten acres, was part of a large estate called Barrows owned by Gervais Plummer, non-executive director of an electronics company founded by his grandfather. He commuted to London on most weekdays and played the country squire in his free time. In season, shooting parties coincided with eclectic gatherings for corporate hospitality and the equine-dominated acquaintances of Fiona, his wife.

Police records, from seven years back, detailed an emergency call-out for a house fire there when an inebriated guest, one of many, had been arrested for suspected arson and the charges withdrawn by his host on the following day. The affected wing of the house had subsequently been pulled down and replaced by an orangery at present used as a music room for occasional concerts or amateur dramatics. Since that time no untoward incidents had been whispered abroad or splashed on the *Buckinghamshire Recorder*'s front page. Yeadings had recently heard on the Thames Valley grapevine that the chief constable had attended, and mildly enjoyed, a performance of *The Pirates of Penzance* there. This circumstance emphasized, if need be, that a certain delicacy must be used in the police approach to the Plummers. Not Salmon in that case; nobody lower than Angus. And this was a bad time to have Rosemary Zyczynski missing from the team.

The superintendent's immediate concern was to notify her lover, Max Harris, that she was injured. He was out when he visited and for some time unreachable by mobile phone. The columnist answered on the fourth attempt and Yeadings recognized the susurration of a printer working in the background. Good; he was

19

back home. Max wasn't often so hard to catch up with.

'Mike Yeadings here, Max.'

'What's wrong? Is it Rosebud?' A steely, snapping tone to cover his alarm.

'RTC on the M4, I'm afraid. They've taken her to Reading A & E. I'm on my way now.'

'I'll see you there.' Max hesitated. 'Her condition?'

'Not known at present.'

'Well, thanks, Mike.' He rang off.

'Stabilizing down here, while a suitable bed's found for her,' the nurse at Emergency said crisply.

Yeadings wandered off to find someone less likely to hold him at bay. He ran Dr Wells, consultant haematologist, to earth in the restaurant.

'I'll get a report,' he offered, phoned through and came back with the news that Z was already on her way to X-ray. Waiting in the corridor outside, Yeadings was joined by Max.

When she was wheeled out it became clear it was going to be a long wait. The detective's face was partly covered by gauze padding. She was unconscious and surrounded by nurses with emergency equipment and an IV stand holding saline and blood bags.

'I'll stay on,' Max insisted, 'and ring when she's come round. I guess you've come straight off a case.'

There was little point in staying. 'I'll get back

then. Tell her we're all with her, and to take her time.'

'I'll walk you to the door. They'll be a while settling her in. You're sure this was a genuine accident? There's no danger for her here?'

'I'd put a guard on if I thought so. From present accounts she was trying to get through a snarl-up and was hit from behind; the car rolled and she knocked herself out on the door. We're holding the trucker involved for questioning. He was barely scratched. No alcohol level.' He squeezed the other man's proffered hand. 'She's a tough little cookie, Max. And they're good at the job here. I'll keep in touch.'

DCI Angus Mott stayed on at Bells Wood for a further half hour, overseeing the cutting down of the body, its bagging and removal. Professor Littlejohn, the Home Office pathologist, had arranged tomorrow's post-mortem at High Wycombe Mortuary. Salmon and the first-on-scene uniforms would attend it while he allocated staff and an office manager from the augmented team.

When Yeadings returned to report on Zyczynski he sent Angus home with a résumé on the additional team members. 'I'll have a word with them tonight. There's little more can be covered at the crime scene before daylight. I want you out there early. Salmon, as first CID on scene, will attend the post-mortem; and I'll look in on it myself after the briefing.'

21

In his element, Angus thought. Nothing the Boss liked more than quitting his desk for a part of the action, even overshadowed by his evident concern over DS Zyczynski. Now he'd brought forward the initial briefing and staked out a full-time role for himself. Angus grinned and accepted dismissal home.

Paula had read his note and so didn't expect him back, but she heated up soup and leftover shepherd's pie.

'Joining me?' he enquired, pouring wine for them both.

'No. I lunched out. Rather well, I'm afraid.'

He cocked an eyebrow, but she wasn't intending to expand on that, appearing to have something on her mind. She had curled up in her chair and was staring into the embers of the pretend log fire. Well, he had enough to occupy him, with this weird new case. The press were going to slaver over the Tarot implication. The Boss would be working on it himself tonight, preparing a PR statement.

It was while he was brushing his teeth in the bathroom later that he remembered the girl he'd walked in on at midday. Paula hadn't brought up the subject herself and when he slid into bed after peeking at the as-yet-unnamed baby, his wife had turned on her left shoulder and appeared to be asleep.

The girl was altogether too pert; she'd have to be replaced by someone older, reliable and discreet. Before they'd discussed having help in the new house there'd been no need to take special precautions, although everything on their computers was automatically secured under passwords. With police work you could not risk a motormouth picking up restricted information. He'd have to stress this to Paula in the morning.

Idly Angus wondered who she'd had lunch with. In the maternity ward, she'd met several new mothers who might in time become friends. He was glad she'd have backup in this new phase of her life. It had probably been one of those collective baby-worshipping sessions at one of their houses.

He closed his eyes and instantly was haunted by the image of the murder scene: the wood, the oak tree in the clearing and the macabre, sheet-draped figure hanging from a branch. Whatever bizarre behaviour lay behind the display, the perpetrator had certainly intended to cause a sensation. Mott hoped the theme wouldn't keep recurring in his dreams. He didn't need an overworking subconscious, with a heavy day promised ahead.

DI Salmon had taken grim pleasure in informing DS Beaumont by mobile that his remaining days of leave were instantly cancelled, while suppressing details of the emergency.

'Suits me,' the detective sergeant answered laconically. 'I'd only one whole day left, and anyway the fish aren't rising.'

'You should know too that DS Zyczynski is off this case. You're needed to help organize the augmented team,' Salmon snarled. 'Briefing from DCI Mott and myself at eight thirty a.m. tomorrow. Be early.'

So they had a new body. And what indiscretion had our Rosemary committed? Beaumont asked himself. The news was welcome. In her absence he could hopefully produce a master stroke of detection that would put him a pace ahead of her in the long and agonizing trek to promotion.

There was a text message unopened on his phone, which he'd deliberately ignored, but now might prove important. He read it to find that Mott had ordered him to an apparent murder scene over at a private estate called Barrows, near Beacons on the Bucks/Oxon border. He should familiarize himself with it before attending tomorrow's briefing.

Now why couldn't Salmon have passed on that info? The miserable old fish, treating his sergeants as if they worked for the opposition. Heigh-ho, it meant an early rise to get over there at first light.

He remembered seeing SOCO's photos of an arson case there several years back. He'd been a DC then, not yet a member of Yeadings' select team. Barrows was a plush country estate with several hundred acres owned by one of those city moneymakers playing at country squire. Too many of the stately homes round here were getting snapped up by chancers and politicians, to run as tax losses balancing their questionable gains.

Sometimes he thought he was in the wrong job, until the next time he enjoyed the blood-pumping relish of putting the villains away. Had he been better at maths he could have aimed for the Serious Fraud Office. He'd admit the hunt for white-collar criminals was the up and coming thing, even while he mocked SFO as the Seriously Flawed Outfit.

He parked his car on the road, his driveway being blocked by the refrigerated van of his wife's catering partner. He deposited his fishing tackle in the cluttered garage, and followed a spicy aroma indoors. In the built-on, space-age kitchen the two women were bent over a collection of saucepans on the hob. 'No uglies to sample,' warned his wife severely. 'We're into sauces today, not baking.'

'No nosh going, then?'

'Salad in the fridge.'

He moved towards it.

'Not that one. The one in the utility.'

All these rules and regulations, he fumed silently. An Englishman's home was once his castle. Now Health and Safety had usurped his domain, dividing family areas from those intended for Higher Things.

He wasn't sure he was in a salad mood anyway. If there were eggs, bacon and beans he'd do a fry up and to hell with the cholesterol input.

In due time he snapped off the TV late-night news, grumbled at Stuart's homework books scattered all over the dining room, and belched his way up to bed. There he closed the curtains on a misted night and set the alarm for five fifteen. Tomorrow there'd be another viewing of man's inhumanity to man: anything from a boring old blunt instrument job to the increasing excitement of a labyrinthine puzzle. He hoped this time it would prove a brain-teaser.

The morning was a brisk reminder that the best of the year was almost past. The air had an autumn bite to it, not far off true frost. And whoever the source of man's inhumanity, as Beaumont learned from the constable on guard at the site, the victim was not man, but woman. A description of the scene, received second-hand from an eyewitness colleague, suggested that his wish for a real challenge was likely to be granted.

'Yuh, a right weird one, this. Can't say I enjoyed night duty, expecting all sorts of ghoulies and ghosties to come out of the wood.' The PC gave a dramatic shiver.

Beaumont walked the perimeter of the crime tape before ducking under and approaching the tree. It was a deciduous oak, old and gnarled, standing in isolation. There were a good hundred yards of space all round it before the mixed woodland began, sloping towards a little lake. At some time, he guessed, a deliberate clearance had been made. The surrounding grass, fairly short and free of weeds, had probably been kept close-mown during the summer. Considering the prolonged drought through August, it looked surprisingly fresh. Was there a sprinkler system out here so far from the house and outbuildings? If so, for what purpose? Picnics *al fresco*? Genteel ladies' tea parties? Even croquet? Surely the location made those uses unlikely. There weren't flocks of servants these days to cart out all the paraphernalia required. Nowadays it was usual for outside entertaining to take place round the swimming pool. To reach the wood he had driven past one with a Japanese tea-house affair, a five-metre diving facility and a paddling pool for the kiddies at one corner.

So why the clearing round the oak tree? He'd put money on something a bit naughty going on here from time to time. It would be worth getting friendly with staff up at the house, find someone with a taste for gossip.

Plenty of evidence indicated recent police and forensic presence. Grass round the tree was flattened where the body would have been cut down and bagged before being trolleyed away to the lane winding through the woodland. Marks remained where an upright ladder had disturbed the earth and later been dragged some distance away. That would be SOCO's

27

doing, when they'd taken the body down.

Voices cut through his observations. A relief had turned up for guard duty. Beaumont strolled across and nodded to the new man. Not so new, he learned: Constable 3159 Graham had been here when SOCO were operating. From him Beaumont extracted the way they had covered the job, photographing in close-up and distance, putting tree bark under magnification, dusting for fingerprints, setting out numbered markers where they had come across objects that might later prove significant. Apart from the burnt patches of grass there were only five of these. It wasn't a place for discarded litter.

The beeper on his phone warned him to get moving if he wanted to be on time for the briefing at Area. He nodded thanks to the man left on duty and made for his car.

When DCI Angus Mott entered the crowded hall he noted the Boss already seated at the back by a window; Beaumont had yet to turn up.

'Let's get straight into it,' he ordered.

Crisply he gave details of the crime scene, aware that most present would have accessed leaked information. 'You'll have gathered this is not a run-of-the-mill crime, and what we bring to the investigation will need to be of the highest order. It demands total commitment by everyone involved.

'An incident room has already been set up in this building, with an analysis room adjoining. Relevant photographs are already being posted there, also colour-coded evidence sheets as they come through. Sergeant Harry Deakin is Office Manager and all information gathered should go directly to him. A mobile office van will be parked at Barrows for interviewing witnesses. New members of the team should seek advice where necessary from DS Beaumont, who has just entered, or DC Silver to my left. We are badly hampered by the absence of DS Zyczynski who is recovering in hospital after an RTC. As substitute feminine light to shine on the findings, CID will be joined by Constable Holly Hughes as acting DC. Any questions?'

There were several, ranging from pretentious to frankly idiotic. Mott dismissed them with a few words, finally handing over to a uniform inspector as Allocator.

He waved Beaumont outside with him and beckoned to a young woman in plain clothes. 'Beaumont, Hughes. Hughes, Beaumont,' he introduced them. 'Holly, I want you to stick close on this. You can pick up a lot of valuable tips.'

Then, aside to Beaumont: 'Keep her away from Salmon, for God's sake.'

Beaumont went po-faced as the DCI walked away. He turned to the still overawed youngster. 'Looks like we've no choice in the matter.

Come along then, Limpet. Let's see if we can get in on the post-mortem. I haven't seen the body yet, so we might as well get acquainted.'

Yeadings, watching from his corner, contrived to overtake the couple in the corridor. He nodded to his DS. 'I take it you're going my way, so you might as well drive us.'

He nodded to Holly. 'My name's Yeadings. Welcome to the team.'

'Yes sir, I know, sir. Superintendent, I mean.' She wasn't sure she was going to be comfortable with this secondment. A post-mortem was deep enough water to be plunged into, and she hadn't counted on meeting the Big Man face to face.

Three

DC Silver required no directing. His computer in the CID office was his personal action station, and already his head was buzzing with subjects to search. First in line was the Barrows estate. He logged on to area contour maps and scrolled through. Something familiar came up.

He recognized it at once, a large country house set in mixed woodland, pasture and open heath. This was one of the supposed millionaires' mansions he'd observed recently from the hot-air balloon. Then, altitude had disguised the lie of the land, but here everything was clearly marked. The contour lines indicated that house and outbuildings were sited on the slightly lower of two pronounced crests, with woodland between which sloped to a small lake. The other, consisting of bare heathland, was marked as an ancient monument, maybe connected with the area's name, Beacons, being the high point from which great bonfires were lit in ancient time to warn of dangers like plague or threatened invasion.

It had been used that way more recently if he

31

rightly interpreted the clump of ugly buildings as a relic from the Cold War period. New RAF warning stations had been established inland after the Wall went up in Berlin and atom-bomb threat was perceived to come from a new direction. Some of these bunkers, later converted to emergency Regional Seats of Government, had been kept on and were fully maintained. Others still held the tall aerials and radar installations of the period. Please God they'd never need be used for their original purpose, he thought.

As they dropped height, the grey concrete buildings of the bunker had become clearer, and the protective fencing was the sort he'd seen on film surrounding camps for prisoners of war.

A double-gated entry between tall stone pillars gave on to a concreted road which led to the squat buildings, past a global listening-post which, from the air, appeared grubby grey and unused. The entire site was isolated, but seemed to contain a solid-looking bungalow and a Portakabin with a little plot of what looked like vegetables to the rear. So, despite the appearance of neglect, the establishment still merited a modest guardhouse.

Nostalgia threatened to crowd out the present. How could he forget that idyllic day — floating on cloud nine on his first date with the wonderful Jo? He had picked her up from her shared London flat and they'd driven back west. The Pimlico streets were not yet fully awake. With the roof down and low sun warming their shoulders, the breeze teased at her chestnut curls. A fine September morning followed by late drizzle had been forecast after almost a week of porridge skies constantly darkening to threaten rain but never quite delivering. The CID office he shared with the two detective sergeants faced north and he'd been working for days in artificial light.

It should have felt like a glorious release but, venturing in unfamiliar country, he'd suffered first-date qualms. He was conscious that, when swashbuckling genes were allocated, the Silver family had lost out. His mild-mannered parents having married late, he was a last-minute child brought up with old-fashioned values. He had applied to Thames Valley Police as soon as his height was acceptable, with a vague preference for aligning himself with the angels rather than the rogues. He then found his IT skills had real value, honed as he preferred computers to roistering with his more sparky college mates. He saw himself as a dull guy, but his new fellow squaddies found the geek amiable enough and, although no great drinker, he would sometimes be persuaded to go along on a 'jolly'.

So it was by chance, rather than choice, that he'd found himself at a village disco, dancing with a shy-seeming girl with chestnut curls, large brown eyes and an occasional slight stutter.

Her name was Jo and she drank mineral water with a touch of lime. It was also pure chance that she'd found herself there. Living and working in London, she was staying overnight with a great aunt recovering from a hip replacement. Aunty had insisted that she get out of the house that evening and find some entertainment.

The final coup of the triple chance was when the charity raffle ticket Jimmy bought her won second prize. It proved to be two tickets for a Champagne celebration flight by hot-air balloon at a date and time of their choosing. There was no question: they had to use it, and together.

That day had changed his life. He could still barely believe the series of lucky breaks that had brought them together that morning, driving west into Thames Valley, shoulder to shoulder in his beloved vintage MG. And she wasn't just sweetly pretty. She was responding to his efforts to amuse her: laughed at what he found funny; didn't giggle, or flap, or go embarrassingly sexy; stayed quiet when there was nothing to say.

Every detail of every minute was imprinted on his mind. Jo had been the first to see the orange windsock blowing in the Buckinghamshire field, and had squeezed his arm in excitement. He'd followed the sandwich-board sign, bumping across stubble to the temporary car park adjacent to the Iron Duke pub. They were early.

'Coffee?' he suggested. They went in and he ordered at the bar.

The pub's interior was dim and almost empty. Two early drinkers, both youngish men, left the rail as a third filled the low doorway, a big guy with a big grin and a vividly scarred left cheek. The trio grunted in recognition and joined up, huddling over a table beyond an archway draped with dried-out hop vines. Their low voices rose occasionally in moments of enthusiasm and were followed by a deal of belly laughter. They reminded him of the little groups that collected in the police canteen, with few concerns in the world, Jimmy guessed, beyond planning their next laddish foray.

'See they're going up again s'morning,' the landlord interrupted as he delivered cappuccinos to their table. 'It's been a day or two.'

Jimmy nodded agreement, refusing to be drawn. The man got the message and moved off to check his barrels.

Outside again, there was magic about the morning, making the early autumn colours sing. A green and white striped marquee now overtopped hedgerows blood-spotted with hawthorn berries. There was a warm scent of ripening blackberries. Ahead, among moving figures in blue overalls, he made out a slim female in a sandy-coloured flying suit. Strands of her long blonde hair escaped on either side of a close-fitting leather helmet.

She was hunkered with her back turned, hands dragging on the length of jazzy fabric that stretched for some fifty yards from where the blowers were being set up. Men in blue overalls were unloading three other balloon carcases in parallel from trucks across the field. Jimmy, keen to get cracking, dropped off his jacket and went to lend a hand, climbing on to the nearest pick-up to get a grip on the basket's steel superstructure.

'Thanks, mate,' said a second balloonist as he joined him. Together they swung the heavy square basket over, and the man below eased it to the ground. A little way off, the small sandy-coloured figure stood astride with hands on hips, watching.

More cars drawing into the parking space disgorged passengers. The woman balloonist went into hospitality mode, ushering them into the marquee to check tickets and fill in consent forms. Jimmy and Jo followed.

Four balloons were to launch from the village that morning. Across the field giant blowers had begun inflating the jazzy carcases. Intending passengers crowded around, chatting in loud party voices.

Jo grinned at him. 'Natural ground-huggers who've talked themselves into being heroes,' she whispered.

'You're not nervous?'

'Slightly. More excited, though.'

Good, because that was how he felt.

As it inflated, the nearest carcase stirred on the ground like some immense wild beast recovering from sedation, and finally rose erect, dragging the basket upright.

With check list completed, passengers scrambled to mount via square footholds in the wicker walls, heaving themselves in. Each of the four compartments was to hold a couple, with the central, larger space, for the pilot and equipment. Jimmy checked with the windsock and led Jo to what would be a forward section. She went up lithely, making room for him alongside. There was a deal of good-natured joshing as the other passengers settled, surprised there were no seats but only threaded rope to hold for steadying themselves.

As the jets fired, the whole contrivance stirred restively. Guy ropes were released. Spectators below waved furiously and the basket eased off the ground, swayed, and started on its gently slanting journey. Jimmy stared up through the roaring blaze at the inflated fabric, its garish colours pale now against the vivid flames.

They were airborne; he had never felt so happy. Beside him, Jo moved closer, lifting her smiling face to the sun. Far below, the field's stubble streamed underneath, striped as though coarsely combed. The temperature noticeably began to fall. He wished he'd brought his car coat to put round Jo's shoulders. He found she didn't object when he used an arm instead, moving close.

Nothing below was real because it was so reduced in size: the fine ribbons of roads and waterways, insect-like traffic, peoples' lives being lived in miniature. The three other balloons began to rise from the now distant field with the windsock, and followed behind them.

'You've a great morning for it,' the woman pilot announced in a pause between the burners' roars. 'There are sixteen balloons going up today from four separate points. Quite a rally.'

Jimmy found himself reversing familiar map-reading habits of relating flat print to three-dimensional forms. The land below had clearly suffered from the prolonged summer drought. He started picking out half-familiar landmarks in terrain diminished by distance and perspective. He had passed over the rivers Chess and Misbourne, recognized the Regent's Canal crossing a wooded valley before opening to a chalky plain with its chequer-board pattern of blonde-streaked stubble and lopsided squares of dark green vegetation. Then they were floating over open country with irregular crowns scarred greyish white, either balding with outbreaks of limestone rock or speckled with straying sheep.

They had stared down in delight as their huge shadow, shaped like an inverted pear, preceded them north-westward over the deceptively flattened world below. He remembered startling silence as the loud bursts of the burners cut off and their pilot controlled alternating rises and floating. And then he would become aware of distant lowing from a toy farm, the faint sound of recorded music floating up from partying at the side of a turquoise swimming pool, and once the two-tone hoot of a toy turbo train approaching an anonymous station.

He tore his mind back from remembered enchantment, printed off the pages he needed and focused on the area required, enlarging the Barrows estate. The main house was extensive, with outbuildings grouped at the rear round a square farmyard. On the south side lay the turquoise swimming pool. Beyond that lay fields dotted with sheep and then woodlands.

The office manager appeared in the doorway. 'Incident room's set up. What have you got for us?'

'Locality of the Barrows estate,' Silver answered shortly. 'I'm searching for the owner's family next and then press covering of the arson. I'll send it through.'

That special day in Jimmy Silver's life had had a significant outcome for others who watched the balloons' lift-off. The raising of the orange windsock had been instantly observed in the village and the word passed round. Singly or in pairs the locals had begun to drift into the Iron Duke, order their pints and take them into the village street to gaze in its direction. 'Lift-off at ten,' one informed them.

Drawn by their interest, the three young men inside quit their table and followed. 'We missed out on that,' muttered Jeff Wills. 'If we'd known, we could have booked flights, got our own aerial shots. Wind's in the right direction.'

'Nah, it's too late.' Phil Duffield shot him down scornfully. 'In any case I can access all the official info we need. We'll take our own pics later. It's the interior shots that count, and we don't want you prematurely sticking anything on the web till we've completed the series, Geeko.'

Barney Bullinger grinned amiably at the pair of them. Not far short of a giant, the firefighter from Acton was happy to leave argument to the Brains, always out to upstage each other. Nobody would be challenging his own vital role in the partnership; nobody had the body for it. Or the technical equipment. He looked across at his newly resprayed green Ford Transit which gleamed as proudly as any engine of London Fire Brigade, polished and refurbished in the long hours of waiting between call-outs and training.

Career-wise he reckoned he had got himself the best job of the three: bags of risks, with guaranteed adrenalin rushes; a team of great mates all joshing along together, even the butch girl who'd recently joined Green Watch, poor cow, and tried hard to fit in. He couldn't imagine life chained to an office chair like the other two poor sods.

40

Jeff Wills was an IT expert employed by a retail chain and fancied himself as a universal hacker. He must be stoned out of his mind with boredom on the job. Small wonder he needed a dash of excitement now and then. As for Phil Duffield, he worked for the MoD in Whitehall – a bit of a softy. Nothing remotely military about him. He had more to do with supplies; one of those desk-warriors sending out equipment 'unfit for purpose' to our guys fighting in Afghanistan, like the papers claimed.

Barney's own union would rightly raise hell if the firefighting service got treated that way, although there'd been some dangerous cheese-paring in recent years, due to the economy's downturn. You had to watch what those clever dicks in government got up to, feathering their own nests while screwing the taxpayers.

A faint cheer interrupted his reverie as slowly a gaudily striped dome rose majestically above trees a quarter-mile off.

'It's the girl piloting,' said one observer lowering his field glasses.

'Not my idea of fun,' Phil Duffield muttered. 'I hate flying. And airports worse.'

The other two exchanged glances. 'Trot back inside for a noggin?' Barney suggested before something sarky could slip out. Mustn't risk hurting the Whitehall wimp's feelings. They still needed him in the team.

'Four balloons up already. That's the local lot then,' said one of the onlookers. 'Day like this,

41

some'll be going up over Aylesbury way too. Who's for driving over and watching the rally?'

The little group broke up, some falling in with the suggestion, others with Saturday jobs dragging them off, but arranging to meet for a ploughman's lunch before the airstrip's returning passengers crowded in the pub, champagne-charged after the binge in the marquee.

The three outsiders resumed at their table, ordering jacket potatoes with ham and cheese filling. It was time they needed to fill, not their stomachs, but they hadn't long to wait before the expected old man limped in with his elderly German shepherd at his heels.

Not much opposition there, Barney considered. It might end with them getting him sacked, but he must be over his shelf life anyway. He'd been at it so long the authorities had forgotten he was there: just a name on a computerized wages list that no official bothered to bring up to date. This was the second weekend in the month, when the old guy regularly came over to look up his married daughter in Missenden. That duty served, he'd stay on here until he was pretty well pissed before driving home to sleep it off, hopefully till morning. So far, it seemed he was keeping to routine, so they could soon push off to the bunker and find themselves some fun.

Four

Sheba the elderly German shepherd sniffed at the breeze and her hackles slowly rose. She barked twice, startling Chaz Sowerby plodding alongside. The old girl hadn't sounded so alert in years and he'd assumed that the guard dog part of her brain had gone soft over time.

'What's up, girl?'

She turned to her master and barked again, more excited now that she'd raised some response. For a while, as they patrolled the bounds, she'd been picking up faint traces; and now that they'd reached the north-west corner of the compound, with the wind blowing in her face, she was certain. Three separate human scents were being carried down from the ridge: youngish males, moving stealthily beyond the fencing, and that could mean trouble.

The light was already fading. Chaz wouldn't be able to follow her uphill and across the rock-strewn field. He slipped her collar and shouted, 'Go, girl, go!'

On the higher ground, hiding by a bulky gorse bush, Barney Bullinger watched their approach through his prized night-vision scope.

43

'Oh, crap! The dog's on to us. We'll have to hoof it.'

The other two swore, starting to collect the equipment and pack it back in their neoprene backpacks.

'Hang on, though. The dog's stumbling, it's stopped running. Yes, it's limping back to its master, tail between its legs: looks beaten.'

Phil Duffield gave a little choking laugh. 'There's a case of paying peanuts and getting monkeys. In this case a geriatric, fleabag mutt. Sure enough, there it goes, defeated.'

He smirked at his co-conspirators. 'Gentlemen, I do believe we're still in the bunker-beating business.'

Back on level ground, Sheba limped in shame back to her master, flanks heaving from the effort of the chase. The fifty-yard run uphill had brought back the cramping pain in her hind quarters, and with it the memory of a brutal beating she'd received on catching up with intruders all those years ago.

By now the temperature was taking a dive and drizzle thickening to rain. It seemed far better to go home, curl up in the warm. Her chasing days were over.

As she lay at his feet, head on muddy paws, Chaz bent stiffly to scratch behind her ears. 'Just another rabbit, was it, girl? Not got the sharp nose you once had, eh? Us old 'uns ain't as sharp as we once were. Let's head back for a bite of supper.'

Inside the compound the man and his dog hobbled away as the three Urban Explorers moved silently down from their observation point and towards the unclimbable fencing near the point they'd chosen for entry. They were already familiar with the site's layout, having researched it thoroughly. With both Phil Duffield's MoD plans and a satellite picture of the old RAF camp buildings found on Google Earth, each man knew where he was heading, as well as the most direct exit route in case they were detected. The only unknown factor had been the location of CCTV surveillance, but now, with dusk, the infrared lamps had automatically come on, revealing the cameras in a bright red halo as the gusting rain swirled round them.

'Great!' said Barney, lowering his glasses. 'Those cameras can't hide. If the day comes when infrared lamps can be made to emit no light, that's when we'll have to retire. We're clear of them as far as the old RAF canteen, where we'll get in, crawl inside the major power duct and cross under the road to the maintenance shed, so avoiding the CCTV.'

'How tight a fit will that be?' Phil asked doubtfully. 'I don't fancy getting wedged.'

'No sweat, mate. It's a doddle.' Jeff positively smirked. 'There'll be bags of room down there. I got this on the web from that Mancunian bloke, Moonstruck. He did a recce of the site a couple of months ago. He didn't get inside the bunker itself, though. Luckily for us, he couldn't access all the info we have, so we're sure of notching up this one's virginity. With detailed internal shots, it's gonna look a wow on the Urban Adventure website.'

Bullinger frowned. 'Hold your neddies, lads. Moonstruck is one of the best. I've explored several London sewers with him, including the mighty Fleet River, and if there's a way in he'll find it. What info do we have that's so exclusive?'

'Obviously,' said Jeff, nodding towards Phil, 'we have the edge with a man on the inside. It's all MoD archives stuff on the Cold War. These ROTOR bunkers were built at enormous expense in the 1950s. They were intended as an integral part of a radar system to foil Soviet Tu-4 bombers armed with atomic bombs flying in from Europe.'

'What – to bomb leafy Bucks?' Barney laughed. 'What was the Soviets' secret plan – world domination by flattening all the shoe shops, hairdressers and estate agents?'

Phil stuck out his chin. 'You must know how it is. Since the first ROTOR stations were all facing out to sea, their radar would lose the invaders once they crossed the coast. So, further installations were located inland on high ground to pick up any bombers getting past RAF interceptor planes. And who knows? Maybe at that point we would have picked off the last baddies with Bloodhound missiles.

'Anyway, this is one of those deeper inland developments which cost the earth in money and manpower, while the old UK was still reeling from the war. Our second line of defence. Sadly, by the time the whole system was set up and working, small atomic bombs had been replaced by powerful hydrogen ones capable of far more damage and widespread fallout. Also, radar technology had advanced beyond original designs. So, the grand idea was already out of date and unfit for purpose; which should have caused an enormous stink, except that the shit was covered up by Official Secrets. That's when these deeper refuges were ordered, and while nuclear wipe-out still seemed imminent, a whole rat pack of politicians and civil servants, determined to survive the holocaust, decided to turn these places into the twentieth-century, underground equivalent of Crusaders' castles – or, in officialese, Regional Seats of Government. Many of them stayed in service right up to the destruction of the Berlin Wall in '91. Some are capable of practical conversion even now.'

'So much for history, but it doesn't explain how we're going to penetrate the bunker,' Barney insisted, impatient for action.

'OK, kids, here comes the science bit.' Jeff took over again. 'As any good computer hacker could tell you, the way out is the way in.' He was enjoying holding the floor while Barney got to work with wire cutters on the outer rim fencing.

'Yes, folks: poor old Moonstruck was bang-ing his head against the armoured front door. We, on the other hand, will ease ourselves gently into the beast's backside. Or, more sedately, enter a filtration exit.' He paused, debating with himself whether to admit to the stuff he'd picked up on the website used by Tankgirl.

She'd been boasting of her intention to take this bunker, and hinted she had access to similar info herself. But that was a year ago and no report of a successful mission had ever come up since. Originally he'd contacted her offering to join in, but she'd brushed him off; saying she had a partner in mind she could trust with her life. They'd take it on together.

But she had never posted a site report of her 'explore'. Obviously Tankgirl was one of those wannabes – all big talk but actually gutless. Not surprisingly after her fiasco, her name had never appeared on the forum's website again. That meant that the site was still virgin for the taking.

The other two were waiting impatiently. This was the vital part of their project, only plaus-ible because Phil had photocopied detailed plans from archives at MoD.

Now Barney, expert at hacking his way through infernos, was sceptical. 'You're not telling us that this bunker, which was con-structed to withstand a near miss from an atomic bomb, has a back door made of three-ply?'

Phil stuck in his thumbs and twanged imaginary braces. 'Nope, but this is how the Whitehall Warrior here scores on this trip. There's something special Jeff and I have discussed but we didn't disclose to Mister Muscle here.'

He surveyed the firefighter cockily. Barney might fancy himself a Rambo, and the other was a mere geek. It took specialist knowledge to save them from attempting this project ham-fisted. And he had the necessary info in spades.

'While most of these bunkers now appear abandoned, a few remain on Care and Maintenance. This is one. Every mothballed bunker like this gets an annual visit from civilian contractors. There's a twelve-day schedule for this and it involves two engineers starting on a Monday, working all through the week and weekend, to finish on the second Friday. Their first week covers checking water and electrical services. The second week is spent on the air-conditioning plant, and replacing the nuclear, biological and chemical filters located in the tower above the emergency exit.

'Times are slack. There's a whisper that these contractor's teams have a wee fiddle set up, working late every evening for the first week, so they can leg it off home for the weekend. What's of special interest is that they've usually removed the blast-proof grilles for the air-filter stack before they take their unsanctioned leave. Now perhaps you understand why I told you both to keep this particular date free at all costs?'

'But why keep that much under your hat until now?' Barney asked. 'So, you're saying that our entry will be blocked by an impenetrable tank-metal door with absolutely no way anyone can get past – apart from a gaping four-foot hole in the top of the bunker, which they've conveniently left open for us?

'Wow! It sounds a doddle. In short, you say we're entering a site patrolled by one arthritic old codger dozing in a Portakabin, guarded by an equally fearsome dog; an unlocked nuclear bunker with nobody inside and a ruddy great welcome mat. Slack maintenance giving us a whole weekend to explore. Now that is really cool.'

'Hats off to our firefighters. They sometimes grasp the point in the end. But listen, guys, this special offer is for one weekend only in each year. It's open house, but only for those Urban Explorers who're in the know.' He tapped the side of his nose. 'So let's keep it that way.'

Knowledgeable, yeah, thought Jeff Wills sourly; but that doesn't make him Top Cat in our alley. Who set it up in the first place, searched the websites? Without me doing all the hacking, Mister Duffer Duffield from the MoD would never have known what to dig for in the archives. And he's a wally if he thinks lording it over Rambo Bullinger isn't going to find him flat on his face before long.

'Well,' Barney announced, dumping the wire-cutters and standing to his full six feet four, 'the fence is open, ready for entry. No one will spot this hole behind the bushes, and the van's nearly two miles away down the farm lane.'

He tore his sleeve free from a branch of rain-spattering gorse and grinned at them. 'But a theory's only a theory until it's put to the test. Speaking for myself, the adrenalin's up and pumping. Let's go for it!'

Once inside the perimeter fence, they'd headed over rough ground to the old RAF canteen. No cameras covered that non-vital area. From that point they could make out the Guardhouse that covered the two-storey underground bunker, but a direct approach was out of the question. Externally it resembled a sturdy brick bungalow, but on near sight the mock windows would be revealed as solid black shapes.

Inside, they knew from their similar previous explorations elsewhere, there would be an armoured turnstile, decontamination facilities and a square stairwell topped by a powerful electric hoist serving the floors below. A 100-plus metre tunnel would lead to blast doors behind which were the control and communication rooms, domestic offices and living quarters, each floor identified, for safety reasons, by colour-coded walls and doors.

Beyond the squat shape of the bungalow they picked out the group of four ventilation towers which stood above the filtration bank and air-conditioning plant. The updated MoD info on all surface structures promised that this was a vast underground site, at one time of vital importance.

Gaining entry to the old canteen was no problem for Barney with his practised skills. The major power duct led them under the road to exit into fresh air again after leaving the unguarded maintenance building by its push-bar exit. Now they had the cover of overgrown conifers to reach the four ventilator stacks where Duffield had promised the opening left by the skiving maintenance team. They climbed a grassy mound to reassemble at the foot of an eight-foot stack.

'And now's when we find they've suddenly gone efficient and replaced the blast grilles,' Barney growled.

Even Phil had been unsure until then that their luck would hold, but getting away with slackness in the past had made the workmen overconfident. The gap in the filtration towers yawned darkly.

'No shots of that for the website,' Duffield warned. 'We can't risk using flash. And this'll remain our little secret. We don't want a procession of Urban Explorers stealing our thunder in later years, to make it look like child's play.'

Barney pulled the climbing rope from his backpack and stood ready to drop it into the filter chamber below. 'Stand clear,' he ordered. 'I'm going in first.'

In his Portakabin old Chaz nudged Sheba with one slippered foot. Ever since their return she'd been fretting.

'Shut it, girl. I dunno what's set you off moanin' that way. Mebbe something you ate. I better have a look at that old dump you been nosin' into for days. It's not as if I doan' give you decent meals, but you 'ave to go diggin' up a lotta filth.'

He adjusted his bifocals and shook out his newspaper. He didn't want to face the thought that the old girl could be on her way out. Was something nasty going on inside her? They'd been working together for a good fifteen years now, ever since she came as a pup to replace the retiring Jezebel.

He preferred not to be reminded that he'd have to make arrangements for his own retirement before long. His daughter over at Missenden wouldn't want him there, sitting around indoors, getting in her way. She'd more than enough to cope with: three teenage kids and one of them in trouble with the police. She wouldn't say what he'd been up to, but he'd guess it was something to do with cars. Other people's, that was. Kids these days had no respect for grown-ups or their property.

Sheba sat up expectantly, ears pricked, clumsily got to her feet and limped across to the door.

'Want out?' Chaz grumbled. Bladder trouble, he supposed. He stood there waiting for her return, but the wind reminded him it was September. The day had started well but turned to rain, and now, after weeks of drought, the radio was putting out severe weather warnings.

'Come on, girl. Can't stand here all night.'

But despite obvious weariness after that fruitless bunny-chasing uphill, it seemed she'd a fancy for staying out. He slammed the door shut. Let her scratch at it when she was ready to come in.

Chaz settled again with his newspaper, bent to switch on the single-bar electric fire and in a few minutes was sound asleep.

For Jimmy Silver that day of their balloon flight had continued to be perfect, even as he had later struggled to raise the soft top on his vintage red sports car. For a late lunch they had shared a quiche and takeaway coffee, huddled together under its roof. Later, after a meandering drive round picturesque villages which Jo recognized from a television series on the Chilterns, he had taken her to a restaurant in Old Amersham and they'd lingered cosily over dinner, sharing a half-bottle of Californian Merlot which Silver hung back from.

'Do you want to drop in on your great aunt?' he suggested. But it was too late. She was recovering well, Jo told him, but she went to bed prompt on nine.

Time, then, to think about taking her home. As they started on the motorway to London she fell quietly asleep with her head gently resting on his shoulder.

Would she invite him in when they got there? A relative newcomer to the dating culture, he was tortured with doubt. So much hung on it. She'd told him she shared the penthouse apartment, but hadn't mentioned her flatmate. He imagined it was a girl of the same age, working as she did in some office, but for all he knew it could be a man, and she was in a standing relationship. In the next hour or so the romantic dreams that had possessed him could be utterly dashed. All those happy accidents that had brought them together would be frustrated, mocking him with an empty illusion of what might have been.

She awoke as they turned at Sloane Square, and smothered a yawn. 'That was a wonderful day, Jimmy. I'll never forget it.'

He drew up by her door and she turned to kiss him lightly on the cheek. 'Th-thank you so much.' That was dismissal, and her slight stammer had returned.

'Perhaps we might do something like it again?'

'Oh, yes. I'd like that.'

Since then he'd seen her three times. They had gone hill climbing, taken a boat up the Regent's Canal and pruned a lot of dead wood off Aunty's apple tree.

He'd learned that she shared the Pimlico apartment with her divorced father and worked part-time as his secretary. Alarmingly for the undistinguished detective constable in Thames Valley, her father was a backbench Member of Parliament representing a constituency in Lincolnshire. It was a detail Jimmy hadn't shared with colleagues who'd joshed him about the burgeoning relationship. Let them go on marvelling at him squiring a pretty redhead. They'd commented how she seemed to have brought the dinosaur geek out of his computer cave.

She had never mentioned politics: he'd no idea which party her father represented, and he kept an equally tight lid on anything concerning police work. Why not, with so much else to find out about each other?

Certainly he would never refer to this sensational new murder case, although she was bound to pick it up in the national press and guess he was involved in the investigation. *Suspected* murder case, he corrected himself. Superintendent Yeadings had insisted on his overall Rule One being respected: *suspect everyone and everything, but assume nothing until proved.* Although in this case the spectacular way the body had been displayed surely made an alternative out of the question.

He walked through the incident office to the analysis room and examined the new photographs from the crime scene. The dead girl had been slight, like Jo, and perhaps pretty too when alive. She wasn't now; her mouth agape in a wolfish snarl. The way she was hanging, her long hair, dyed a fierce rust colour, almost touched the grass. Whatever her hopes and fears and pleasures had once been, they were all wiped out. A warm, living girl, and she'd become nothing. It horrified him.

'Sickening,' said the office manager, coming in and staring over his shoulder. 'We'll be putting everything we've got into finding the monster that did that to her.'

Five

'Mmm, this'll be a subject to write up in your memoirs, Mike,' said Littlejohn as he bent over the body on the slab. 'A cold case, in any sense of the term.'

'A Misper, then? From how long back?' demanded DI Salmon, impervious to the Home Office pathologist's dislike of undue haste and badly timed questions.

Littlejohn stood erect and fixed him with a steely eye under ebullient greying brows. 'Shall we await events?' he enquired mildly.

Superintendent Yeadings settled more comfortably on braced legs. This was going to be a long wait. At first sight the pitiably thin body could have been taken for an old woman's. There was distinct shrinkage of the toughened outer skin, which had a curious, waxy texture. But he had seen X-ray photographs of the body when first brought in and the distorted, occasionally fractured, bones, glowing white against the grey of soft tissues and black of film, were those of someone considerably younger.

He had queried the distortions, and the lab

technician – the Prof being absent at the time – had suggested the cause as sudden trauma: a violent collision with a large, solid object, or a fall from a considerable height. Nothing, apparently, connected with the reversed hanging position in which she was found. The bones in that tensed leg showed no fractures.

'The body,' Littlejohn explained now, 'had been, either deliberately or by accident, preserved; but not – as we more frequently find – through refrigeration. This is a case of mummification due to enclosure within an impermeable wrapping, and remaining under dry conditions without access to it by egg-laying insects. The recently removed covering, having created a mini-convection oven about the body, was sufficiently flexible to avoid hard surfaces causing bone to break through flesh and become externally visible.'

He began a wordless humming as he gently probed the surface skin of the face and neck. Yeadings had to suppress the recurring horror he always experienced at the inhumanity of the necessary invasion. 'Shall we give this young woman a name?'

'Why not? Your choice.' Littlejohn resumed his humming.

It was a half-recognizable tune. An aria from some opera? Yeadings had a fleeting impression of a spacious theatre and himself in a seated audience all focused on a single tortured soul centre-stage. And then the words came to him. *Oh, how I sigh to rest me/ Deep in the quiet grave.*

Dolorous enough. Littlejohn was not as unfeeling as he contrived to appear.

'Leonora,' Yeadings murmured.

'As you wish. For myself, we have the body of a Caucasian female between twenty-five and thirty-five years, of disputable weight before death, but not more than one hundred and twenty pounds. She stood five feet four to five feet five inches in height. External examination reveals an interesting occurrence of both mummification and surface saponification together. The latter condition, which is quite mild, not being the result of immersion in water, but effected by fluids seeping from the body itself over a considerable period.'

He straightened and swept the watchers with a mocking eye. 'On internal examination we are also likely to discover extreme putrefaction, suspicion of which must by now have reached you. You may later find the stench overwhelming.'

There was an embarrassed shuffling of feet as the two uniform officers first called to the crime scene moved a little distance away. Salmon glared back at them.

Unperturbed, the pathologist cut a long strand of tousled dyed hair from the girl's head for chemical analysis, watched it bagged by his assistant and then deliberately made the first curved diagonal cut into the chest, ending below the sternum and joined by a mirror image from the opposite side. Everyone else drew breath, regretted it, and steeled themselves to endure the worst part of the operation.

Littlejohn reached for a saw. 'The body was first wrapped in the supine position,' he explained for anyone who'd not seen it in the wood, 'and retained enough flexibility to allow it to be fixed in the reversed crucifixion display.'

'Well?' Angus Mott demanded as a sickly looking DI Salmon returned to base.

'Professor Littlejohn believes that the death is an old, unreported one. The unidentified girl, in her twenties or early thirties, died anything from one year to eighteen months ago.'

'Are we dealing with a case of sexual assault? Impossible to say, due to the internally decomposed state of the body. It had originally been clothed in dark man-made fibre and then sealed in something like heavy plastic sheeting until exposed within the past thirty-six hours, when the dark clothes had been replaced by a single white sheet and the hanging scene was rigged. There was no sign of strangulation, either manual or by ligature. The cord indentations on the left ankle were made long after death and at the time she was – er, suspended. So the theatrical staging had no discernible connection with the cause of death. Which remains open. Accident is not ruled out. Nor is murder by person or persons unknown. The Professor actually suggested the final outlandish exhibition was the result of "high jinks by an immature and solipsistic personality".' Salmon's dour features twisted to indicate more than usual disgust.

Mott hid a smile. Littlejohn had been mischievously sending up the easily offended Inspector who continued. 'Unfortunately the more spectacular aspects have turned the media into ravening wolves. They're determined to create some superstitious hocus-pocus out of it. I had almost to fight my way through the camera flashlights on my way out.'

Mott looked owlish. 'I hope they got some flattering pics of you – for your wife to display on the piano.'

What they'd been after, of course, was the Boss. He'd have had the wit to escape from the morgue by an alternative route. Salmon's sour features would get widespread airing instead and add to the lugubrious flavour of the mystery.

'Anyway, there's no great pressure on this one,' Salmon said decisively. 'We can hand it on to Cold Cases.'

'The presentation is active,' Mott corrected severely. 'Some unknown is either demanding we do something to clarify the death or is flaunting an ability to get away with concealment of a killing. You'll find Mr Yeadings putting this case right at the front of his priorities. He knows a challenge when one's thrust under his nose.' He frowned. 'And the Professor suggests one or two years back for the time of death?'

'Yes. Greater precision's impossible until it's known where, and under what conditions, the body was kept concealed.' Salmon disposed of his overcoat on DS Beaumont's empty desk. 'So what has been going on here in my absence?' He sounded like a Victorian father preparing to discipline his unruly children.

Mott rattled off the answer. 'Considerable media pressure on PR; briefing of the augmented team; study of missing persons lists for Thames Valley over the past five years; HOLMES searches nationwide for similar offences; listing of likely suspects in female abduction cases. And, of course, further forensic examination of the site where our body was found, with Uniform responsible for supervised fingertip searches of an increasingly wide area in Bells Wood.

'I've had initial interviews with the two family members available at the house and need you now to follow up with any domestic or estate staff DS Beaumont has yet to question. But first, report on the post-mortem as fully as possible to the office manager and familiarize yourself with updatings in the Incident and Analysis rooms. Refer to DC – sorry, acting DS – Silver for maps and local info.'

Salmon was tempted to point out that it was already four thirty, the light would shortly be failing, and he had worked tirelessly since eight thirty without interruption for lunch. All that prevented him was the knowledge that he'd have shot down anyone of lesser rank airing such a feeble complaint. Scowling, he picked up his coat again and made for the corridor outside, barely persuaded that a cold case merited so much fuss.

The incident room was buzzing with activity – all these needlessly drafted-in outsiders trying to get themselves noticed! He was jostled in his efforts to pick up the details he required, but eventually emerged with sufficient background on the area to supplement whatever scanty interviewing Beaumont would have made of Barrows' domestic staff. It was time that that casual waster took note of an experienced investigator in action.

After his return from the post-mortem to his office, Superintendent Yeadings had emptied and refilled his coffee machine, noted the supply of filters was running low, and settled to sort his observations on the present case. His views on little Leonora, he corrected himself.

The first question he scribbled on his pad was WHO was she? Followed by WHEN? and WHERE? The next two had to be BY WHOM? and WHY? But he didn't see yet which of that last pair led to the other. And weren't there two

64

distinct sections to all those questions, because there were two possible crimes to be exposed? – first the death and then, much later, the body's public exposure after deliberate concealment.

How much easier if the same person was responsible for both. But something in his water warned him not to assume that too soon.

He always allowed a little leeway in his ruminations for the intuitive faculty. He disliked the word hunch, but self-mockingly would refer to an inherited gene from his late Welsh grandmother renowned locally as the last in a long line of Wise Women. It might have helped to know what she'd have made of the Tarot reference, if one really was intended. He doubted she'd have had recourse to the cards herself, was more a herbalist and palm-reader, but surely she'd have come across their use, the varied interpretations, and the effect they could exercise on superstitious people.

Laboriously, with fountain pen on his thick desk pad, he began to itemize the impressions he had formed throughout the day, noting alongside the approximate time at which each was made. Old-fashioned, he would admit, but how many times had these jottings proved invaluable on rereading, when they revived some half-recalled fact which was nuclear to the final solution. Computers had their place, a vital one by now, but their combination with human fallibility allowed something to get lost.

They insisted on domination, were therefore stultifying in some way. To keep retracing his faltering passage throughout any investigation refreshed the reality of each detail as it had come to light. It allowed a creative mental parallel between the perpetrator of a crime and himself: the hunter working blindly alongside the hunted.

He had picked up a nuance that Littlejohn was reserving judgement on something. It had come to him when the pathologist had paused, stared into space over the rim of his spectacles and sighed. 'What I should like is for you to bring me the covering she was removed from. It could provide a great deal of something I'm curious about.'

Yeadings thought there was little chance of that happening. Given the state of the body, the plastic sheeting or whatever, and the clothing underneath, would have been pretty disgusting. The normal reaction would be to destroy it totally. Or submerge it, weighted, in the not too distant lake. But if that, why not the body too?

Because, of course, it had to be put on show. As bravado then, or as a warning? And for whom? The answers to that lay in the most complex part of the puzzle – the perpetrator's psyche.

DS Beaumont was in his element. At Barrows he had found himself comfortably installed in the large but surprisingly cosy kitchen which transported his mind back to the old television series of *Upstairs, Downstairs* to which his wife had been addicted.

The cast was different this time, but their functions were easy to recognize from the characters' appearance, uniforms and demeanour. Yes, there *was* a butler, Edwin Bowles, and a motherly, bustling female cook, called Mrs Bradshaw. Two younger girls, Molly and Barbara, shared kitchen and serving duties. Apparently two women from the village came in daily as chambermaid and general cleaner.

Neither the gardener, Holt, nor his trainee-assistant, Mervin, lived in, but took their midday meal in a room off the kitchen. They were there drinking tea when Beaumont chose to interview the staff *en masse*, believing they would feel more relaxed outnumbering him and the note-taking Limpet. Hopefully they might incautiously strike sparks off each other, dropping some semi-precious gems of gossip.

Regarding their employers, they were guarded. As would I be about mine, Beaumont granted. They saw little of Gervais Plummer, and perhaps a little too much of their mistress, Fiona. There was a daughter, Geraldine, whom everyone called Gerry. She was 'all right', a bit of a tomboy, had started to read Law at Cambridge, dropped out after getting involved in an affray which earned her a minor criminal record. Since then she had taken up with a young man of mixed race her parents disapproved of, and moved out. The pair were understood to be somewhere in Africa at present.

How old was she? Beaumont asked. Twenty-five, she must be, Mrs Bradshaw, the cook, thought, because it was four years ago that she'd made that massive cake for her twenty-first birthday ball. If he'd wait a minute she'd look out the photograph of Gerry cutting the cake with a cavalry sword.

'And when did she leave for Africa?' Beaumont asked the butler.

'Ten days ago.' Good; so that eliminated her from being their present body.

After a brief absence Mrs Bradshaw came back with an album of photographs which the DS was determined to wheedle from her for deeper perusal at leisure. Gerry was a real smasher, fine-featured with her long, blonde hair whipped up into a sort of knob behind a tiara set with either diamonds or quite convincing paste, her clinging evening gown a shimmering aquamarine. The cake was equally ornate, rising in three tiers and topped with icing swags and pale-pink sugar roses.

'Lovely,' Beaumont said, to cover the whole pretentious lot. As a disillusioned parent himself, albeit of a teenage boy, he wondered how Gervais and Fiona felt about such high promise crumpling into the kind of pedestrian disappointment that seemed endemic nowadays in any middle-class family. Perhaps wealth and social standing helped them overlook their collapsed expectations.

'No other family?' he asked.

'Except for the little boy,' Mrs Bradshaw murmured, and was obliged to explain how seven-year-old Freddy had been drowned years ago in the lake. After that Beaumont passed on to the gruesome finding in the grounds.

'Yes, it was me that found 'er,' admitted Holt droopingly. 'Give me an awful shock, it did. Poor lass. That anyone should do a thing like that to 'er!'

'You didn't recognize her?'

'Never seen 'er before in me life.'

'She didn't remind you of anyone?'

'Nuh. Not that way up. 'Ow could I? I was real flummoxed, came straight up to the 'ouse and got Mr Bowles, the butler 'ere, to phone the perlice.'

'Not Mr Plummer? Wasn't he here?'

'No. 'E was. 'Ere, I mean. But 'e wasn't about, like.'

'It was early morning,' Mrs Bradshaw excused him.

'Yes, and misty. I couldn't rightly see what it was at first. I thought, oh they've started 'anging things on the tree again.'

'You mean that's an established habit?'

'Was once, years back. The Wishing Tree, see? It's donkey's years old. People used to hang things up and make a wish for something they wanted real bad. Only it stopped after the

69

old vicar preached so 'ard against pagan rites. A real 'ellfire and damnation parson 'e was. Anyway, nowadays folks don't make so much of the tree. They got other ways of getting what they want.' His voice carried disapproval and the DS was curious to know what he meant.

But somebody was still mindful of the old ways, he thought. What had that someone been wishing for, hanging a near-naked human body there, upside down from a cross branch?

DI Salmon arrived late at Barrows to find the staff had all been interviewed, and were rigidly determined not to observe his presence while continuing their routine duties of plating-up and serving a four-course meal to a distant dining room he was barred from entering. It had him fuming with barely concealed contempt for such feudal remnants as kowtowing to supposed superiors.

Beaumont reminded him that Mott had already conducted an initial interview with the Plummer couple, so he promised himself to confront them later with specific requirements regarding police use of their land.

'How's Z doing?' Beaumont demanded as they made their way out to their cars.

'I've no idea.'

Well, he wouldn't have, the DS told himself. He'd have to get any news of her by phoning Max Harris.

In the discreetly dimmed lights of the Intensive

Therapy Unit, a nurse unwrapped the BP band from Zyczynski's arm and recorded the improved result. Pulse improving, temperature still a little high. Tomorrow Dr Samways was going to check the position of the broken ribs, one at a bad angle to the left lung, but for the time being she was best left resting and sedated. So far there were no active signs of concussion but after a car crash there was always a doubt about the state of the spleen. She had lost a lot of blood, so must continue with crossmatch transfusions.

She went across to the man standing, back tactfully turned, as though looking from the window. It was too dark for him to see out. The glass only reflected the lights of the small ward and the pale figures of the nurses moving between the beds.

'Why don't you go home?' she suggested. 'Get some rest, and tomorrow you'll be fresher to see her when she's awake.'

He looked blindly through her. 'She's everything to me. If anything happened...'

'We're here for her. We're taking every care. You've left us your number, but we shan't need to use it, truly.'

Max still stood on for minutes watching for any flicker of life on the sleeping face. Then he bent to kiss her cheek, whispered in her ear, and quietly left the ward.

Six

The next morning Mott, in conversation with the office manager, broke off to take a call. It could be serious. Why otherwise would Max Harris need to get in touch when he'd posted himself full-time at Zyczynski's hospital bedside?

But it wasn't as he'd feared. Z was fully conscious now and Max was with her, having slipped home for a few hours in the early hours and returned, picking up their mail as he crossed with the postman in their driveway.

The little bundle had contained an anonymous letter addressed to the DS that she wanted ed passed immediately to CID working on the hanging girl case.

'On my way,' Mott assured him, and rang the Boss who swept up Beaumont and followed on. If Z had become involved, even in her present state, she'd every right to be included in any consultation the team held.

The DS had been moved from ITU to a small single room where they crowded in.

'Strictly police business,' Max greeted them scrupulously, 'so I'll make myself scarce, much though I'd love to be a fly on the wall.

I'll get someone to bring some chairs in.'

'Strictly ten minutes. And don't excite my patient,' a nurse instructed them.

'What a turnout,' Z appreciated faintly. 'I'm impressed.' Her right temple was covered with a gauze pad and a number of small white strips partly hid crimson gashes on her forehead and nose.

'It's good to see you,' Yeadings said for them all. 'Are you sure you're up to this? We've been concerned.'

'I'm going to be fine. A dislocated shoulder, but they've put it back in place. A couple of broken ribs and some bruising. I'll be out in a couple of days. Max told you about the letter? It was addressed to me at home. We've kept the envelope. Anonymous, obviously, from someone who guessed I'd be on the investigating team. But why choose me? I don't know.'

'Celebrity status,' Beaumont suggested, po-faced. 'Have you ever noticed you've got a stalker?'

'Because you're the only woman among us?' Mott suggested. 'Could it be from someone who'd prefer not to deal with a man?' He lifted the single sheet of paper from the bed. Max must have wheedled a plastic freezer bag from one of the hospital staff to preserve it from further fingerprints.

'POWERS OF DARKNESS,' he read from capital print. In lower case there followed a dire warning of occult influences at work among

73

the locals of Barrows Village – witchcraft and devil-worship – with orgiastic dancing at full moon round the Wishing Tree in Bells Wood. It picked up a Tarot reference in the display of the corpse, and incorrectly referred to the Hanged Man as a death card. More and greater evil, the writer predicted, was to follow.

Mike Yeadings grunted. DS Beaumont rolled his eyes. Rosemary Zyczynski silently admitted it was all a bit over the top. She pointed to the foot of the letter. *Copy to all main national newspapers.* 'A pity there are no spelling mistakes to pick up on,' she noted.

'Powers of Darkness,' Mott repeated. 'We could have panic stations with the locals, and our crime scene turning into a tourist attraction. We need to do something about it.'

'Or be seen to,' Beaumont modified. 'Groping in the dark, as it were. Our cue to be luminous.'

'We'll get forensics to examine the paper,' Mott promised, 'but the print used looks like any common or garden computer job. It's essential to trace the writer and get a retraction, but I don't see it's relative to the investigation. It's just another loony aiming to achieve his fifteen minutes of fame.'

'The writer specifically targeted Z,' Yeadings reminded them. 'He, or more likely she, knew Z's position in the team and her private address. Possibly she was the one chosen to receive it because of a personal connection with

74

a household name in the newspaper world.

'I find that amount of personal information disturbing. Too close for comfort. And that final bit about greater evil to come – is that more than a warning? Even a threat? Is this a hysteric stimulated to display dangerous socio-pathic tendencies?

'I'm not happy about Rosemary staying on here without special security measures. I want a uniform on duty outside this room whenever Max can't be here. And the sooner he can get her away on a recuperative break the better.'

Max, once consulted, agreed. He could work just as well abroad as at his London office. He'd book in for the two of them somewhere off the beaten track – maybe Lanzarote or Madeira – for at least a couple of weeks, once she was discharged.

The group broke up. Yeadings – seeking time to catch up on the morning newspapers and having missed his customary elevenses – heading for the Costa Coffee house across the street from the local nick.

He had consumed a skinny latte for liquid bulk and his stomach's satisfaction. Now countless taste buds screamed for undiluted caffeine.

The waitress, black apron to her ankles, was clearing the next table. She hesitated beside him. 'The usual, sir?'

'My chaser, thank you.' He nodded, enjoying the flattery of being recognized as a regular.

She carried off her loaded tray, bound to fetch his double espresso. When he looked up again, someone else was standing there. A man of about his own age, of a little less than medium height, with fine, sandy hair, and leaning on a stick.

'Superintendent?'

'You have the advantage of me.' Yeadings hesitated to offer him the vacant chair. This coffee break was almost sacrosanct.

'Gervais Plummer,' the man said. He didn't offer a hand to shake, but gave the merest hint of an old-fashioned bow. 'Of Barrows. The unfortunate incident in Bells Wood occurred near my home.'

Yeadings noted the carefully chosen words: 'incident' not 'death'. The man hadn't said 'on my land', although the wood was part of his demesne. 'Home' could have applied equally to a tenement squat or a semi on a housing development. Perhaps he wasn't as overwhelmed by his own possessions as some others equally privileged.

'Yes, unfortunate,' Yeadings echoed. He declined to be drawn on the case.

Plummer's eyes were the warm brown that often goes with carroty hair. The left one drooped. His smile was a little crooked. At some time he could have suffered a mild stroke, or was soon to have one.

Reluctantly Yeadings closed his newspaper and moved it to one side. 'Will you join me?'

76

Gervais Plummer sat, neatly, hanging the stick by its crook on the back of his chair. 'A pompous forename, I've always felt. It embarrasses me rather.'

'We aren't responsible for what our parents pass on to us.' This conversation had a quirky beginning, and the policeman in him was alerted.

The waitress had arrived with his espresso. Plummer ordered a small pot of Darjeeling tea. 'I'm in business,' he offered. 'I work in London. That is, I go in most weekdays and sit at a desk. The real work is mainly done by others.'

Yeadings was tempted to suggest his own life followed the same pattern. 'I tend to be deskbound myself,' he granted.

'But you enjoy your escapes into active policing – as I understand from press accounts of your achievements.'

'I sometimes remind myself I'm still a copper.'

'Which is why I presume to approach you. Regarding, of course, the present case.'

This was almost an invitation for the superintendent to interview him, but Mott had been there already and there was no reason to doubt he'd done so efficiently. Yeadings refused to double up.

Instead, he pursued the personal line the man had introduced. 'So, how do you occupy yourself at your desk?' he enquired.

'Not excessively.' He hesitated a moment,

then confessed, 'I'm writing a book. I get more done there than at home.'

'And the subject?'

'Religion – for want of a better term.' He screwed his eyes small. 'Not relative to any one organized faith, but as something intensely individual.'

Curiouser and curiouser, the policeman thought. I'm really down a rabbit hole with this one. 'Quite a vast subject,' he said, tempting a reply.

'Germane to the entire world and its present troubles.'

'Indeed. Or to any time.'

'Yes. My thesis is that everyone creates his or her own personal formula – a central tenet that holds one together – for some the comfort zone afforded by familiar observances or rituals; others by raw superstition; emotional satisfaction; the pursuit of money or power, or of eccentricity or even of common decency. I'm tracing patterns in various characters from history – Hannibal, Napoleon, Mohammed. I shall get round to more contemporary obsessives in time, or so I hope.'

'Such as...?'

Plummer's eyes went bright with laughter. 'Elvis, Tony Blair, Jeremy Clarkson, the Marx brothers. There's no limit to interesting subjects.'

'Even the perpetrator of the obscene hanging in Bells Wood?'

'Ah.' All the humour fell off him. 'It's not clear as yet what that is about. And I'm not sure I would welcome any further manifestation to give us a lead.'

Yes, Yeadings told himself, I share his unease. It may not be an isolated act, and something worse could follow.

'And in your study of religion you avoid any assumption that the supernatural is being evoked? You accept no likelihood of paranormal influences?'

'The religion I am concerned with is a human concept which we allow to inform and control our lives. Certainly the person who devised that scene in the woods is moved by some powerful motive outside my experience. But perhaps not yours, Mr Yeadings.'

His tray of tea arrived and they dropped the subject. Again Yeadings reminded himself that Angus Mott had interviewed Plummer already, concerning any connection he might have with the case. He doubted it would have followed such an eccentric route as this highly subjective meandering that he'd allowed the man to inflict on him.

He watched the precision with which Plummer poured the tea, added milk, stirred once and laid down the spoon at a right angle to the edge of the table. Here was a disciplined man with an impulse to control, whose 'religion', as he employed the word, could even be manipulation. Had he happened upon Yeadings entirely by chance, or was this an ambush, with Plummer intent on presenting an impression that differed from one already made elsewhere? Was he eager to be fixed in the superintendent's mind as some kind of bumbling amateur psycho-philosopher with a harmless bee in his bonnet?

Yeadings assumed an appearance that would suggest to Plummer that he was losing interest in the subject. He knocked the back page of his closed newspaper with a knuckle. 'Doesn't look good for England's cricket openers.'

'I'm not sure they've got the right captain,' Plummer doubted, apparently willing to be diverted from concerns closer to home.

'Hey, Jimmy!' The call came as DC Silver hesitated at the kerb edge. When the queue of traffic had cleared he made out a lanky figure at the far side of the crossing, apparently about to hurl himself across. He waited, reflecting that the impetuous Baz Noble appeared not to have changed one whit in the five years since they were at college together.

'I thought you were living in London now,' he said mildly as the other bounded up and whacked him heartily with a high five.

'Sure do. I run a CCTV outfit. I'm white-van man himself. Own a small fleet of them, complete with extending ladders. I provide the eyes that make your job so easy, man. I guess you're still with the Old Bill?'

'DC, acting DS at the moment,' Silver confirmed. 'Are you working locally?'

'Sure am. Hicksville this week, Edinburgh the next, the world any moment now. How about we drop in somewhere for a pint and catch up with all that's flowed under the bridge?'

It was his lunch break, as Silver had been reminded by the enticing aroma of hot steak pie reaching him from a kitchen grille of the nearby Crown Inn.

'Why not?' He led the way.

Baz told much the same stories as before: frequent romantic entanglements and last-minute escapes from anything permanent. 'And how about you?' he drew breath to demand.

Silver hesitated. It didn't seem quite decent to bring Jo's name into the conversation. 'Well, there is someone,' he admitted. 'It's pretty new and I'm treading on eggshells.'

'Man, that sounds serious.' Enormous dark orbs within startling whites rolled in his ebony face. He gave a wide smile.

'I'd like it to be.'

'Yeah, that'd be right for you. How'd you meet?'

Silver told him about the chance village dance, the raffle ticket and the hot-air balloon flight.

'Reads like a fairy tale. Something to save and tell the grandchildren.'

Silver had to admit it did make a good story, but he wasn't quite ready for the rest. It was one thing to hope Jo might start feeling the way he did, but beyond belief that so much could follow.

'So, what are you working on here?' he demanded, to change the embarrassing subject. 'I thought we were easing up on cameras now the locals know where the dodgy spots are.'

'Nothing like that. Some counties round here are pulling out of public surveillance now, so it's good we've picked up some government contracts updating MoD security. Hush-hush stuff I wouldn't admit to, except that you're Old Bill and I know you're discreet. I start surveying locally, solo, tomorrow.'

Silver ran through in his mind the known establishments he might be referring to. There was Military Intelligence at Wilton Park, of course, and one or two suspicious country houses for which Special Branch call-out was a priority; then Halton – the RAF technical training base beyond Wendover. He recalled the geometrical layout viewed as the balloon had passed over it, heading west by north-west. And then that other more isolated place which had been a Cold War bunker still designated for a Regional Seat of Government if Putin, or a successor, reinforced some of his spasmodic threats against the West.

There was a time when Silver had considered applying to train for Video Forensics, but it had seemed too specialized and he liked being a valued part of Yeadings's Serious Crimes team. He mentioned it now to Baz. If he'd made the change their paths might well have crossed before now.

'That so? In that case, why not seize the chance to see in the flesh what you might have been dealing with on your goggle-box? I could get you in on your warrant card when I do my initial inspection tomorrow. It's not far.' He reached for an unused table napkin and wrote down a map reference.

Silver stared at it. It was one he'd looked up only days ago: the old RAF bunker, just eight miles from their present crime scene in Bells Wood.

'I'd like to take you up on that,' he said slowly, 'if you're certain you can get me in.'

'Sure thing. Might just be extra persuasive if you claimed you are from Video Forensics, dazzle the old guy on the gate with science. Have you any paperwork left over from the training programme?'

Silver was an inveterate filer. He knew he'd several pages with the required official headings. Deception wasn't his style, but he'd every confidence in Baz's ability to pull off whatever he set his mind on.

He had run up some overtime during these last two weeks, so, whatever the present pressures, he would put in for a free weekend and leave it to chance whether it came off.

Seven

'Isn't it time you knocked off, love?' Nan Yeadings asked, pausing in the doorway with a mug of hot chocolate.

'Too many floating ideas,' he told her. 'I'd never sleep till I've put something down on paper.' He had a whisky sour on the desk beside him and a pad of his favourite squared paper. There was a single word heading the top sheet, but she couldn't read it from the doorway.

He waited until she had moved off calling back, 'Well, goodnight then.'

He murmured a reply, leaning back, eyes closed, and allowed his mind to run free. Tarot cards – the Hanged Man – attached upside down – by a single ankle – from a gallows or tree branch – his expression serene, almost entranced. He wore medieval court dress. That was all he recalled of the picture without consulting an encyclopedia or his computer. It was, he believed, the twelfth trump card.

There had been a fortune-teller's murder after a village fayre at Fords Green about eight years back and he'd had to look the Tarot up then. It had been a complicated case of jealousy and revenge, but not as complicated as working through the ambiguous interpretations of the way the cards had been displayed on the woman's blood-drenched table. There were so many versions of what each card stood for, and then ambiguous readings of how they combined. The Delphic Oracle had been plain speech in comparison. In the end the cards had led only into dead ends, and not to solving the death under investigation. In court it had been presented as a case of aggravated theft by a mentally unbalanced fellow traveller.

Yeadings reached reluctantly for his laptop and consulted Wikipedia. The picture card came up much as he remembered it, but there was a halo, or nimbus, about the head in this version. Did that imply saintliness, and the act of hanging a form of martyrdom? If so, did that concept relate to the death of the girl found hanging in the wood?

He picked up the copy of an 8 by 10 photograph supplied by SOCO. There were too many differences: the body female, and pathetically draped in a white bed sheet. She looked anything but calm. Agonizing death throes stayed etched on her face. The free leg hung loose behind her, not tidily crossed in what the Tarot account described as a 'fylfot' cross. A second shot, taken from behind the girl's body, showed the wrists loosely tied with stout cord apparently similar to that around the ankle used for suspension. This could have been in deliberate imitation of the Tarot figure or simply to facilitate handling of the lifeless body.

What had been the intention of the killer in making such a display? No; that was assuming too much. What, actually, was the intention of the person or persons who thought up this presentation? Because they might not be one and the same at all. The display could even be in protest: *see what X has done to this innocent!*

He returned to the Internet account of the enigmatic card. Yes, 'martyr' was one interpretation of the figure. But another was 'traitor'. Plenty of oracular choice there!

Twelfth card; the screen entry suggested significance in the number of solar, as against lunar, months, which implied – would this wild fiction never end? – that another cult had replaced that of the ancient Earth Mother. There was even a reference to Nordic myth through Odin, who had hanged himself upside down for nine days to attain wisdom.

Do I need to do the same? Yeadings questioned. He reached for the tumbler, found it empty and considered a refill. He decided he should indulge. His mind was by now sufficiently awash with way-out theories to guarantee no clear solution was on its way. A further top-up could at least guarantee that once in bed he'd drop off more rapidly, as a way out of the mental maze.

He examined the handwritten notes he had scribbled on the pad. His last reference had been to 'twelve'. There was another number at the back of his memory. *Seven.* The number of candles that had been lit around the display and removed before Holt had happened on the scene next morning. It wasn't the five he'd have associated with an occultist's pentacle. Had seven been meant as a commonly accepted sign of good luck and well-wishing? Or was that simply the total of spiked candle holders that could be found at the time? And who had assembled there to observe the presentation? Did this imply a local coven?

World of the weird, he consoled himself as he closed the laptop. But suppose it was all simply a joke in abominable taste, and someone somewhere was imagining him sitting up past midnight trying to make sense of it all.

Well, he'd grant that unknown the last laugh of the evening, retire to bed and leave his subconscious to grapple with the enigma overnight.

The white van was there to pick Silver up prompt at eight thirty the next morning. He'd rung Jo and fixed a meeting for tomorrow, Sunday. By then he'd have something of special interest to tell her, safely free of any connection with work.

Baz appeared in well-pressed white overalls with some kind of badge on the breast pocket, and he'd brought along a similar outfit for Jimmy.

The government establishment's double-gated entry was between tall stone pillars at a break in a wooded lane. The nearest dwellings were at a considerable distance. Within the compound a concreted road led to squat buildings past a looming golf-ball-shaped structure. Tall meadow grass was rampant everywhere, and the roadway had potholes. At this point nothing gave the impression of a vital defence fixture. A Portakabin appeared to act as guardhouse, with smeared windows and a little plot of what looked like vegetables to the rear. Beyond it, on a grassy rise, stood a large gabled bungalow built of stone and brick with a taller cubic extension.

There was to be no problem with gaining entry to the site. An elderly man wearing a dark uniform emerged from the Portakabin where he must have been watching for their arrival. A leashed German shepherd kept to heel and growled quietly as its master examined the papers which Baz presented between bars in the iron gateway, stepping aside as the man dropped the leash to work the electronically operated gates. Silver, remaining at the wheel, drove the van between the stone pillars and parked where directed.

'Got the kettle on,' the old gaffer offered. 'Tea or coffee, is it?'

Silver had been warned: these lone guardians

craved company. Baz was keen to get on with the initial survey but knew the value of good relations on the job. Carrying only laptops, they followed Chaz in, the dog bringing up the rear, still slightly suspicious and sniffing at their shoes.

'Steady, girl,' the old man warned. ''Er and me been on this job more years than I like to tell. She'll not 'arm you.'

His visitors found two upright chairs and drew them up opposite the man's recliner. On the wall above the electric fire a bank of monitors showed views of the compound with nothing stirring. Old Chaz ignored them, but the bitch, nose on paws, remained watchful, growling low once when a scrawny dog fox was shown limping across a patch of rough grass marked with a well-worn trail. It seemed that even the wildlife here was ripe for pensioning off, trailing home late after a fruitless night's hunting.

'That'll be Reynard,' said Chaz, not looking up and busy pouring mahogany-dark tea into three mugs. 'Don't look much, but 'e fathered fifteen cubs back this spring.' His voice held all the pride of a licensed breeder.

The newcomers had no need to make conversation. Chaz was still full of the doings of the maintenance team that had paid its recent annual visit. 'Nice to see a human being now and again. Coupla jokers, but they're a 'ard-working couple for all that. Live on the site, see. Not that I get to see all that much of them. They got their own television and like a 'and of poker of an evening. I doan' play that no more. Too 'ard on the pocket.'

He wanted to know everything about Baz's job and the travels it involved. Jimmy got off more lightly once he'd admitted he was mainly concerned with computers. That much at least was perfectly true, he thought gratefully, and the quoted Video Forensics was obviously a world the old geezer knew nothing of.

They extracted themselves eventually from the enforced hospitality, and Chaz, with the bitch alongside, accompanied them as far as the bungalow structure which Silver now saw was in fact a dummy, with what had appeared as windows merely blacked-out rectangles. At that point the old man left them to find their way around.

Baz slipped the two sprung catches on top of his van, allowing the long ladder to slide off under the force of gravity. Then, with skill honed from years' experience, smartly swung it on to his shoulder.

'Some weight,' Jimmy commented. 'Do you want a hand with that?'

Baz laughed. 'No, thanks, mate. It's all about technique. Once it's up, it's nicely balanced, and easier to move round than if we both carried it.'

They set off towards the first building on the site. Beside the concrete plinth of what had originally carried a large radar dish, Baz pitched the ladder under a camera housing. 'The ground's a bit dodgy here. Why not employ your weight and foot my ladder while I zip up?'

'So what exactly are you looking for?'

'Well, the video system used in the Portakabin is as old as the hills. The picture's pretty dire. But I'm hoping to find the cameras are much more modern, so they'll perform well plugged into my system.'

'So what exactly is this system?'

'OK, so I'll keep my voice low. Because the whole point of the upgrading is to remove any need for an on-site security guard. The cameras will be plugged into a computer which digitizes the picture and sends it over the Internet so that the site can be monitored from a remote location. And, now being digital, the pictures can be made to do motion sensing. So if someone walks in front of a camera my system will both set off an alarm at the remote monitoring point and text the mobile security guard's personal phone. As a result it's the death knell for old gaffers and their dogs. Someone as inexperienced as a school-leaver can monitor hundreds of locations from his nice, dry, air-conditioned office.'

'But we've just picked up a fox on the old system. With yours, wouldn't it set off false alarms when the thing's already run off?'

'No, because the system here will send a

video file to the monitor station and any mobile phones set up to receive. So if it is Reynard, everyone alerted will see a video of a fox. And, if it's intruders, that's exactly what they will see.'

Jimmy nodded. 'And as they move around the motion sensors will track them from one camera to the next. That's when the Old Bill will nip in and pick them up.'

'Exactly.' Baz was pulling the heavy casing off the camera mount. 'Ah, as I thought, this is a decent resolution job which will plug straight into the computer and give a very sharp picture. All we need do now is zip round and check on the state of all the other cameras.'

Jimmy's face displayed disappointment. 'Don't we get to go down into the bunker itself? Aren't there cameras there?'

'None I'm involved with, I'm afraid. The bunker may be equipped with whatever system the Civil Defence people set up themselves.'

'Oh, bummer,' Jimmy regretted.

The routine Saturday morning at home was not conducive to the pondering Superintendent Yeadings would have wished for. Promising the children should go 'somewhere special' after lunch, he left the interpretation to Nan's ready imagination and escaped to his office, guiltily aware as ever that a young family acquired in mid-life brought its own chal-lenges.

He was unsurprised to see that DCI Mott had called in the full nuclear team, with the exception of Z and young Silver, excluded in view of overtime already claimed on recent cases. They assembled in the incident room where new photographs of the extended crime scene were on display and results of the fingertip searches in Bells Wood listed.

There was less than the usual unpalatable collection of refuse found in public places. It was hardly the season for picnics, and any recent romantic rendezvous would probably have been inside cars parked off the circular route surrounding the wood. There were several speed warnings indicating the free movement of deer.

Although it was part of a private estate, reasonable public access was permitted in certain areas where the only fencing erected was as a safety measure at the deeper end of the lake, with a padlocked gate to the little jetty and an adjoining slope on which lay an upturned rowing boat.

'Used recently?' Yeadings asked, examining the close-up shots of this.

'No external evidence of fresh weed,' Mott told him, 'but we're awaiting results of a humidity test on the exposed timber. We've been dragging the shallows, but I'd like permission to call in divers, if the cost's acceptable. A dog-handler thinks there might be something of interest in there.'

'Six daylight hours,' Yeadings allowed, mindful of cheese-paring at Kidlington HQ. The decision would require exhaustive negotiation with Finance.

'We need to find what happened to the young woman's clothes and wrapping. There's nothing relevant in the way of fibres from the ground search at the crime scene. What outbuildings are there in the surrounding area?'

'In a smaller clearing there's a good-sized locked shed for equipment. It contains single- and double-handed saws, axes, pruning tools, spades, mowers, sacking and so on. We've taken samples of heavy cord from there, both used and new, for comparison with that used in the hanging. There's also a hut nearby where pheasant chicks are incubated and cared for. The padlock's not been tampered with and the head gamekeeper has the only key not kept at the main house.

'Then, nearer the domestic offices at the rear of Barrows there's an ancient ice house, stone-lined and cut into a slope. It's no longer in use since refrigeration first came in. Apparently it was an underground refuge and campsite for the children of the family when they were young.'

'Children – plural?'

'Gerry had an older brother who died at age seven, drowned in the lake. That's when they had the fencing erected.'

He seemed to have everything well in hand,

Yeadings thought. His own best bet was to leave them to it and see what solitary brainstorming could achieve in his office.

With the cafetière burbling on his office window sill, he settled to draw up his customary schedule of basic questions. Who was this girl he'd named Leonora? Was her death accidental or murder? Who had needed to kill her? Who had displayed her on the tree? What did that spectacular exhibition signify? And the white bed sheet used as a shroud: where had it come from? Was it new or did it have a history?

He stared at the words. As yet the first question offered no clue: the supposed lapse of time between death and display had brought up a considerable list of missing persons of suitable age and appearance from within Thames Valley. A squad of uniform officers were following that up with edited photographs of the dead girl. But the second question at least suggested a lead. Littlejohn had offered a choice for the extreme trauma suffered: she'd been either violently struck by a large moving object or had fallen from a considerable height on to a hard surface.

Her body, the bones crushed in several places, had shown no specific marks of a vehicle such as car or train. A demolition crane's chained ball seemed physically possible, but hugely unlikely.

So from what height could she have fallen?

The church tower in the village was a good five miles from where she was put on display. The trees weren't tall enough and the woodland ground too soft to produce so much damage.

He decided it could be useful to pay a personal visit to Gervais Plummer at home and show an interest in the house: particularly the rooftops and the terraces that lay below.

Eight

Yeadings produced a warrant card as the lodge keeper approached the ornate gates, but the man had no need of it. 'Mornin', sir,' he said, removing the padlock and opening up by hand. Not for the first time, the superintendent regretted the local press's generous use of a personal photograph.

'Your lot are all over the place,' Holt grumbled mildly. 'Won't let me get to my work no 'ow.'

'And you are...?'

'Adam 'Olt, sir. 'Ead Gardener by profession. But I doubles 'ere when need be. You doan' need to introduce yerself, sir. We all know 'oo you are.'

'I'm bound for the house, Mr Holt.'

'Straight a'ead then, sir, near on 'alf a mile.'

Yeadings followed the instructions, the driveway ending in a gravelled circular sweep with a central fountain which was not playing. Was it switched off out of respect for the dead, Yeadings wondered, in lieu of a flag at half mast? Automatically, his gaze swept up to the central roof. Plummer didn't go in for flags,

97

not even a flagpole. Did that mean he lacked pride in country or family?

He told himself to reign in his idle curiosity about the man. Wasn't that exactly what Plummer intended he should feel?

The double front doors stood open and a tall, well-built woman in jodhpurs came out to greet him. She could have been forty-five or sixty-five. Her salt-and-pepper hair was strained back in an elastic band to end in a graceless knob. Her face was broad-boned and still showed summer tan. She wore no make-up.

'Superintendent.' A whiff of the stables came off her.

'Mrs Plummer? I don't think we've met.'

'Lady Alice,' she corrected him, 'but everyone uses my second name, Fiona. Come along in. I hope I can persuade you to stay for lunch.' It sounded almost a command.

'I'm afraid not, but it's kind of you to invite me.'

'Gervais mentioned he met you yesterday and thought you might follow up with a visit.' The claim sounded almost smug. Spider and fly stuff. 'Actually you've just missed him. He's gone down to Gloucestershire. He'll be back tomorrow.'

'Then perhaps I can talk with you, and take a look at the house? It's impressive. Queen Anne, I imagine?'

'You're out by a year, Superintendent. It's William and Mary.'

He was quite prepared to waffle on at that level. His time was his own and he could afford to play along, letting her derive a certain pleasure from correcting him on details.

He wondered, as so often on meeting a couple, what had attracted them to each other and how the passing years had mellowed, or modified, that first experience. In this case, so disparate – horsey upper-class social dominatrix who had mated with solipsistic philosopher. Was it the attraction of opposites? Or had they at some time assumed these roles and revelled in playing them? Certainly he suspected each of a sly type of humour. Was it playing intimate games that kept them together?

'You'll at least take coffee,' she ordained, leading him into a large, elegant but untidy, morning room. They had scarcely seated themselves in sunshine by a window when a maid came in carrying a loaded tray and started setting a small table between them.

Yeadings considered mild retaliation by declaring himself staunchly a tea man, but the aroma was working on his weakness. The coffee was a distinguished blend. He allowed her to lead the conversation – briefly covering the estate history and the three families who had lived here until Gervais's step-grandfather had taken it over at the end of World War One.

'Armaments,' she dismissed the circumstances coolly. 'Dreadful business really.'

And only then did she refer to the recent

nastiness in Bells Wood, having demolished a jam-filled cream horn in three inelegant bites. She could make nothing of the incident: locals were quite unaccountable, almost medieval in their superstitions. 'There are all sorts of rumours about what they get up to.'

She had told Gervais he was far too lax, allowing them free range over his property.

Yeadings – who was considering her feet, which were large and covered only by beige woollen socks after she'd eased off her riding boots – was startled by the term 'free range' and had an immediate image of the inhabitants of Barrows Village restrictively caged like battery hens.

He pulled himself together to murmur a discreet observation on the shocking nature of the incident and declined to be drawn further.

She gave up on him after he had refused a second coffee and steered wide of the pastries. She'd learned nothing new and he wasn't the challenge she'd hoped for. Quite the country Plod in fact, seeming unaware of being subtly taunted. Gervais had been more impressed by him.

She flicked a glance at her wristwatch. 'Ah, the house. I'm afraid I must leave it to Bowles to do the tour with you. I'm sure he'll make a more thorough job of it in any case. He almost arrived with the foundations.' She rose, scattering pastry flakes, and held out a hand.

Dismissed, Yeadings discovered the butler

had quietly entered behind him and was waiting to act as escort.

'Where would you care to start, Superintendent?'

'I'll leave it to you.' There was more chance that way that he'd pick up on anything the other contrived to skate over. But Bowles wasn't evasive. He clearly loved the building and was accustomed to showing visitors around. A modern lift swept them to the top floor where, besides the servants' bedrooms, which were closed off, and a well-equipped laundry with linen cupboards, he found two small studios, one equipped for photography and the other for art. The first had been used by Miss Gerry, now abroad, and the other was Mr Plummer's, where he painted in watercolours and occasionally produced political cartoons, line and wash, some of which had been published in national newspapers under the pseudonym of Fugit.

The walls of both rooms displayed examples of their work and Yeadings would have liked to spend more time there enjoying them.

'Do you have access to the roofs from here?' he enquired.

'Indeed, sir, and I think you will agree that the panoramic views from there are quite outstanding.'

He opened what looked like a cupboard door and they went up by a twisting stone staircase to a steel door at the top. 'Is this always left unlocked?'

'Except at night, sir. For fear of sleep-walking. Nobody has ever done so, to my knowledge, but one must abide by safety regulations.'

They emerged behind the main gable on to a flat area across which were strung wires to take drying laundry. The height of the three-storey building and the waist-high stone balustrade would have hidden from eyes at ground level the pegged-out tablecloths and bed linen, aprons and intimate underwear ballooning in the wind here.

They walked the entire rooftops, and no-where along the balustrades was there evidence of damage or repair that could explain an accidental fall from this height in recent time. Yet what an open opportunity for someone with a mind to murder.

Yeadings leaned over and surveyed the ground below. Stone-paved terraces were un-softened by flower beds or shrubs to a distance of some fifty feet. He closed his eyes on the image of what might happen to a human body falling from here.

Bowles led him through the rest of the house, only pausing at the open door of any room currently in family use. Ever the policeman, Yeadings noted the couple's separate sleeping arrangements. Their rooms were quite differ-ent: Plummer's simpler, almost monastic, and Fiona's grandiose as though a further reminder that she had been raised as the daughter of an earl. As in her person, it showed a lofty indifference to appearances. The mirror at her dressing-table had mildewed silvering and the heavy silk curtains showed stripes of fading due to the southern aspect.

She didn't reappear, leaving it to Bowles to see him to the main door. He noticed the small formal garden was empty of human or animal life as he drove back towards the lodge. He might have expected a couple of over-friendly dogs, or even a winter-grey peacock trailing a dispirited tail. He assumed his hostess was now reunited with her horses and employed on something pretty vigorous. Near the lodge he found Holt occupying the time waiting for his return by riding a powerful motor mower over grass already approximating to a number-two haircut. He broke off to operate the gates and give a nodded goodbye.

DCI Mott's report of his interview with the Plummer couple had been brief and mainly covered their initial reactions to the incident in Bells Wood. Gervais had been content to let his wife manage the conversation, smiling at her casual complaint that the villagers were 'a strange, inbred lot'. Coupled with the opinion Beaumont had picked up of the servants' attitude to the family, it presented an old-fashioned picture of upper-class detachment from what any of his police team might consider real life. But Yeadings wasn't prepared to write them off as types. Nor did he miss the fact that that had most probably been the casual impression the couple had formed of his anything-but-typical team.

At the bunker Silver had been impressed by the thoroughness of Baz's survey. He remembered then that at college, for all his reputation as a gadfly, his one-time classmate had reached top grades through spasmodic bursts of brilliance, well outshining Silver's results gained through keeping his nose to the grindstone.

The place had been impressive, showing a marked contrast between the obvious intention of installing updated technology and the neglected appearance of the outer setting. Old Chaz and the failing guard dog would shortly be replaced by the modern automated surveillance system Baz was introducing. That could imply that recent press warnings of a return to Cold War conditions were being taken seriously by the present government.

Baz had supplied a light packed lunch for two from the pub where he was staying, and on leaving after a three-hour examination of the complex they dropped in on Chaz where he again plied them with tea.

The elderly guide dog tried to rise as they entered and fell back on her side among blankets on the floor, panting. 'She bin so sick,' the old man told them. 'Gawd knows what muck she bin eating out there. Gone for ages she was.

I 'ad to go and search for 'er.'

They sympathized.

'Won't eat nothing. Which reminds me. Either of you two like baked beans? Because there's a tin the maintenance men left with me. Funny business. None of them could account for it. Found it in the bunker, they said. It just turned up on the floor, almost under some kitchen equipment in the bit they're not meant to use for eating their sandwiches.

'Jest appeared out of the blue, like magic, and they swore it 'adn't bin there on the Friday. Give them a bit of a turn, it did, thinking some-one coulda got in there while they'd gone off, like. Not that they found anything else different from 'ow it was left. Couldn't decide if they oughta inform the authorities, only they'd be in real trouble about slipping away. Might lose their contract, see? Wouldn't do me much good neither for letting them scarper weekends and saying nothing. I jest 'ope some nosey official don't get to 'ear they didn't use their room at the Travelodge for them two nights. They always put in for full expenses and make a bit on the side by going 'ome in the middle.

'So, in the end, they decided not to mention it in their report, and they left me the beans for the dog. Only at present she won't eat noth-ing. So what about you two? I can't stand the things. They make me gassy.'

Silver and Baz exchanged glances. Being offered what the dog had refused! It was as old

105

as a mother-in-law joke. Baz would be busting himself not to laugh out loud.

'Me too,' he claimed solemnly.

Silver wasn't too sure. *Suspect everything* was ingrained Law. He looked at the tin, considered the circumstances – MoD establishment intended to be secret, and the trusted men going on unofficial leave over their duty weekend. They appeared to have taken seriously the possibility of a break-in, so maybe they knew how it could have been done. This smelled definitely off, even if the unopened can of beans looked safe enough.

Both would have handled the can; old Chaz too. So any vital fingerprint evidence would be overlaid. Nevertheless the thing's existence bugged him. He picked it up. 'Maybe I'll give it a home. Thanks, Chaz.' And he slid it carefully into a pocket of his parka.

Baz's engineer was due to start installing the computer system on Monday, and Baz had decided to stay on at the pub where he'd dumped his personal luggage. It seemed only civil for Silver to act host to him in return on Sunday, despite it overlapping with the arrangement he'd made with Jo.

It would mean the two meeting. What would they make of each other? Would Baz's familiar manner offend her? Would Jo, fatally, assume the two college mates were birds of a feather?

Even worse, would he charm her, as he did

106

most women, and it would end with Silver losing her to him?

He had already booked the morning's programme for the pair of them. With fine weather forecast, he proposed to pick her up from the Pimlico flat, enjoy a pre-booked circuit on the London Eye followed by a boat ride up the Thames to Boulter's Lock at Maidenhead. There Baz would collect them, and Silver would stand them lunch at the Angler's Retreat.

The main drawback, he discovered, was that his two-seater MG must be left in London for picking up later. And this meant that Baz would need to drive them back to her home address. After hours in his company, would she be won over by his bouncy personality? Would it be adieu to Jimmy Silver?

Pondering these doubts, and still uneasy over the minor mystery of the beans, he decided to cut short any evening socializing with his friend and seek a sounding board for his new suspicions. DCI Mott was busy with fresh stuff on the hanging girl case and would have no time for this sideline, so Silver headed for the CID office and found DS Beaumont painfully pecking out a report on his day's activities.

'Jimmy, just the man. What'll it cost me for a fair copy, brilliant grammar and faultless spelling?'

Actually that might resolve his dilemma. 'Deliver a verbal on something I picked up today?' he suggested. 'It might be something, or it might be nothing. That'd be up to you.' He slid the tin of beans on to Beaumont's desk.

'From Information Received?'

'Something like that.' Silver retailed the unexplained appearance of the can without admitting how he came to be involved.

'You say he reported it to you, this old geezer who's the guard?'

'Yes.'

'No harm in passing it on, I suppose. Anyway, I promise not to scoff the beans. Sure, get cracking on the keyboard then, if you can read my writing.' He slapped down his notebook and vacated the chair.

Relieved of the responsibility, Silver settled at the laptop, replaced a missing 'r' from the word 'perpetrator' and completed the report in a quarter of the time it would have taken the DS. In Beaumont's absence he sent it through to the incident room.

At home, his father looked up from his book by the fire and surveyed him over the top of his half-spectacles. 'I don't suppose we'll be seeing you for Sunday lunch?'

Silver gritted his teeth, prepared for an interrogation. 'I'm afraid not. I ran into an old college friend today and we set something up together.'

'Not taking out this new young lady of yours then?'

'Oh, she'll be coming along too.'

There was a loud silence.

'Your mother's been wondering, lad, when we might be meeting her.'

Silver felt colour rising up his neck. Why must they treat him as though he was eight years old? He bit back a retort. Voices were never raised in this house. As ever, he had to try and see things from their point of view. But it was a helluva way off the real world. They watched fearsome television crime and pictured him defenceless in it, a prey to scheming women and crazed gunmen.

How could he get them to see he was a white-collar scribe at a computer, in his free time biting his nails over thinking up ways to entertain Jo so she wouldn't discover what a dull dog he was? Her London life had so much to offer, dining out at fashionable restaurants, attending debates at the House, mixing with famous people met through her father's contacts.

He loved his dad and mum. They were his folks and he would face fire and flood to defend them, but once she met up with them she'd see how ordinary he was, and that the treats he'd thought up to entertain her were just desperate attempts to hide how he fell short of what she deserved.

Nine

Monday dawned and Yeadings discovered there had been no giant leap forward in the Barrows hanging case. Considering how the first three days of any possible murder investigation were the vital ones, he regretted that in this instance not only was identification no nearer but the lapse of at least a year from time of death made it, as Salmon had gloomily predicted, a cold case. It was not even certain that they were dealing with a deliberate killing.

Cold, but not closed, he reminded himself with grim determination. If he couldn't directly attack the circumstances of the death, he could work on the way in which the death had been brought into the open. It took a certain kind of mind to be behind it, because the act of hanging the body had no connection with the way in which death had occurred. There had been intentional manipulation.

So perhaps his time spent with Plummer and his wife, enduring their quirkiness and indulging his curiosity about their mode of life, had not been as inexcusable as it might seem. The man, he believed, could mentally be capable of setting up the scene with its possibly mock implication of occult practices. Fiona – Lady Alice, with false modesty calling herself Mrs and answering to her second name – was surely muscular enough to carry out the hanging and was apparently accustomed to dealing with practicalities. He suspected too a detachment that allowed her to plunge into unpleasant situations which would have others recoiling with distaste. Could this melodramatic set-up even have been their combined effort?

But why? Were they likely to bring un-savoury attention to their own home ground?

The present musings were getting him no-where. What he required was factual evidence. He settled afresh to examining the papers on his desk, hoping to find that overnight some hint of advance could be uncovered in them. Apparently not: Sunday inertia had settled over the world and was still hanging around today.

Nevertheless, Angus Mott would at present be briefing the augmented team, and no further press release was to be made yet. Journalists and paparazzi would still be abed after their weekend's liquid exertions.

Someone from the PR office had left him relevant cuttings from the Sunday newspapers and today's which further fanned the public's flaring curiosity about the dead young woman, varying with each imprint's taste for prurient suggestion. In one an artist's impression of the supposed scene showed a Page 3-type exposure in exaggerated detail.

Yeadings scanned and binned the lot, relieved to find DS Beaumont's Limpet hovering shyly at his open door. He waved her in, ready to be distracted.

'Sir, something DC Silver dropped off last night. Nothing to do with present interests, but he thought it was worth a mention.'

The object she placed on the desk between them was covered in a plastic freezer bag. It appeared to be a can of beans. It wasn't a brand he'd ever come across in Nan's store cupboard.

The girl blanched as he swung his gaze back to her. 'Is this some complaint about the canteen?'

'No, sir.' She knew the hazards of being the novice on the job. There were many police versions of the apprentice carpenter being sent for a rubber hammer. But she'd guts enough to accept the challenge and do as she was ordered.

'Sir, it was handed in by the caretaker out at the old Beacons RAF Station. It's been closed down since the Cold War ended, but there's just been a maintenance check there and this came to light where it shouldn't be.'

He was silent, watching her.

'Bit of a lost-cat job, sir, I know, but DC Silver was insistent it meant something.'

'Why didn't he deal with it himself?'

'Free weekend, sir.'

Yeadings remembered then OK'ing the

application over Mott's head. The acting DS had been putting in a lot of overtime and was a valuable team member. 'And he channelled this through...?'

'DS Beaumont, sir.'

Whose sense of humour would have seized on it to plague the girl, of course. It might be only a lost-cat case to the DS, but it would do no harm during the present hiatus if he took a look at this maybe not-so-minor matter himself. The Beacons site had been ranked an emergency Seat of Regional Government and should have been secure against break-ins. 'Do you have the caretaker's name?'

'Charles Sowerby, known locally as Chaz. I wrote down the landline number, sir.'

'Thank you. Is that all?'

'Yes sir, I'm going across to Barrows now to see how far they've got digging in the ice house.'

'Good. I'm hoping ... Excuse me.' He broke off to lift the external phone. 'Yeadings. Yes, well, you know what to do.' His voice sounded unnaturally calm. 'Thank you, Angus.' He replaced the receiver and smiled at the girl.

'A little progress at last. The divers have retrieved a weighted bundle of clothing from the deep end of the lake. Would you care to come with me and see forensics open it up? If the ice house's pull isn't stronger.'

He handed her the BMW's keys. It would be good to get an all-round assessment of her

113

abilities. As she drove he explained why he considered the can of beans not to be the non-starter Beaumont could have thought it.

'Have you ever heard of Urban Explorers?' he asked her. 'They run a forum on their website where they record their exploits, breaking into restricted premises. Illegal actions, of course, but a minor blight. They claim to do it for the sheer buzz, taking nothing and leaving only their footprints. It could be that they've made a successful entry into the Beacons site and this time also left an unwanted part of their picnic.'

'A sort of lads' day out, sir?'

'Exactly, except that there are "ladettes" too among their number. Don't confuse the Urban Explorers with Subterranea Britannica who are legitimate and also run their own website. Their official parties visit the old Cold War installations and write them up for historical interest.'

'I'll look them both up, sir,' she promised earnestly.

Arriving at the Thames Valley forensic labs, they found that the discovery from Barrows Lake had just been handed in. A smaller version of a body bag was unzipped to reveal a rope-bound plastic parcel still mud-smeared with pond water and showing in places the outline of hard shapes bulging through fabric. The object's weight, including these bricks, was found to be near 11.3 kilos. The clothing appeared to be dark-coloured, possibly black. From a glass-panelled observation room Yeadings and Holly watched white-coated experts detach the contents and bag separately for intensive examination.

'Black sweater and black jeans; once-white or cream cotton briefs and brassiere; white cotton ankle socks; black canvas, rubber-soled boots,' was listed through the intercom.

'Female underwear,' Yeadings noted. 'We'll leave it to them to decide how long they've been immersed in water.' He turned away, more than half satisfied that these had been the dead girl's. Forensic scientists would now work overtime to analyse organic traces needed to confirm the DNA matched the victim's. But until he had some reliable list of missing persons for the period in question, that valuable information would lead nowhere.

He recalled the way Professor Littlejohn had regretted that the body was naked. It was essential that he should be informed at once that the forensic lab now had the clothing he had needed.

Yeadings rang the Home Office pathologist, interrupting him during an inquest for a fatal car crash on the A416. Only Littlejohn would have dared to leave a coroner open-mouthed in mid speech.

'Hold everything,' he snapped at Yeadings, 'until I get there,' and abruptly cut the call.

Yeadings passed on the message, consulted

his watch and decided there would be time for a snatched lunch. Over ham and salad sandwiches he hoped to discover a little more about the young policewoman's background. He learnt she had spent two years at Brunel University studying metallurgy before dropping out.

'Had you chosen the wrong subject?'

'No, I loved it, especially the middle of the sandwich course, which was microscopic analysis. Metals can be really beautiful, you know.'

There was no denying her enthusiasm. 'So what happened?' he probed.

She hesitated and he thought he detected a slight flush rising up her neck. But it hadn't been any misdemeanour of hers that finished a promising career. Her father had been fatally injured in a furnace accident and her mother, suffering a mental breakdown, refused permission for her to continue in the same line.

'So you became a PC?'

She nodded, almost shrugging. He made no comment, determined to see that in future she was given some greater challenge than manning a phone which some civilian could easily take over.

They returned to the labs to find Littlejohn's red Porsche parked illegally in a bay reserved for the disabled. Inside, he was already overseeing the initial examination of the clothing.

'Same blood group, AB rhesus negative,' he

told them, looking up as they entered.

'So we've a pretty good guess that it was the hanged girl's clothes?'

'It's rare enough. But what I need now is a chemical analysis on the sweater. If I were a religious man there's something I'd be praying for.'

Yeadings knew him well enough not to press for further explanation. The minute the pathologist had his answer it would be passed on. But that might not be until tomorrow. He guessed that the needed substance would contain traces from the place she had died.

A slammed outer door announced Beaumont's arrival. 'What have we got?' he demanded, bursting in.

Yeadings nodded to Holly Hughes and she reported succinctly.

'So now,' he said, 'I'll relinquish your assistant who has opened up a separate promising can of worms. Or should I say "beans"?'

He caught the swift look of unease in Beaumont's eyes as he turned to leave.

Yeadings chose to seek a private word with a senior clerical officer at the Ministry of Defence. It was two or three years since they had worked together and high time, he decided, to renew the acquaintance.

'Now what are you up to?' was Pete Crabtree's instant reaction. 'Admittedly I'm intrigued, on reading current press reports from your patch. Some kind of devilry going on there?'

'I can't promise there's any connection. Just a little something that's come my way from the neighbourhood.'

'Concerning my department?'

'Could be. Though I think you may share responsibility with Civil Defence. It concerns an old Cold War bunker situated a few miles from the Barrows estate.'

'I know the one you mean. The site's called Beacons, from centuries back when fires were built to pass alarm signals cross-country or to celebrate great victories. As you say, the underground defences were added in the days of atom bomb scares.'

'So what's its security rating now?'

'Ah, for the answer to that you'll need to reach higher up the tree, Mike. It's a bit special, one of the sites reserved for immediate reuse in the event of national crisis. Sorry, but I can't say more. Don't actually know.'

That was meant to keep me quiet, Yeadings appreciated. But it had told him nothing new and he was far from satisfied.

Professor Littlejohn's interest in the black sweater retrieved from the lake had caused it to be passed to Chemical Analysis, where they found examination less complicated than expected. Apart from some slight gritty deposit, minute traces found on the polo neck were no more toxic than a commonly available cosmetic for cleansing the facial skin. It contained glycerine and citric acid, among other substances.

A phoned enquiry to the pathologist – whether a specific brand name was required – was met with an irritable growl. 'Of course it is. I want full details of the maker's name and production address; whether it's a current preparation; the degree of penetration; likely date of application. Everything watertight against courtroom challenge.'

'Got a bee in his bonnet,' the recipient of the message relayed to his lab assistant. 'You've got to watch that one. He's a stickler for accuracy.'

'Just because some sheet-wrapped unknown female chose to remove her make-up before she took her sweater off,' was the sour response.

'Watch it, lad. Littlejohn's one ferret who seldom explores an empty rabbit hole.'

Littlejohn was satisfied that the clothes had produced something more promising than human sweat and blood likely to confirm the DNA samples already under analysis. He decided that Yeadings might appreciate the general finding even before the cosmetic's details were known. He rang through and dangled a suggestion before the superintendent.

'A cleansing agent used on the face *after*

recovery from the plastic wrapping?' Yeadings repeated, puzzled.

'And the same smears on her sweater as applied on the dead woman's face.'

'A mortician's aftercare. Presumably part of the special laying-out – or, rather, hanging up – of the body. But done before the clothes were removed? Any chance of a second DNA there – that of the person who cleaned the body and organized the display?'

'We'll try for it, but my guess is that gloves were worn. Damage to the body was extensive. Nowadays few would dream of attacking blood loss with bare hands. I'm awaiting specific details on whether a professional cleanser was used or the sort every woman has in her beauty box.'

Most females over twelve, Yeadings agreed. But he'd make the exception of Fiona (Lady Alice) Plummer, recalling the leathery texture of her weathered skin. And if someone, possibly a female, had taken such care, first for the face and later for the dead girl's body, wouldn't that imply respect, even love? In which case, it would hardly be the killer. Unless, of course, the motivation had been repentance. And there was still no positive proof that the death hadn't been suicide or even accident.

'Was skin cleanser the only foreign substance found in the clothing?' Yeadings pursued.

'There were also traces of a silver-grey grit on the sweater, jeans and canvas boots. No efforts appeared to have been made to remove these. The same plastic sheeting which once protected the fully dressed body over a considerable period had been used to wrap bricks inside the clothing when dropped in the lake, but these traces were not from them. On first sight they appear to be some form of aggregate. This seems to confirm that the considerable injuries were due to a fall on to a hard surface like concrete, rather than collision with a mechanical object.'

'And chemical analysis of these grains could match them to likely surfaces and lead to the high point from which she fell.'

'So I would assume. At this point,' he added cautiously.

'But whoever picked on the lake as a safe way to conceal evidence was curiously naive. It was surely an obvious place for us to search. Perhaps time was of the essence, and the lake could provide a red herring to divert attention from the person involved.'

'On to the family owning the estate or their staff? Perhaps, but that little quest is not in my remit,' Littlejohn said prissily. 'I leave it to you.'

Quite so, Yeadings agreed silently. And for the first time he felt some positive belief that they might be getting somewhere. Perhaps he should go looking for a local building site with raised scaffolding, where cement fragments could be found. That 'little quest', as the pathologist saw it, could excuse his absence from the executive desk and briefly offer a return to active field work.

He checked for messages on his mobile and discovered that the ACC (Crime) had advised him that he would be visiting at three p.m. He'd want an update on the main investigation, and the fact that he hadn't summoned Yeadings to Kidlington for this meeting meant he expected a personal escorted visit to the site which the national press was feeding to the public as central to his most quirky case to date.

Ten

Yeadings was privately amused to find that the ACC's visit was as much motivated by a relish for the unusual as by a need to check on the investigation's progress. He appeared disappointed to find the site of the hanging was a normal clearing in a rather pretty wood of mixed deciduous and conifer trees with an aged oak at the centre. The crime-scene photographs he'd been shown of the display had been more exciting.

'No bipeds with cloven hooves and forked tails, I'm afraid, sir,' Yeadings apologized, without displaying a flicker of humour. 'Just a normal country house estate. Since we removed the protection tapes I see they've even had the grass close-mown. Nothing of special interest was found. You might care to take a look at the lake, and the ice house which we had hopes of, but was never used to store the body for the considerable period between death and display.'

They lingered at the lake and Yeadings pointed out the padlocked access to the jetty at the deep end where many years back the son of the house had been accidentally drowned.

'Sad business, that,' his visitor commented. 'I remember the fuss made in the local newspaper. The then chief constable attended the child's funeral. I assume you've made full enquiries about possession of keys to the padlock. There's a generous amount of barbed wire on top, but young rascals have their ways of overcoming that.'

He'd been thinking of the scraps of old carpet abandoned on spiked fencing by graffiti artists who'd fled from Aylesbury railway sidings. British Transport Police had sprung a recent ambush there and temporarily cleaned up the gang activity, if not the extensive damage to rolling stock.

As they walked back to the superintendent's car, they were overtaken by the lady of the house at a smart gallop on a handsome, large-boned grey. Yeadings made the expected introductions.

'Tony,' she said shortly and, at their blank reaction, flicked her crop at the snorting animal to include it.

'Er, quite,' murmured the tall assistant chief constable, unused to be stared down on from a superior height. He disliked the smell of horse-flesh, considering the only proper form of sport to be regular weekend golf at Denham Club.

Fiona shook the reins, Tony gave a final contemptuous snort and they were saved further conversation as the lady trotted off.

From a distance Yeadings pointed out the balustrades atop the house and confessed little faith in the girl's injuries having been caused by an accidental fall from there. 'And so far,' he admitted, 'we've no clue to where the body could have been kept concealed for a period of up to twelve or eighteen months.'

'I'm surprised pathology hasn't provided some pointer to that.'

'The body had originally been carefully wrapped, the clothes and covering recently removed and weighted down in the lake. No one on our local list of missing persons fits the description for the probable time of death. She could have come from Land's End or John o'Groats, except that CID there can't offer an identity either.'

'Doesn't a stately home of this period have a chapel in the grounds with vaults for the family? A body could surely have been concealed there for the year unaccounted for.'

'There is a small chapel but the lock was rusted and won't turn. It's dilapidated; hasn't been used since a quiet family wedding back during World War Two. I agree that it would have been the ideal place with the right conditions to account for the body's physical state. But, no, I think we must look for somewhere equally cool some distance away.'

He refused to share his disturbing inability to picture the personality behind the macabre display on the tree. He still felt there were two persons emerging from the imagined scene: one sympathetic enough to the dead girl to take some care for the body, and one with the detachment of a jester, perhaps even malicious, who took over and completed the macabre presentation. Or was it a single complicated character in two minds – either in the psychopathic sense or metaphorically?

'You haven't requested the services of a profiler?' the ACC demanded. His cautious tone implied reluctance to take on extra expense.

'Not at this early stage,' Yeadings reassured him.

Only today the post had brought a curious letter from someone claiming to be a 'forensic psychic'. This lady, mundanely named Maud Button, dismissed the idea of Norse, Druidic or classical references. Nonetheless, her assumptions had been filed along with other odd characters attracted to the exotic case. The killer, she claimed, was an avowed enemy of the state, an anarchist who regarded the victim as part of the Establishment to be removed.

Yeadings had granted the letter five long minutes of consideration and decided that the writer was immature, highly imaginative, possibly politically obsessed and basically patriotic. He was surprised therefore to find that a sombrely dressed matron answering to the name had called at Area in his absence demanding to see him and adamantly insisting on waiting until such time as he should return.

This was a moment when he could have done with passing the interview to Z, but she was on her way to Madeira with Max. Holly Hughes, her female replacement, was as yet untried in diplomacy. There being no one else available he must take on the self-styled forensic psychic himself.

Maud Button showed no offence at having been kept waiting. She apologized for demanding his valuable time, but the psychic message coming through to her had been so strong in this instance that she could not ignore it.

'You claim to be able to profile the person responsible for what the press are calling the "Tarot killing"?'

She tutted impatiently. 'What a lot of nonsense. That connection is mistaken, introduced perhaps as some kind of cover-up.'

This was so close to his own intuitive feeling that Yeadings was tempted to take her more seriously. 'You speak of a "message". Can you describe how this came to you?'

She frowned, pursing her mouth. 'In an unusually personal way. Not as though I caught glimpses of what occurred, from without, which is how it usually happens. This time it was as though I were the one involved. Not the victim but the perpetrator. It was an act of terrible anger, sudden and quite overwhelming, as though in an instant my experience of this living girl was totally wiped out and she appeared as something detestable I had never

dreamed of. I felt terrible disillusion, a posses-
sing fury, a reaction so unthinkably vicious that
I was unable to believe it of myself.'

She covered her face and her hands trembled.
'I'm sorry, Superintendent. You must think I
am out of my mind. But, believe me, I have
never been so moved by any experience in my
lifetime of sharing in others' experiences. It has
left me quite unnerved.'

Her distress was convincing; the outline of
her story less so. He decided the poor woman
was suffering from some repressed toxic memory partially recovered from her own young
life which had returned on her reading of this
bizarre case. She badly needed counselling and
comfort, but he knew that suggestion would be
strongly resented.

He nodded. 'Can you describe the surround-
ings where you say this happened; whether it
was day or night; in rain or bright sunshine?'
His voice was gentle.

'An enclosed space,' she said falteringly.
'Darkness, but there were two points of light.
One moved as I moved. No windows, so I can't
say what time of day or year it was.'

'No windows?' Yeadings picked up. 'Do you
mean you were indoors? Not *outside* a building, on a roof, looking down? Or in open country near cliffs or some steep place?'

The woman shuddered, both hands covering
her eyes. 'I was looking down into a square
pit,' she whispered. 'It was hideous. I could

only just make out her shape below me in the dark. And I knew I had to go back down there, be with her. But I don't remember doing that. The experience ended suddenly. I never saw her close up.'

Yeadings sat silent for half a minute but it didn't provoke any need in the woman to fill the gap. She sat with her head bent, her hands loosely clasped in her lap, like someone expecting a rebuke.

'Mrs Button,' he said gently, 'have you discussed this with anyone before now? Other members of Thames Valley Police, or the media?'

'No one at all. I had to wrestle with myself before asking to see you.'

And the press releases had contained no specific description of the dead girl's broken bones. It had been left to the public to assume the cause of death was some variant on the act of hanging. Only the pathology report had led to the assumption of a fall from a considerable height. There was always the chance of some loose-lipped minor member of the team having divulged the findings, but in that case he would have expected it to result in blazing headlines when he, or she, exchanged the information for hard cash.

'Thank you, Mrs Button.' Yeadings closed the interview. 'I will make a note of what you've told me and I must ask you not to mention our conversation to anyone else. Don't leave this area without informing me in advance. I may possibly need to speak with you again.'

When she had left he made a few rapid notes on his desk notepad and dialled DCI Mott's mobile. 'Angus, I want a list of all lift shafts in buildings within thirty miles of the Beacons estate, domestic and industrial, currently in use or supposedly out of service. Put someone reliable on to that, will you? No fuss, but regard this as top priority.'

Health and Safety regulations were strictly observed for the most part, wherever buildings were suspected of being left in a dangerous condition, but experience had taught him that exceptions slipped through because of construction firms' fear of extra costs. A faulty lift system where the gates had no fail-safe link to the current position of the working mechanism had been reported from time to time on the regional fire chief's reports after random examinations. Failure to ensure instant repair in half-derelict buildings was usually due to confusion over ultimate responsibility.

Much of Maud Button's story might be due to overactive imagination, but somehow, without access to information that only the investigators held, she had happened on circumstances that fitted the material findings. While not claiming any great faith in the claims of the paranormal, in this case Yeadings was willing to meet them – not for the first time – with an open mind.

There'd be no harm, though, in checking the background of the woman who had just insisted on seeing him. He rang through to Acting DS Silver. 'Everything you can find on a Maud Button,' he ordered. 'She possibly has some reputation as a medium, either on stage or in private practice.'

Dawn had always been the favourite time of day for Gervais Plummer and this, as he approached his home county, promised well, darkness lightening into pale silver grey gently shot with primrose until, suddenly the sun shot brilliant gold darts from behind a bank of low cloud straight ahead. Such a scene in earlier years would have challenged him to attempt some watercolour imitation, but he was past that sort of inspiration. It made him melancholy now, when he was at the end of so many things.

He decided not to take the short driveway direct to the house but go by way of Bells Wood and spend a few minutes of farewell at the little lake which had changed his life so tragically.

He would be a young man now; no longer Freddie but Frederick James, maybe in business like himself or in some gentler occupation, taking after Penny who wrote poetry and stories for children.

'My son,' he said aloud. He had been so proud of him. But within hours of his arrival

Penny was gone and the frail little scrap barely surviving, starved of oxygen through the protracted labour. But skilled nursing and agonized prayers had granted him almost eight years of damaged life struggling with cerebral palsy, until at length the water had closed over him and he too had followed the woman his father had worshipped. With him the last trace of her was gone, except in everlasting memory. He didn't need this place any more to remind him. It was all secure in his mind, inviolate. And soon he would be sloughing off all the unnecessary accumulations of the tedious years afterwards. Within days he would be gone, the estate on the market and himself free.

Still several miles away, whether it was sound or smell that first broke through his distraction he couldn't tell, but he knew he was heading towards a burn-out. And then he was suddenly upon it all – the mixed smoke and steam, breathless air, the still flickering distant trees, dark figures rushing with hoses; the huge structure of three fire appliances blocking his path ahead. Dear God, what now?

Staff at the Plummers' home had been roused by an urgent phone call at three fifteen a.m. Revellers returning from a wedding party in Windsor and taking a short cut through Barrows estate, informed them of a great cloud of smoke and flame rising from inside Bells Wood.

By the time emergency services arrived on the scene the whole area of trees was a roaring inferno. Three fire appliances were called, but due to widespread use of accelerants the blaze could barely be contained until well into the evening. Two firefighters had been injured by falling trees.

By dawn, when it was possible to see through steam and smoke between the twisted and blackened trunks it appeared that the central oak in the clearing was undamaged, standing alone among the devastation. The surrounding ground remaining dangerously hot, no approach could yet be made, and forensic examination was delayed until later that day.

'Never seen anything like it,' was the general opinion among the experts as they approached the wood's centre. It appeared that the beeches and birches encircling the Wishing Tree had been devoured without sparks blowing in from any direction to ignite any part of the old oak.

'We've got a weird one here all right,' was the local fire officer's cautious assessment. 'No one's ever going to persuade me this is other than arson. First, there's the residual smell of petrol. And then, as isolation, a concealed sprinkler system set in the grass surrounding the oak had been activated.'

A ripple of excitement ran through the assembling press corps held back by the new barriers. Already they were set to record further headline judgements alongside spectacular shots of the mutilated trees around the sole survivor.

Embers were still smoking when late that afternoon Yeadings ducked under the exclusion tape and followed the single beaters' track through to the white-overalled SOCO team crowded about the oak tree's roots. Disgust filled him as he saw what lay at their feet.

In a pool of congealed blood lay the decapitated body of a white cockerel. The head was separate, nailed to the oak's base as it emerged from the soil.

Eleven

Jeff Wills watched Phil Duffield hesitate at the door, look cautiously behind him and then bolt into the dim interior. He gazed swiftly round the snug, saw Jeff's raised hand and joined him in the secluded corner. 'Barney?' he demanded.

'Ordering. Did you imagine you were followed?' His voice was heavy with sarcasm.

'Can't be too careful. Security's hotting up at work. We don't want talk of a leak from Cold War archives. The check-up's general at present, but too close for comfort. God knows what's alerted them. Nothing they can trace back to me.' Nonetheless, he looked apprehensive.

'Let's hope not. Barney's got the wobblies enough for the two of you.' As he spoke, the firefighter's broad shoulders came into view, pushing back through the wall of bodies hugging the bar counter. He balanced the three pint tankards on the table with a minimum of spilling and, with a grunt to the newcomer, seated himself opposite.

'Cheers,' he said unconvincingly.

They drank, their movements synchronized;

Jeff the first to sit back, wipe his upper lip and scrutinize the others. 'Well, here's a pretty kettle of fish,' he said with heavy humour. 'The Three Mouse Quitters, eh? So what've you been up to since we fled the scene?'

Neither volunteered an answer.

'You deleted the website, like I said?'

Both nodded. 'Not that that's foolproof,' Barney warned. 'It's all still there on the hard drive.'

'There are means. Only nobody's coming to look for it, are they?'

'I'm ditching the laptop,' Phil admitted, 'just the same.'

'Much like Tankgirl musta done a year ago,' Jeff pursued. 'Only she had a bloody sight more reason to do so than us. We shoulda caught a real bad smell off her pulling out of the bunker-breaking. There's no doubt she'd been in there. Only it sure wasn't her body we found. We all saw the pics she'd already posted on the web. Only a back view crawling through a tunnel, but when she picked Tankgirl for a name she musta meant a Chieftain. So the body we stumbled on was the friend she took along: the one she'd "trust with her life". Ironic if the dead girl felt the same!'

'For God's sake,' Barney exploded, 'do you have to go on about it? Do you think I've been able to get it out of my mind? Every night when I'm dropping off I'm back there, bending over that open drawer. Hell, I've found bodies enough in my job, but that ... so unexpected. And it was meant to be a fun day.'

'You didn't have to go stark bonkers and start "rescuing" her, all the same,' Phil ground out. 'It got us all shit-scared, but at least Jeff and I had the wit to grab our stuff and scarper. I couldn't believe it when you came lumbering up that ladder after we'd got out. You and your bloody fireman's lift! What the hell did you think you were at, Superman?'

Barney shook his head. 'It was instinct. Training. No time to think. First rule, you gotta get the bodies out. You've done it dozens, hundreds, of times in practice with dummies; almost as often with the real thing. Adrenalin pumps in. A life-threatening situation – and sheer habit takes over.

'I could see it was crazy when I got out in the open, but I was damned if I was going back. Not for anyone. There was no choice but to get the body taken right away.'

'Well, I'm bloody glad we used your van and not my new Volvo. Have you flogged it?'

Barney's head sank between his shoulders and his voice came out muffled. 'Cleaned it out with bleach next day. Nobody saw us any-where near the bunker or driving over to that wood at Barrows. Hidden by undergrowth, she should have stayed safe for weeks, maybe months. There'd be nothing there leading back to us.'

'Only somebody did find her, didn't they?

Just a matter of days later, there's this weird thing with a girl strung up on a tree there. Didn't it get through your dumb skull it could be the same body?'

Barney groaned aloud and men at the neighbouring table stared across. Phil kicked him viciously on the ankle. 'Well, didn't it?'

'That was none of our doing,' Barney hissed, 'any more than the death was. Like the papers said, it was some twisted devil's sick joke. What kind of psychopath would do a thing like that?'

'Devil or devils, like the papers say – with a spare body turning up to play black magic with. Do you think the police will stop at discovering who did the hocus-pocus stuff? Once they've solved that, they'll dig deeper. They'll want to know how a dead girl got to be there and who killed her. And it could all lead back to us.'

Jeff stirred wretchedly, knowing that Phil took a mean pleasure in baiting the big man. 'It's all covered,' he insisted. 'We've cut our web links with the Urban Explorers forum. Barney's cleaned the van. No witnesses. Nothing left behind at the bunker...'

'Can you swear to that? We took a lot of foodstuff and booze. Did we pack it all back when we scarpered? Try and remember. Go through it move by move. Visualize – we've got into the catering department: the ruddy space-age kitchen the Civil Defence lot had

138

fitted at the ratepayers' expense. All chrome and slate; cookers, dishwashers and waste-disposal units.'

'We'd dumped our backpacks on the floor and started to unpack,' Jeff strove to remember, 'ready for a meal. Camp stove, frying pan, sausages, bacon and beans.'

'Only you'd brought the wrong kind of can,' Barney said scowling. 'It wasn't a ring-top, so we started looking for an electric tin-opener.'

'That's when Phil pulled open that long drawer under the counter.'

'And scared the living daylights out of us.'

Phil grimaced, set his jaw. 'At first I didn't see what it was wrapped in all that plastic sheeting. Then I made out a white face with blood streaks and I knew we'd found a body!

'So what happened next? I know I grabbed my stuff and started packing it back. I never saw what you others were doing. I just made for the ladder back at the opened air filter tower, lost my way once, and then you got in front and were first out. Barney was left way behind.'

Barney's face was in his hands, his voice muffled. 'I remember lifting her out, putting her over my shoulder. Maybe I thought the place was on fire. I kicked the drawer shut and ran for it. She was so light I could hoist her up beside my backpack. I nearly tripped on something rolling on the floor, but I made it back to the top floor, then the passage and the ladder to climb out. When I slid her to the ground you were both already there, laid out and panting.'

Jeff was recalling more. 'Your fingerprints would be on the drawer, Phil. If ever the police get that far...'

'Mine aren't on their records. Why should they be? I've never been in trouble.'

They stayed silent, remembered their drinks, downed them.

Jeff said, 'My round, I guess.' He went to fetch refills.

Barney scratched thoughtfully at his chin. 'That thing I kicked against on the floor. I just wonder: could it have been the can? Did it drop off the counter?'

'Or was it back in someone's pack when we got home?'

'Who knows? Anyway, it was just an ordinary supermarket bean can. The maintenance men could have left it.'

'Except that checking the Civil Defence utilities isn't in their remit. They're a strictly MoD maintenance team. No reason why they'd have access to that area. I should be the only one knowing the electronic entry code. Could be the bean can's still down there, kicked half under a cupboard.'

His face twisted sourly. 'May not be found until World War Three and the bunker's actually in use. Unless, of course, the maintenance team did get hold of the entry code or break it for themselves. Only eight figures and letters.

It wouldn't amount to rocket science. They were only halfway through their job when we...'

Barney scowled. 'You said there's a security scare on at work. Some bright spark may have worked out that some archives stuff had been photocopied.'

'Don't be so bloody cheerful,' grunted Jeff, arriving with another three brimming tankards. 'Actually I was thinking this ought to be our final meet-up for a while. Let things quieten down. Last thing we want is to get dragged into someone else's mischief.'

'Cut connections,' Phil agreed. It made good sense, but it still sounded like the other two were rats running down the ropes, and he could be left on a sinking ship.

Nobody suggested they stay on for a meal. Group games had gone sour on them. On consideration it had always been a pretty naff idea. Trouble was that on their first meeting they'd got pretty pissed at a friend's birthday bash, and seen themselves as three of a kind: laddish buccaneers fit for any challenge. So when Jeff went on about these competitive bloggers he'd found on the net who organized unauthorized entry to semi-secret government installations, they'd got caught up in the craze, recognizing how their individual specialities combined could supply much of the knowledge needed to wipe the board with these mere amateurs.

141

DCI Mott had picked up Sergeant Beaumont
on his way to the new incident at Bells Wood
but, returning later to the nick, suddenly
screeched to a stop, ordered him out and he had
to find his own way back.

It had started to rain, the slow, dogged kind
that warned it could keep it up indefinitely. The
DS was far from gruntled, turned up his collar,
hunched his shoulders and let body language
loudly complain at the unreasonable treatment.
There appeared to be no crime-in-action on the
streets that could merit Mott's incivility; but
there he was, double-parking in a busy shopping area. Serve him right if he got the car
dragged off.

Angus was unaware of any offence, far too
concerned with horrific recognition of the large
plum-coloured pram parked outside a fashion
boutique. That Babe was inside it he never
doubted because a couple of grannies were
bending over waggling their fingers and making all the usual coochy-coo noises. Paula must
be out of her mind, leaving the child unguarded. Anything could happen – baby-snatchers, a
car out of control mounting the pavement...

He bounded across the flagstones. Yes, no
mistake; it was his pram, his baby under the
recognizable covers.

The women made fluttering protests as he
whipped Babe out and cuddled her close. The
little knitted bonnet went askew over one ear.

142

Babe, who had been perfectly contented, wailed in protest. That, surely, should be enough to bring out any neglectful mum.

The shop door remained closed. Angus peered between the swathed models in the window but could make out no familiar figure inside. Could she be actually *trying on clothes* while Babe was left to the mercies of the street? He shouldered the door open and the bell gave a pathetic little *ping* of welcome.

Or was it of denial? Two spindly saleswomen in black and a young blonde customer stared at him agape. They were all strangers. 'My wife...' he started to say but the blonde interrupted. 'Oh, Angus,' she cried, smiling broadly. 'Now you can give us a lift home.'

At her voice he knew her. Last time – the only time they had encountered each other – she'd had brown, curly hair. It had been wet from the bathwater. This, slightly transformed but every bit as unwelcome, was the outrageous girl Paula had employed as a cleaner.

He looked desperately towards the row of curtains that hid the changing rooms. 'Is my wife in here? Why was Babe left outside?'

'Babe,' echoed one of the black-clad women and giggled. 'Like that pig in the Australian film!'

On closer sight, under the make-up, she was no older than this slip of a girl Mott found himself detesting more every moment.

'Pram's too big to get in. And it's heavy.

What you really need is one of those little...'

'Where's my wife?' Angus pursued.

The girl – she'd called herself Giselle, he remembered now – gave a chic shrug, arms akimbo, palms upwards. 'She went out.'

'You took B— the baby, out on your own? Does she know you do this?'

'Well, of course. That's what I'm for.'

Not a cleaner then, but a paid baby-minder, untrained, unprincipled and hideously incompetent.

'Get in the car,' he ordered through clenched teeth. 'I'll see to the rest.'

'Just a tick,' the girl said. 'I've got to have it wrapped.' She gestured towards a pile of silky fabric lying on the counter, the main colours jade green and orange.

Babe had ceased wailing and was snuggling close now, turning her lips hopefully to his chest. He realized there was no proper seat for her in the car. He'd be breaking the law if he tried to drive the pair of them home. Never in a lifetime would he trust the girl to nurse his precious Babe on her knees.

He struggled to get at his mobile and call Beaumont. 'Get back here,' he commanded. 'At the double. I need the car removed. Pick up a passenger from the dress shop opposite and drop her off at my place.'

The Giselle girl was fiddling with a credit card, decided against it and dug in her handbag for a substitute. He left her to it and carried

Babe back outside, transferred her to her own transport. The two elderly ladies were still there a few paces off, awaiting events.

He faced them doggedly. 'I'm taking my baby back home.' Almost echoing Nat King Cole, he thought foolishly.

One woman nodded. The other looked doubtful. What's the betting, he asked himself, that she ponders it all day and finally reports a suspected male baby-snatcher to the police?

Ignoring persistent hooting from traffic beyond his abandoned car, he tucked the covers snugly in the pram, raised the rain hood further and set off, pushing briskly. Halfway down the block Beaumont passed him running all out.

I would think it's just one of those days, Mott told himself as his rage began to subside a little; except that starting with the diabolical practices at Bell Wood, and now this, there never has been another day like it. I hope to God there never is again.

He almost threw his car keys at the DS.

Beaumont arrived before him, the car parked before his front door and the girl just inserting a latchkey in the lock. So Paula must have come up with a replacement for the back door one he'd confiscated. He followed her in, carrying the baby.

'Wait in the car,' he told Beaumont brusquely as he made to join them in the hall.

He felt anything but ready for dealing with the situation, drenched to the skin because he'd been driving in his shirtsleeves. The damp cotton clung to his flesh. Even Babe had given up nuzzling for a teat. He laid her, protesting, in a deep armchair, knowing it wasn't ideal. She started bawling at full lung power.

Giselle had marched straight in and was heading for the stairs. 'The door,' he bellowed. 'Go back and shut the bloody door.'

His mobile had been left in his jacket which was still in the car outside. He reached for the landline, flicking back damp tendrils of hair, and pressed in Paula's number. There was no answer.

It meant leaving a message. He took a deep breath. 'Wherever you are, Paula, for God's sake get back home right now.' His urgent tone reinforced by Babe's vocal backup should bring her running – if and when she picked up the call.

The girl had disappeared upstairs clutching her wrapped purchase from the boutique. Just as well. He couldn't trust himself yet to sort her out. And wasn't it Paula anyway who'd let this situation arise? *She* was the one who'd picked on this wretched incompetent to look after Babe and casually leave her at risk in the street.

He went through to the kitchen, seized a towel and started rubbing at his hair. He tore off his shirt and threw it in the sink, switched on the kettle, reached for the instant coffee.

It was then that he heard a key in the front door and voices as Paula let herself in. He walked into the passage and was confronted by his wife and an unnecessary visitor.

'What on earth...?' Paula began. 'Oh, heavens, the din!' She ran into the lounge to pick up the squalling infant. 'Angus, you know not to leave her howling like that. What were you thinking of?'

He stood shirtless facing the detestable Oliver Goodman, one-time fellow student with Paula at King's, junior partner in the firm working on her to return to active court work.

'Come on in, why don't you?' he snarled as Goodman started shedding his overcoat.

'Bit of a domestic fracas?' asked the solicitor silkily. 'Bad time to call. Just returning the wife after a business brunch. How's yourself then?'

Angus received a full blast of alcohol on the man's breath. He'd thought the day couldn't get much worse.

He'd been wrong.

Twelve

He wasn't allowed to go beyond the outer police tapes, but when the local fire officer recognized Gervais Plummer, he ducked under and came out to have a word. On hearing the landowner's name mentioned, DI Salmon eagerly followed. His eyes narrowed at sight of the man's appearance. Here, he told himself, was someone who'd slept the night in his car. And someone with a more than comfortable home to return to would normally have no need.

Plummer made no attempt to straighten his jacket or return his MCC tie to a seemly knot. He felt comfortably crumpled, and some of the pleasure of his leisurely drive through the dawning countryside remained undimmed by the sight and stench of charred woodland. He even felt a wry humour at the secret thought of what he had had in mind for it. Salmon noted the faint smile and decided that here was someone worth looking into further.

He placed a hand on the car's radiator. The heat given off was evidence enough. 'Have you driven far, Mr Plummer?' he probed.

'What's that?' Vaguely he turned his gaze from the ruined woodland and took in the inquisitorial face. He rightly assumed that this was a mid-rank policeman.

'I asked if you've come some distance. Overnight.'

'Quite far enough, but a pleasant run mainly, thank you. Not a lot on the roads by the route I came. I prefer the leafy lanes, avoiding heavy goods traffic.' He sounded totally relaxed.

His gaze returned to the devastated trees of his own estate. 'Not so leafy here at the moment. How on earth did this come about?'

He had addressed this to the fire officer whose blackened cheeks were marked with wet trickles of sweat.

'That'll be for us to find out, sir: source and origin. But you can safely rule out spontaneous combustion.' Vic Grant had his own brand of grim humour.

'Human intervention?'

'That's one way to put it. A spot of midnight mischief, at a rough guess.'

'There was more than the fire?'

Grant hadn't a chance to answer. Salmon darted in first. 'Do you have any reason to expect that, Mr Plummer?' It was suspicious how unfazed the man was over what must be a considerable financial loss, apart from the spoiling of his amenities.

Plummer turned mild eyes on him. 'As a policeman, you must be aware how a pattern

149

seems to be emerging from incidents about here. Fire attracts attention. For what purpose? What is on display here this time?'

It was uncanny, Salmon decided. Or else the man had pre-knowledge. It seemed unlikely he'd have had a hand in it himself, but it wasn't beyond belief that he'd been receiving threats and so expected hostile acts. It was of prime importance to get some information on his business affairs; see what enemies he'd made on his way up.

'Amazing,' Plummer murmured as if to himself, 'how fast nature reasserts itself. Not the best time of year for new shoots to start up, but a couple of years on and there'll be a pretty little copse of young growth.' He nodded to the two men, climbed back in his car and drove carefully off.

Salmon scowled after him, frustrated. He was eager to take questioning further, but uncertain as yet in what direction to steer it. Plummer was not his run-of-the-mill suspect and had a way of looking through you that left you feeling almost uncomfortable.

There seemed nothing left to do here. Mott and Beaumont had already pulled out, leaving only himself from CID. Uniform were assembling, prepared to get on with the next fingertip search of the area between the devastation and the untouched oak. The SOCO team could be left to bag up whatever they could find of traces from the vandals. This time there was no call for a pathologist, with a cockerel for victim.

Vandals or something more? Salmon was distinctly uneasy about what had been done around the old oak tree. An unquestioning Methodist of the old school, he had once accompanied his wife to a crowded service in a little country church where people had suddenly started 'speaking in tongues'. While stoutly disapproving of the ostentatious self-display, and the readiness of others to stand up and authoritatively translate the content of the meaningless jumble, he had been left disturbed by something outside his personal experience.

Even while condemning the whole business as theatrical hysteria, he had had to accept that those involved appeared to be totally convinced that they were possessed by 'The Spirit'. Was it so much beyond acceptance that others equally suggestible should see themselves as servants of an evil power that required animal slaughter and destruction by fire? The world had deluded fools aplenty.

And if so, what connection had there been with the Tarot-like hanging of a woman's broken body on a tree which for decades had been considered to have magical properties? And where had she been hidden away between death and this display so much later?

Yeadings could be wrong in dismissing the strange happenings as mere mischief by village lads stirring up undeserved fears of devil-worship in order to put Barrows on the map, exciting wild press speculation with made-up stories of chanting figures spied dancing naked by torchlight at full moon. Such mischief did happen, young people being what they were, but there still remained the possibility that others were involved with quite different motivation.

His mobile vibrated and he clapped it to an ear. Young Silver had been unable to raise DCI Mott and wished to pass on new information. 'Hold on until I can get in,' the DI snapped.

It was starting to rain steadily, which made staying on here out of the question. And if Angus Mott was off the scene, Salmon decided that this could be an opportunity to get a step ahead of his over-promoted young boss.

Oliver Goodman was quietly relishing the situation. Briefly he'd thought of accepting Paula's assumption that he would stay on for coffee, but then thought better of embarrassing Mott further. It might, after all, be expedient to butter the man up in case Paula needed to overcome his strong opposition before taking on the Sylvester Carling defence. Her baby was only a couple of weeks old and it seemed Angus was falling into the role of besotted new father. There had always been the possibility that he would oppose her returning to the courtroom before the infant was of school age.

What a waste that would have been. With all

that London experience at the Old Bailey and Law Courts, she stood head and shoulders above anyone available locally to take on his potentially profitable case. It could last for months and establish a new reputation for the family firm when she became an established member of Chambers.

The police had built a strong case with CPS backup and thankfully, since it was a charge of fraud, the Yeadings team had not been involved in its preparation. Having the married couple slog it out face to face in a protracted court-room battle would be, he accepted, almost impossible at present. But give it a couple of years for her success here to spread and the financial benefits to circulate, then Angus would give up trying to persuade her into the ill-paid Crown Prosecution Service.

Another aspect was that Oliver hadn't lost any of the fondness for Paula he'd felt when they were students together. A gradual easing apart from the ambitious detective chief in-spector who'd swept in and prised her off him couldn't come amiss.

'Look guys,' he offered now, 'time's a-wast-ing and I know you've a lot on your plates, just as I have. So I'll be off. We must meet up again soon. Maybe do a meal out together when you can both fit it in.'

Mott clamped his mouth tight and saw him to the door, shivering there at the cold slap of wind on his bare flesh. He resisted the temptation to say, 'See you in court.'

Back in the lounge, Babe had ceased wailing and was being rocked in Paula's arms. She looked hard at him. Angus hardly knew where to start. He suspected that behind her annoyance his wife wasn't far from repressing a giggle at his appearance. He paused opposite the staircase, one hand on the newel post, and opted for dignity before catechism. He could deal with the Giselle situation better when fully clothed.

DI Salmon was prepared for spectacular revelations on Jimmy Silver's computer. Instead, his researches appeared to have been based on a tin of baked beans. It was incomprehensible and had nothing whatever to do with the principal case under investigation. A further connection with a flight by hot-air balloon, taken in Silver's free time and involving aerial shots of an equally irrelevant area, had him almost choking with irritation.

There were so many other directions in which the young geek could turn his technical skills. Paramount at present were the significance of ritual slaughter of white cockerels and the business history of Gervais Plummer, a man of some substance who must in his business career have stepped on many toes and probably profited at others' expense. Salmon delivered a stern reproof on time and expertise wasted.

'The Boss thought it was worth following up,' Silver dared to protest. 'He's such a stickler for detail, and it struck him, me too, that there were too many coincidences turning up.'

'Such as?' Salmon demanded witheringly.

Jimmy refused to be withered. 'The yearly visits from a maintenance team under MoD instructions at a one-time defence bunker not more than nine miles away from Bells Wood. The possibility that an intruder or intruders had broken in and overlooked the can on leaving. The time lapse between the last two visits being about the period the body could have lain hidden in a place with the atmospheric conditions required to preserve it in the way that it was...'

Salmon's fist came crashing down on the desktop, causing a mug stuffed with pens to rattle dangerously near the edge. Jimmy reached out a swift hand to steady it.

'I never heard such far-fetched nonsense. It's birds' nests from China,' Salmon ground out. It even topped the ridiculous suppositions he'd entertained for a few minutes about devotees of some pagan god worshipping round the oak tree and torching the woodland on leaving.

But at least that had been based on observation of actual events. This rigmarole was all the frenzied invention of an over-imaginative and over-promoted lad barely out of his teens and good only to sit at a computer.

To think that this wild theorizing had caused

him to quit the site of the most recent incident in their central case made him furious. He felt hot blood rising up the back of his neck to flood his face. It was such diversions that wasted police time, ran up astronomical bills on overtime.

He should have stayed on, followed Plummer back to the house at Barrows and satisfied himself about what the man had been up to overnight. It wasn't beyond belief that he had set up the whole business himself to extend publicity, driven some way off to establish an alibi, and then returned to be spectacularly unamazed on seeing what had occurred.

Yes, Plummer was certainly worth investigating. Too much time had already passed since they spoke together. He'd been allowed to get home and sneak into fresh clothes. What excuse had he produced to account for being out all night? Might there even have been a notable flare-up between husband and wife over his absence?

The DI slammed out of the office, barely catching what Silver shouted after him. Something about Superintendent Yeadings getting in touch with someone at the Ministry of Defence to try out the bunker theory.

Waste of time, Salmon grumbled silently. But then he knew the Boss welcomed quitting his desk to look up outside contacts, dissatisfied watching the paperwork pile up there. Even worse the computerized data, because he belonged to the pen and ink generation; hand-wrote copious diary notes, no detail too small. Maybe he hoped one day to publish them like minor politicians did to drop their colleagues in the mire.

'This Giselle,' Mott challenged his wife, less steamed up by now but determined to be firm. 'She has to go.'

'Giselle? Do you mean Gabriela? She's invaluable, Angus.'

'Is that what she calls herself to you? I'm sufficiently practised in remembering names, Paula. She's quite a fantasist, thinks she's settled in as a member of the family. Do you know where she was when I saw the pram unattended and Babe in it?'

'No. I'm sure she'd have been nearby.'

'In that boutique in Saxby Street, trying on a dress.'

Paula was silent a moment. 'That's not good. So you mean you snatched the pram and wheeled it back home?'

'In a downpour.'

'Leaving Gab— whatever she's called, to drive your car?'

'Beaumont was to hand; he drove her back. The point is she's totally irresponsible. She has to go. Didn't you ask her for references, testimonials?'

'They were impeccable.'

More fictions, he supposed. 'D'you know

157

where she was when I first met her?'

He was unaware of a light step on the lower stairs as the girl hugged the newel post, smiling her pussy-cat smile.

Angus poured out his complaints. 'What's more she'd been sleeping in our bed. Her underclothes were still in it. For all we know she's had a man in here while you've been out.'

'Angus, I don't make a habit of leaving the baby with her. It was just twice. Oliver had a proposition. A very important case coming up and he wanted my opinion.'

'A criminal defence?' he asked, at last openly suspicious. 'He wants you to take it on.'

'Fraud. Nothing in your line. It would mean such a lot for his firm as they've been having a hard time since the credit crunch, and I owe Olly. He's been very good to me in the past, when we were at King's.'

'I bet he was. And he hasn't given up, has he?'

'I hope you're not implying anything nasty. Anyway, this isn't about me. It's about your *Giselle*, who's standing right behind you.'

He turned. The girl stood there doing cheesecake in the new orange and green silky creation.

'Like it?' she asked Paula. 'I think it really suits me now I've gone blonde.'

'Is this right, what my husband says? You left our baby in her pram on the street while you were in a fitting room? Anything could have happened. And our bed – you actually slept in it while you were supposed to be looking after her here?'

'She was in her cot. Went down like a lamb after her feed. No trouble at all. I think she rather likes me.'

'I'm not sure that I do,' Paula decided after a moment of closed eyes and an attempt to suppress her temper. 'Angus, pay her off for the rest of the month, will you? And get back the door key.' She turned a freezing glance on the girl. 'And whatever your real name is, I don't want to come across you again, ever.'

Salmon need not have hastened his departure from the nick. Gervais Plummer had entered the house, observed only by the butler-valet, and enjoyed a leisurely hot bath and shave, presenting himself downstairs just a little late to ring for afternoon tea. As if by telepathy Fiona came in dressed in a sweater and jeans to peer inside the sandwiches on offer. 'Hmm, egg and cress or smoked salmon and cucumber again. They've no imagination in the kitchen.'

'You could try ordering something more to your taste,' Gervais offered mildly, thinking that perhaps hay and raw carrots would suit her. He doubted she'd noticed he'd been away for a couple of days. 'What have you been up to of late?' he enquired to start her off.

'Perry's gone lame on his right forefoot. Not a case for the vet though. I'll deal with it.'

'Of course, who better?'

'Oh, and vandals set light to Bells Wood in the night. Did you know? I tried to get a look at it, but the place was swarming with police and firemen.'

'I noticed something as I drove back from my visit to Gloucestershire. Were you going to ask how I got on there?'

He was interrupted by Bowles's polite cough, entering to announce the visit of yet another member of the CID. He hesitated, uncertain whether to hand over delicate china for the visitor's use. Gervais waved it to the table. 'Ask him in.'

Perched on the edge of an upright chair between the two loungers, Salmon was embarrassed by double handfuls of fine china and the requirement to help himself to thinly cut sandwiches. It was easier to opt out. This wasn't what they called teatime at home, which was set out with knives, forks and more substantial fare at any time after six thirty.

He clattered the filled cup, saucer and plate together, stuffed the linen serviette underneath and found a small space on the table to get rid of them. 'I need to ask you some rather personal questions, Mr Plummer,' he threatened. 'Such as where you spent the hours of darkness last night.'

'I thought I'd told you already. Most of it driving back from the West Country, Cheltenham to be precise. I stopped off on the way at about half one to snatch a spot of sleep, well off the road in woodland, which I also made use of for a timely leak. So if you wish to examine my clothes you may well find the odd leaf or muddy twig ground into the soles of my shoes. But no smell of smoke, I assure you. Time was that I indulged in the odd cigar, but gave up eventually on medical advice. The ticker, y'know.'

'Actually, sir, I do require your clothing bagged up for examination, under the circumstances,' he admitted, grim-faced.

'There now, I'm a suspect. Isn't that really something?'

'And I shall require names of reliable witnesses who can vouch for your presence up to your driving back. Am I to understand you were alone in the car?'

'Apart from the pair of call girls I picked up before leaving,' Gervais exclaimed merrily. 'No, that's a joke. I was alone under the stars and blissfully content.'

'What *were* you doing in Cheltenham?' Fiona demanded, showing some interest at last. 'We don't know anybody down there.'

'Exactly. I was just about to tell you when Inspector Salmon was introduced. I was buying a small property, quite modest as befitting a retired gentleman with no family.'

'You intend leaving Barrows?' Salmon asked, eyes narrowing.

'Oh yes, I've finally had enough of it here.

Barrows is on the market.' He smiled across to his astounded wife. 'I'm afraid, my dear, that you'll have to turn your hand to house-hunting.'

Thirteen

Mike Yeadings read through the latest reports on printout, Beaumont's referring typically to Murder Most Fowl. But the incident hadn't been humorous. It signalled someone's willingness to encourage the growing reputation of Bells Wood as a place where occult rituals were observed.

Or, remotely, it was the real thing. Nothing could be entirely ruled out. The glaring obstacle to the investigation's progress was the failure to identify the girl's body which had set off the whole inquiry.

On the purely practical and mundane side, complaints received of stolen white roosters now numbered four, and more might be expected once the news circulated. He wondered whether the competing claimants expected compensation, or whether self-publicity in a notorious context was enough.

The investigation's initial report on the fire had been verbal, but Yeadings had made detailed notes of findings to date. The accelerant used had been unleaded petroleum as commonly retailed for the majority of cars locally.

163

No containers had been left at or near the source of the blaze. The clearing and vicinity of the oak tree had been protected by an efficient lawn sprinkler system activated by the presence of heat and smoke. This proved that the cockerel decapitation had taken place before the torching cut off retreat. The surrounding woodland as far as the little lake appeared almost entirely burnt out, which must rank as a hostile act aimed possibly at the landowner but also regrettable for the public who were allowed free access.

The malicious intent angered Yeadings, though he accepted that fire had its creative aspect and in time the land could even benefit from young regrowth.

Nevertheless Plummer's apparent lack of concern, as reported by DI Salmon, was surprising, particularly since it almost immediately came to light that he had already decided to put the entire estate on the market. Such vandalism must have considerably reduced its value.

It was a curious time to have chosen to sell, when markets were still slow from recession and Barrows was gaining notoriety either as a centre of witchcraft or a target for outright malice.

He regretted he hadn't been present to hear Plummer's surprise announcement and observe his wife's reaction. The DI was less capable of picking up the nuances of behaviour and was clearly put off his stride by the man's complex personality.

'Casual' was the bare description Salmon had given of his tone, but Yeadings guessed there were multi-layers of feeling and innuendo beneath the throwaway manner, which Fiona had been meant to pick up. The man had chosen his moment for the revelation with care, and Salmon had supplied a bonus with his presence, making it almost impossible for her to realize all at once the magnitude of the insult contained in the lack of consultation and long-delayed turning of the unconsidered worm. In a single sentence she was sloughed off, left to fend for herself, to start thinking beyond the box of her horsey interests.

There would be no lack of funds, Yeadings felt sure. Plummer would find almost any price worth the prize of gaining personal freedom.

In this single, brief act the quiet man had opened out what intrigued Yeadings from first meeting – the enigma of the couple's relation-ship. On his side it now appeared as veiled hostility born of long-term recognition of their total incompatibility; while she had been con-tent to supply her own needs without any effort at communication.

However the marriage had begun, they had run out of the need to make it work. The daughter they had made together was gone, the stepson drowned when young.

While begetting young should not be the only

bond that held parents together, yet if they had stayed a family the outcome might have been more rewarding. But Geraldine had sought pastures new, leaving behind a soured reputation.

Not my business, Yeadings told himself, but he found it sad and something else – *unnecessary* because, with some effort in common, life could have been so much better.

Once the discomfited Salmon had departed, carrying a zipper bag containing the clothes Plummer was wearing on the previous day and night, the recriminations began. At storm level.

'Think about it,' Plummer cut through quietly, rising and walking to the door. He turned to look at the furious woman. 'Eventually this could be what will really suit you best.'

Feeling he had discharged his duty here, it remained to break his news to the resident staff. That must be more delicately handled. They had given good service and deserved consideration in securing their futures.

He made his way down to the kitchen where they were gathered round the immense Russian teapot; accepted a steaming cup, having left his own untasted upstairs.

'I have something to tell you all, and I'm afraid it may be quite a shock.'

In the superintendent's office, his external phone rang. He lifted the receiver and recognized the studiedly smooth voice of Jock Halliday, at one time his replacement DS in the Met and now working in Special Security for the Ministry of Defence.

'Mike, my apologies that I was not immediately available. Your message intrigued me. I could make it an early lunch tomorrow if that would suit you.'

'Something a little sooner would be better. Can I meet you from work tonight? It's something I don't want to pass on over the phone.'

There was the slightest of pauses. 'Can we do it now by scramble?'

'Sorry. I don't have the facility here.'

'Then I'll be with you within the hour.'

Angus Mott was glad to plead pressure of work and leave the two females to sort their problems. He was angry – no, *disappointed* – at Paula's slackness in not having followed up the girl's references, which experience taught him could be fictional.

There had been too much haste in finding someone to take over care of their baby. Paula had acted without prior discussion. If help was truly needed during these early days then he was prepared to opt for a qualified nanny with a sound track-record. Any expense was better than wearying Paula while she was still in a fragile state. His mother had once said that a first baby took a good six months to recover from physically.

Paula had spoken of part-time help in the house. That was why he had been so shocked at the girl taking over childcare, assuming that Paula had been seeking more freedom to be with her new baby. But apparently Babe wasn't her main priority. Paula had handed her over without due caution to an immature stranger, seduced by the offer to extend her career. And behind this seduction, as he saw it, was the detested smug face of Oliver Goodman.

Beaumont was at the wheel. Angus sat seething beside him, cursing the slow traffic under his breath. For God's sake, he tried telling himself, it's Babe who matters. She has to come first. I see the point now of fathers getting paternity leave. That's why Yeadings had mentioned it to him only a week ago, but he hadn't picked up the point. And 'Babe' – they couldn't go on calling her that. She was a small person with a right to a name of her own.

Among the last three names Paula had suggested was one he'd quite fancied. He decided to regain his office and ring home, make sure there were no brickbats flying. He'd tell her then that he'd fallen in with her choice.

When Paula answered the call there was a satisfying background of quiet. Then he picked up the rhythmic susurration of the infant sucking on her bottle. A pause came while she was given time to take breath, then a tiny cry of frustration before the sucking resumed.

'Sorry to interrupt a feed,' he said. 'I wanted

to be sure everything had gone quiet.'

'Bat ears,' she said, almost fondly. 'I'm glad we had all that settled. That young woman was pretty awful, I agree. Anything else?'

'Only that I've decided Astrid sounds pretty good. Special enough and it'll still be suitable when she's grown up.'

'Astrid it is then. And how about Susannah after it?'

'I'll give it some thought. Something else though: I love you a lot, Paula.'

He caught her murmured reply. When he got a chance he'd speak to the Boss about taking a couple of weeks off. But only after they'd cleared up the present log jam of cases.

Jock Halliday was as good as his word, in fact better. It was forty-nine minutes after his call that the duty sergeant at the desk rang up to announce he was waiting in reception.

'What was it this time? A supercharged Lamborghini?' Yeadings asked, impressed by the prompt appearance.

'Actually we'd a chopper just arrived on the roof. It flew me to Denham and they had a taxi waiting.' He made it sound modest enough, but obviously he was now playing among the big boys. 'So where's the nest of wasps you're about to produce, Mike? I know it wouldn't be anything less.' He seated himself on the window sill, his long, skinny legs outstretched.

'Could be nothing, could be something,'

Yeadings told him and explained a simple can of baked beans had sent his antennae waving.

Halliday listened impassively. 'And this connects with your present supposed diabolical business at Barrows?'

'I don't like coincidences. There are times and places factors. As for diabolical, that's the exotic press version fanning local gossip. However, I'm convinced these incidents started with something more than laddish mischief. We can't discount the cold fact of a death, however it came about. And there's solid motive behind the macabre way it was brought to our notice.'

Halliday nodded. 'And we both have learnt that the devil's in the detail – in this case your modest supermarket can of baked beans.'

'Am I getting fanciful in my old age?'

'We call it maturity, Mike. Remember political correctness. Anyway we're both still well short of the half-century.'

'But how do you rate it?'

'As worth asking some questions in the relevant department. We'll see what comes up on your Cold War bunker, get the maintenance team over a barrel, threaten to cancel their contract. I'll send my best terriers in on it.'

He unfolded from his seat, waved a limp hand and excused himself with, 'My carriage awaits. Good to catch up with you again, Mike. Let's have that lunch I owe you, at your earliest.' And he was gone.

* * *

Paula put Babe – correction: now officially Astrid – over her shoulder and gently patted her back just as the nurses had shown her. Instead of satisfying, resounding burps, a single stream of undigested milk came flowing over the towelling to soak Paula's silk shirt.

'Oh, you disgusting little creature!' she scolded, holding her at arm's length. 'No, really, I don't mean that. I do love you. At least I'm trying hard to. You'll have to learn about compromise. Then we'll get along all right. Just give me a break now and then.' Otherwise, she admitted to herself, I'll end up shaking you, no better than those bad mothers who end up in court because they can't stand a child screaming any more.

Astrid's head was lolling. It did seem that she might be ready to go down in her cot. Paula lowered her in. The tiny legs rose in the air, bunched once, uncurled and subsided. Set flat on her back as the book instructed, her head turned sideways and her eyes closed. 'Brilliant!' her mother told her. 'You see, you can do it once you get the hang.'

She crept away, closing the door softly, to phone Oliver from the staircase. She needed to make her peace with him, explain the demanding circumstances, in case as a mere man he hadn't picked up on it.

'Angus has decided we need a proper nanny,' she ended.

'Splendid! That'll solve everything. And maybe I can help you there. We must have someone reliable we've acted for in the past. Leave it to me and I'll come back on it.'

At Barrows a more distracted woman was also putting through a phone call; this one long distance to a mobile number. She had fortuitously happened on a wakeful hour in Marrakesh and Gerry was about to leave for the airfield. 'Mother, is this you? Whatever's the matter?' she asked sharply.

'Oh, you just won't believe,' Fiona wailed. 'Your father's out of his head. He's selling up here and going off to live somewhere on his own. God, he's as bad as you now. It's the end of everything.'

'Of Western civilization as we know it? You're starting to sound like fucking Monty Python. Pull yourself together, Mother. You know Dad. He won't leave you destitute. Just do the same, cut free. Go your own way.'

'I could come out to you.'

'Swap horses for camels? You're not built the right way.'

'Have you still got that disgusting man with you?'

'He's not disgusting. And no.'

'He's coloured.'

'As you are. Like weathered leather.'

'Gerry, you aren't even trying to understand how appalling—'

172

'I gave that up way back, Mother. Listen, I have to go now or I'll be late for the flight. Like you told me before I left, "you've made your own bed"; now do the obvious thing. Goodbye.'

Fiona tore at her hair. Those accursed hot-air balloons! Her father should never have indulged her, buying out that dangerous outfit. It had encouraged her outrageous sense of rebellion, gave her carte blanche to chase seasonal tourists all over the world. Now there was nobody left here. She was totally alone and quite literally seeing red.

She sat, fists bunched, searching for some way to alleviate the devouring fury inside. Her whole body was shuddering.

Around her the house was unnaturally quiet. If Gervais had dropped his bombshell on the servants they'd be clustered in the kitchen recovering from the blow. God knows what they would produce for dinner tonight, if anything at all.

She went to the foot of the stairs and listened, then two by two she took the steps towards the top of the house.

There was a brief moment when she could have stopped herself. She knew and admitted it at the time. The action then was deliberate. She let herself into his studio which he always left unlocked except when he was at work inside – another insulting example of keeping himself apart. At such times his refuge was inviolate.

She opened the through door to where Gerry used to process her photographs. It was exactly as she'd left it, an open handbag lying on the window seat, her make-up and smoking things clearly in sight. Fiona sat there until the shaking had subsided, but the fury burned on.

It was after eight o'clock when the first alarms went off. By the time anyone could reach it the whole of the top floor was ablaze.

Fourteen

Yeadings had called the nuclear team to his office for what he insisted wasn't a debriefing but a parley, just to round the day's work off.

'Maud Button?' he invited Silver.

He'd turned up quite a lot on her, despite being busy chasing up the origins of the can of baked beans, which Salmon had considered a total waste of time and then set him searching for occult rites involving the slaughter of white cockerels.

Silver rattled the single sheet of printout. 'Born Maud Jones, married George Martin, 1979, one daughter, Cara, born 1982. Second marriage to Philip Button, 2002, now dissolved.'

'Lucky she wasn't called Pearl,' Beaumont murmured aside. 'Maud, I mean.'

The others stared at him, registered it would have been a sort of pun and moved on.

Silver resumed. 'She's been mentioned quite a bit in local newspapers since she's gone public with this ESP business. Originally she trained as a teacher, taught at three separate private schools before adding a nursing certificate and becoming a registered child-carer. She moved in with a succession of well-heeled families with problem children. In the most recent she was kept on after the death of a twelve-year-old girl by hanging. The inquest jury found the child had accidentally taken her own life while playing alone on the staircase with a skipping rope. It had happened on Maud's day off.

'The mother suffered a nervous breakdown and Maud was retained as her companion and confidante. They became very close, Maud encouraging Mrs Fry's yearning to get in touch with the dead child. She joined her in table-tapping and Ouija board experiments and claimed some success. Over a period it seems that Maud organized seances and gained some local reputation as a medium. The mother financed a psychic research group and paid to publish their findings. It was after a police inspector in Dorset called Maud Button in to help trace a missing boy, that she first assumed the description of forensic psychic.'

'I remember that,' said Yeadings. 'She took three shots at describing where the child's body was hidden; hit target on the last, which was a blocked-up culvert under a country lane. The child had been dead for about ten days by then.'

'Go on guessing long enough,' Salmon suggested sourly, 'and you're bound to get somewhere near the truth.'

'Our enigma's in reverse. We have the body, and lack anything leading up to it, despite the lapse of at least a year's concealment. Plenty of scope there for some Delphic theorizing on what might have happened. So, the lady approaches us with an unsolicited offer to help and claims to be a forensic psychic.

'She begins by discounting totally any occultism in the mock-Tarot display of the hanging body, offers no leaked imagery of the dead girl but quotes a "personal experience" of overwhelming anger and standing inside a building, gazing down from a height at something terrifying below. She spoke of a square pit and that she felt compelled to "go back down there" to the body. This implied she had already had access to some lower level and suggested a staircase or open lift shaft. So far, derelict buildings within our area have been searched without yielding any evidence of such an incident.

'*If...*' He paused after strongly stressing the word. 'If we are to accept anything this lady says, it still requires a giant leap of the imagination to tie it in with another curiosity brought to our attention. I mean the supposed, but unproven, break-in at a Cold War bunker now designated as an emergency Regional Seat of Government.

'There again the supposition rests on the frailest of evidence.'

'A tin of baked beans,' Beaumont was heard

to murmur.

'Exactly. I am not entirely happy going along with this connection, but we are compelled to consider it. Investigation at the bunker has been taken over by another security service and it rests with them to report back to us, if and how they think fit. I continue to press for consultation, given the possibility of a mysterious death which could involve a murder investigation. Again we have an input here from Acting DS Silver's networking.' He nodded to Silver, who took up the narrative.

'Over several years there's been a website which records various feats of illegal entry into closed and semi-secret premises. The contributors call themselves Urban Explorers and compete in presenting photographic evidence of their exploits. I have found the record of an intended break-in at a bunker within the Bucks-Berks-Oxon region dated fourteen months ago. This could be the one the Boss is talking about now.

'The entry was signed with the pseudonym Tankgirl. Photographs of other exploits came with interior shots of named underground structures and city sewerage systems "conquered" by her team. I have copies here showing the rear view of a well-built female in heavy overalls and hard hat crawling through a restricted cylindrical tunnel.'

'These so-called Explorers shouldn't be confused with a perfectly legal set of historical researchers who obtain official permission to investigate and record details of wartime structures,' Yeadings warned.

Since his reference to the despised can of baked beans DI Salmon had been growing increasingly restless. Now he broke out in protest. 'All this rigmarole is built up from this woman's claim to be able to conjure up visions of the past,' he complained. 'Are we reduced to asking the advice of charlatans like her?'

Mott drew a loud breath as he waited for the Boss to defend his theory.

'I'd have dismissed Mrs Button's claim, had she not so staunchly *de*mystified the recent incidents in Bells Wood. Her distress over the subjective experience of visualizing the girl's death was in stark contrast. It convinced me that either it was genuine or she was a most impressive actor.'

'Teacher, nurse, child-carer, psychic medium, why not actor too?' Beaumont muttered.

'I guess we're all agreed she's right about the incidents at Barrows being the work of young mischief-makers?' DI Salmon pursued.

'Who, nevertheless, show some familiarity with occult matters?' Mott queried. 'The average ale-quaffing, girl-chasing village lout is unlikely to spend time networking or library-scouring for details of the Major Arcana. I think we need to look elsewhere...'

'Though slaughter of a white cockerel must be widely known as part of a black magic ritual,' Yeadings warned. 'But I don't think that that and the torched trees came from the same quirky mind that contrived the hanging.'

That brought him hard up against the personality of Gervais Plummer. But he could not visualize the man physically involved in preparation of the girl's body for roping from the tree. He recalled him sitting opposite in the Costa café, neatly adjusting the crockery, with finicky precision aligning the teaspoon with the edge of the table. It was true that someone mocking the figure of the Hanged Man roped by one leg had been as fiddly, angling the other to the rear, with the hands secured behind; but had Gervais Plummer the necessary emotional detachment for such manipulation of a pitiable human body? How squeamish was he?

On the other hand, the display had been presented to *mean* something. And wasn't that how Plummer exercised himself – pointing meanings, mocking human behaviour in his witty cartoons?

How much of a joker was the man? Was he capable of what Yeadings half-suspected was a macabre commentary on a particular death? Or, since the man's approach to him had followed that display, was he then deliberately suggesting himself to the earth-based Plod as a viable suspect?

'So what, sir?' Mott asked, bringing Yeadings rapidly back in line. 'This Button woman, need we go further with her?'

He was reluctant. 'Let's wait and see if she features again. She struck me under the quiet exterior as a forceful, positive person. I think she may thrust herself on our notice again.'

'Could well be,' Holly Hughes gave as her opinion. Until then she had been present but silent, sticking to her function as Beaumont's shadow. 'I came across a pile of these on the counter of the Needlewoman shop.'

She presented a single A4 sheet advertising a meeting at the memorial hall for the following evening. It was computer-printed with magenta ink on pale green paper.

CAN YOU BE SURE? a headline demanded, followed by a series of questions set to test the reader's gullibility. Below, in scarlet capitals ran the quotation, MORE THINGS IN HEAVEN AND EARTH ... In lower case underneath, it announced a public meeting in the memorial hall entitled Contact and Comfort for the Bereaved.

The speaker's name was given as Mrs Maud Button, forensic psychic. There was a £35 entrance fee to cover costs.

'This should have been brought to our notice,' Salmon grumbled. 'How widely was this meeting being advertised?'

'That's the only place I saw it,' Holly told him. 'It's a small shop. Only women seem to go there. Maybe fewer men show an interest in seances and contacting the dead. The Needle-woman could act as a sort of *poste restante* for

181

Mrs Button's PR.'

'Does that imply that Mrs Button has a close personal connection with the shop?' Silver asked.

'Possibly,' Mott muttered; 'maybe she's a needlewoman too. No limit to her skills.'

'It's a clever title – Contact and Comfort for the Bereaved,' Yeadings pondered. 'There's no precision on who is to be contacted. It could quite modestly refer to Mrs Button herself. Holly,' he asked mildly, 'are you known to the proprietor of Needlewoman?'

She appeared slightly embarrassed. 'I'm not an embroiderer myself,' she claimed as if it would be considered a weakness by present company. 'I go sometimes to match silks for my grandmother, and just now they're arranging for one of her pictures to be framed. So, yes, I have got to know the two women there fairly well. They're sisters, and seem quite ordinary people.'

Yeadings nodded. 'So if one of us is to attend the meeting it wouldn't surprise them to see you turn up to hear what line the lady's taking?'

'That's right, because they saw me take a leaflet. I'd like to go, sir.'

'Good. Let's hope you'll discover more about Maud Button's interests and opinions. Since the incidents at Barrows are much in the public mind, the subject could come up, and this could be a chance to spread her reputation, striking while the iron's hot.

'If there's any criticism of the police for lack of progress, you can guess the chief constable will get to hear, and we'll be on the receiving end of a tongue-lashing,' he reminded them. His mouth twisted wryly. 'I'm surprised she hasn't sent the team a group invitation.'

'This is all a sideline,' Beaumont complained impatiently. 'Aren't we avoiding the main problem? Namely, who the dead girl was. The last search, extended UK-wide over the year-long period, brought up eight Mispers in the age group of our victim. DNA samples are available for five of them, which should help elimination, but dealing with the others is even more time-consuming and stretches resources. Pressure's on us to consider investigating them when we're already dangerously thin on the ground.'

'I want you to stick with it just the same,' Mott ordered. 'Silver, you can attend tomorrow's meeting separately. If you get an opportunity to question the speaker, you're shattered by your mother's recent death, have refused bereavement counselling. Let's find out whether the help this Maud Button offers breaches the law in any way. Witchcraft is hard to define, but fraud isn't.'

The team was dismissed, leaving Yeadings sunk in unproductive thought. When the external phone rang he reached for it hopefully. He heard Z's voice against a confusion of comings and goings. In the background a loudspeaker invited passengers for Ibiza to proceed to the departure lounge.

'We're at Luton Airport,' she said brightly, 'and I'm on my way back in to work.' He protested, but an hour later she was with him, having sent Max on home with the luggage.

'I can't believe you spent so little time in Madeira,' Yeadings greeted her.

'Well, I'm not a gardener like you; and it's true the floral displays were out of this world. But we kept in touch with the news from here, and I couldn't bear not to be part of it all.'

'I'm not sure I'll allow that. You can't really be fit yet.'

'Believe me, I am. Don't make me waste time getting a medical certificate.'

'That's the very least I want. Go and see your GP now and get them to phone me right away.'

'And then?'

'We'll see. You might manage to sit through a possibly boring lecture tomorrow evening on my behalf.'

'You're joking, sir.'

'Not at all. And rest assured, there will be paperwork arising.' When he explained about the psychic's meeting, she showed enthusiasm.

He smiled as she left. Max wouldn't have allowed her to bully him into bringing her back unless she really did seem well enough. Certainly her enthusiasm wasn't lacking. Mott would see that no strain was put on her too soon.

He was reminded that they hadn't traced the writer of the anonymous letter to her. Another negative in this almost stalled case. Was he expecting too much now from tomorrow's talk by Maud Button? It could seem excessive to have planted three of the team among the audience. The brass at Kidlington would be querying the cost. There was probably more scepticism there than he felt himself about divination and messages from the dead.

Something Silver had retrieved concerning Maud Button's history had added to his doubt about her. Even when she had been here stretching his credence with her performance, he had considered that such a powerfully experienced emotion might have had a source in some personal trauma from the past. Could even the accidental death of the twelve-year-old child she had been employed to watch over have vibrations that conjured up the scene she described? Had she actually been there at the time, although off-duty? Had she stood at the top of the stairs and looked down at the strangled child?

The trance-like state of the medium was not so far from the subconscious mind when dreaming. It was possible that unwelcome memories surfacing had, with minor differences of detail, transferred themselves into her false paranormal experience.

Fifteen

The circular drive in front of the house was crowded with emergency services. Two ambulances waited with rear doors open. Barrows staff looked on dumbstruck as first one stretcher and then another was carried out. The first brought cries of horror from those waiting as young Molly's scorched hair and face were recognized. Mrs Bradshaw ran forward. 'Oh, my little love! I must go with her.'

The second, her features mainly covered by a temporary dressing, caused the crowd to shrink back slightly, allowing room for loading.

Gervais Plummer wasn't there to accompany his wife to hospital. He had driven off half an hour before the fire broke out and it had been impossible to raise him by phone. No one volunteered now to take his place.

Three fire appliances were in action, one hose soaking access by the two lower floors whilst a hydraulic platform jetted water into the still blazing upper floor. Two firemen discarding breathing apparatus were reporting on the rescues. As the ambulances drew away a marked police car and a red Toyota came screaming in from the road.

'Getting to be a regular thing,' Beaumont commented grimly, joining the uniform men. Behind him Holly Hughes demanded, 'How many injured?'

'Two,' someone told her. 'Molly from the kitchen and the missus. Molly hadn't been feeling well and she was upstairs lying down. The smoke alarms must have woken her and she was overcome trying to reach the stairs.'

'What about Mrs Plummer?'

'God knows what she was doing up there. There's only the staff bedrooms and a couple of studios Mr P and Miss Gerry sometimes used. Unless, of course, she was on her way up to the roof for some reason.'

'You don't think that likely?'

'Never known her go up there since Miss Gerry went away.'

'And then only to start a row,' growled someone rear of crowd.

'Have you any idea where Mr Plummer has gone or when he'll be back?'

'He didn't leave any instructions for lunch, miss. Which is just as well, since Mrs Bradshaw's gone off in the ambulance with Molly.'

Beaumont was arguing with the fire officer, hoping to get in on the ground floor. The man in the white helmet scowled up at the bared, glowing timbers of the roof. 'I can't authorize it. In any case we need to preserve the scene for the fire investigation team. They're en route from Aylesbury now.'

'Right,' said Beaumont easily. If it wasn't authorized it would be the other thing. He'd take a shifty round to the back, find a less observable point, break a window if necessary.

The kitchen door was clogged with fire personnel and hoses which snaked through and up the more direct back stairs, but the conservatory was still closed off in hopes of containing the spread. He pulled off his jacket, bunched it over his fist and broke the glass near to the lock. With typical slack country security, the key was in it and turned easily. He walked through the downstairs rooms and observed that nothing appeared to be amiss. In the morning room he turned on his heel to retrace his steps and almost lurched into the Limpet.

'Holy shit, girl,' he spat at her, 'are we joined at the hip?'

'Following orders, guv,' she gave back. 'And there's a red light winking on the answer phone.'

'That's what answer phones do. Like babies crying.' Nonetheless, he returned to the library and lifted the receiver.

'Dad,' a female voice came across. 'Sorry you're out, but I'll be seeing you shortly. Bye.'

'Interesting,' the DS considered. 'I understood he had only one daughter and she's in Africa. Seems there might be another one about. Unless the butler takes his calls in here.'

'Or Gerry is on her way home.'

'Or Plummer's on his way to Africa right now, having advised her in advance.' That gave plenty of cause for thought. Had he set fire to the place as a final eccentric move against his wife? And how had she come to be right there when the blaze broke out?

There was a clatter behind them and two firefighters came in, one who was female and carrying a contraption in a bucket.

'I'm to clear you out,' said the other. 'There's danger from falling masonry. And this time stay out, or I'll turn you over to the police.'

'We are the police, just making sure the crime scene stays secure. And is that a stirrup pump? I thought they went out with the ark.'

'They still have their uses. Anyway, who says it's a crime scene? That decision's premature.'

Beaumont shrugged. 'If it's not, you must believe in spontaneous combustion with daily outbreaks around here.'

They returned to the front of the building where the main action was being concentrated on the central floor. Beaumont sniffed the air. 'Something strange, not petrol. Sort of bitter,' he suggested.

'I've smelled it before,' Holly claimed. 'A film company's offices took fire in Dean Street, Soho, and a whole lot of exposed reels went up. The Boss's notes on this house mentioned that the daughter had a photographic studio up under the eaves. It could have started there.'

'So who would want to destroy all that re-mained here of the girl? Had she left something incriminating among the developed film?'

'Whatever it was, it'll be gone by now,' Holly regretted. 'But if she's actually on her way home, as the message suggested, we'll be able to ask her about it.'

'Not if she's expecting her father to join her wherever she is. You could read it either way. He's more than a touch weirdo. Who's to say he didn't set a timer for the fire, send the wife up there on some pretext and pull out before the whole shebang went up? We've already heard from DI Salmon that the estate's on the market in any case – an intentional bit of malice directed at the wife. No great financial loss for him, if everything's super-covered.'

'So what's next, guv?'

'We hang around the hospital and see how severe the injuries are. Then contact their insurer and see what value Plummer's put on her life.'

'Not again?' was Angus Mott's wearied re-action when he heard about the fire call-out. But he recognized that this later incident was more serious. Malice had now penetrated the house and there were casualties. He doubted that strangers found their way in by daylight. It looked as though the arsonist could be a mem-ber of the household.

Rather than waste time gawking at the

firefighters' derring-do, he settled at his computer and brought up the details of staff at Barrows. For this he accessed DS Beaumont's interview with them after the finding of the hanged body. It was days old and no one had been put on verifying the facts as given.

The butler had given his full name as Godfrey Bertram Bowles, born 1956 in Bristol where he left school at sixteen, trained first as a waiter at the Grand Hotel there and then, following an urge to go adventuring, had joined the P & O Company as a steward. After fifteen years at sea he had sought less pressurized work as a family servant, after suffering a severe abdominal rupture. There had been a wife who had drifted away during his long periods at sea, divorced him, remarried and now lived in New Zealand.

Most of this info, Beaumont noted, had been obtained from Mrs Bradshaw confidentially in Mr Bowles's absence. Her own biography was shorter; age indeterminate but probably mid-fifties; widowed at twenty-three with twin sons brought up mainly by their grandmother while Emma Bradshaw supported the family by working in hotel kitchens. Through part-time study she qualified as a chef and applied for the post of cook advertised by the present Mr Plummer's father, a widower. She had remained here for eleven happy years.

Molly, 19, and Barbara, 27, were both from Barrows Village, vouched for by the local vicar and doctor, and trained by Mrs Bradshaw straight from school. They were, she'd claimed, good girls, but Molly was on the fragile side.

Nothing improper recorded in their pasts, Mott noted, but Molly had certainly been close by when the fire had broken out and they had only her word that she'd been in bed and asleep. Some gentle probing would be needed at the hospital bedsides and he might need to send a uniform policewoman to watch over events. A pity, he'd mentioned to the Boss, that Z was away on sick leave. Dealing with the women would have been right up her street.

'It certainly will be,' Yeadings had replied. 'You'll be glad to know she's back.'

'Working?' Mott queried, incredulous. 'What's Max about?'

'Respecting female emancipation, I hope.' He darted a curious glance at his DCI over the half-moon reading glasses. Young Mott had a lot to learn about relationships if he thought a male partner had the divine right of veto. But then, when it came to job interests, that could be a sore subject in his household if Paula was determined to continue as a defence counsel locally. He hoped there'd be room yet for give and take in that case.

Rosemary Zyczynski emptied her holiday luggage with only a light sigh of regret as she spread sundresses and bikinis over the bed.

That last glimpse of Funchal from the plane window had almost brought misgivings, but the investigation was pulling her more strongly. Already involved through the anonymous letter, she had found the scant news in English language newspapers frustrating. Armed with a copy of the Boss's meticulous diary notes she could catch up with everything as she sat by the hospital bedsides.

All the same, she felt guilty at spoiling Max's well-intentioned plans. In the plane she had reached for his hand and squeezed it. 'We'll come back again,' she promised. Then, uncertain, she added, 'Won't we?'

He'd given her his crinkly grin. 'If you promise to behave yourself next time.' And the tension was over. She'd find some way of making it up to him.

At the hospital she found the two women had been separated. Molly, the less seriously injured would soon be going home. Mrs Plummer, or Lady Alice Plummer as they had conscientiously labelled her above the bed, was in ITU and strictly incommunicado.

'What are her chances?' Z asked.

'We always hope for the best. In her case, perhaps fifty-fifty. However well she pulls through, there will be permanent scarring to face, chest and hands. As soon as she is stabilized she will be moved to a specialist unit in London to receive the most up-to-date burns treatment. They've come quite a way since the

Falklands War, but there's a stage at which soft tissue...' The registrar hunched his shoulders and turned his palms upward.

Z understood, recalling press photographs of survivors of the *Sir Galahad* troopship. When Beaumont had phoned about the recent incident he'd not spared the black humour. She'd asked after the woman's injuries and he'd told her, 'Enough to upset the horses.'

Mrs Bradshaw was sitting by Molly's bedside reading aloud to her from *Heat* magazine.

'This really is the most awful rubbish,' she apologized to the detective. 'I can't imagine what it does to young people's heads.' But clearly Molly hung upon every word of scandal trawled from the so-called celebrities.

The girl's hair had been cut back halfway and the uncovered scalp was stained a vicious orange-yellow. Her hands and much of her face were invisible under gauze pads from which one eye stared apprehensively. 'I never did nothing wrong,' she pleaded when Mrs Bradshaw explained who Zyczynski was.

'Of course not. We just need to know what you saw when you woke up.'

'It was the smell. I couldn't breathe proper. I'd left my door a bit open so's I'd hear if anyone came upstairs, and it was coming in...' She waved bandaged hands in a rolling movement. 'Like in clouds.'

'And did you hear anyone come upstairs?'

'No, 'cause I must of dropped off straight

after I took them pills. I was still a bit dopey and couldn't walk straight. There was flames in the corridor and the missus was sort of leaning against the top of the stairs and her clothes was all on fire.'

'That's how you got burnt yourself.'

'Well, I knew, because we'd had fire drills with Mr Bowles. I beat at the flames and then I pushed her down on the carpet runner and rolled her in it. By then someone else was there. I think it was Holt and his lad from the garden. They must of bin in the kitchen for their tea.' She was silent a moment, frowning. 'Only it was nearly lunch time and they'd of bin in the way.'

'We were all there,' Mrs Bradshaw interrupted, 'because the master had called us together for his news. You were the only one missing. Well, after he'd gone we just stayed there, couldn't take in what he'd said. It must have been half an hour later that the smoke alarms all started going off. Mr Bowles ordered us out, but the men started upstairs to see what they could do.'

'What news?' Molly demanded excitedly. 'Is there going to be a baby?'

'Don't be silly. How could there be? Still, it's nearly as surprising. He's going to sell up, go away and there'll be strangers coming to Barrows. But if any of us wanted, they could move down to the West Country and stay with him. Only it would be a smaller place and less work to do. But we'd get paid the same, plus five hundred pounds each for the inconvenience of moving.'

'Quite a lot to discuss,' Z agreed, nodding.

'Yes. And he said not to serve family lunch, but make our own arrangements.'

'He definitely said no lunch for himself and his wife?'

'Yes. I supposed they'd be going out to some place to eat. And his car did go off sharpish just after.'

Interesting, Z thought. They must have assumed both Plummers were in the car. 'Did anyone know Mrs Plummer was still in the house?'

'I don't suppose so. I certainly didn't. They'd been together when that other detective called to ask for Mr Plummer's clothes from the day before. And that was a funny thing too. Mr Bowles had to go and fetch them from the linen basket in the master's bathroom.'

This was all news to Molly who sat there with a puzzled frown. She shook her head slowly, then covered her bandaged face with her padded hands. 'I think I'd like to have a little sleep now.'

A nurse came forward to remove one of the pillows that propped her up. 'You've had long enough to talk for the present. She's still quite shaken by her experience, poor lamb.'

Dismissed, Z decided there was no point in remaining. By giving Mrs Bradshaw a lift back to Barrows she might pick up further useful snippets. And at Barrows, by then accepted as on the side of the angels, she would be in position to overhear what the staff in general made of the present set-up.

Gervais Plummer did not return that night. Salmon was set to contacting all airports offering long haul to Africa, but his name did not appear on any passenger departure lists.

'Could he have set up a false identity in advance?' Mott asked of the others. 'It couldn't be done overnight.'

Yeadings mused aloud that the man appeared quite capable of involved plotting ahead.

'How about incoming flights?' Beaumont demanded. 'If the daughter was being met at the airport, Plummer could have booked them in overnight at a hotel. Z, since you're all chummy with Mrs Bradshaw, can you get her to call you if they turn up today at the house?'

'Will do. But shouldn't one of us be there anyway, picking up on the circumstances of the fire?'

'I'm keeping in close touch with the fire investigation team,' Yeadings assured her. 'And SOCO are standing by to cover the whole house as soon as the decision on arson or accident is made. A search warrant is on its way. I am particularly curious about the doors to the two studios on the top floor. The fire investigation officer will concentrate on the state of the locks.

'I recall that when Bowles took me around the building the only door with a key on the top floor was to the room where Plummer had occasionally painted or drawn his satirical cartoons. The second studio was walk-through from there. It struck me then that father and daughter might have enjoyed a certain amount of intimacy; at least the freedom to look in on each other while work was in progress. But the outer door could guarantee freedom from any other interruption.'

'Particularly the wife?' Beaumont picked up.

'So yesterday, if the room was left locked, she would have needed to collect the key from wherever it was kept, in order to penetrate the holy-of-holies. I recall Bowles had with him an enormous bunch of the things. He wouldn't have carried them normally on him.'

'I could question Mrs B on that,' Z offered.

A phone on the superintendent's desk rang and all eyes swung on it as Yeadings took the call, naming the local fire officer. He listened in silence, then said, 'Yes. That's interesting. Answers a number of questions. Thank you for letting me hear so promptly.'

He replaced the receiver. 'They've found the remains of a cigarette lighter totally burnt out. It has been identified as belonging to Miss Geraldine Plummer, who gave up smoking some weeks before she left for Africa. The source of the fire was also located in her studio, the farther one, but the lighter itself was on the floor among burnt papers in the outer studio belonging to the father.'

He looked around at the team. 'We are left to draw our own conclusions.'

Sixteen

'We've seen all we need in the bunker,' Jock Halliday told Yeadings. 'It's clear for your lot now.'

The superintendent smiled into the phone. He wasn't deceived by the laconic tone of the message: Jock was a dab hand at understatement. What he meant was *there's something you need to look at there*.

'Thank you. I'll send SOCO in now you're giving us clearance.'

They closed the conversation with enquiries after each other's family. Jock complained about the idiotic surplus of academic testing in middle school years. Hannah was getting quite dithery over the latest lot. Yeadings sympathized, glad that for his own Sally no importance was given to exams at her special-needs private school. Academic excellence wasn't an aim for a Down's syndrome child. Luke's testing time would come, but not for a year or two yet. And, judged from any angle, the lad was not only bright but relatively unflappable.

He hung up and went to make the necessary arrangements in person. 'They'll be expecting you,' he told the scientific team.

He would have liked to go along with them. The possibility of positive evidence at last increased rather than alleviated his impatience. For some reason he felt in his bones that the core of the present case lay there at the preserved Cold War structure, and that the complex events at Barrows were almost incidental. He couldn't escape the suspicion that the team was being deliberately diverted from the action that really mattered. And again he ascribed this to Plummer himself who also appeared to be orchestrating some complicated charade within his own family.

What was it with the man? How much of a nutter was he? How malicious? And where had he disappeared to at the moment? What was he brewing up?

He hadn't long to wait for an answer regarding the man's whereabouts. It came in a phone call from DCI Mott who had received a message from the woman PC left on watch at the hospital.

Gervais Plummer had unexpectedly turned up demanding to see the two women injured in the fire. His wife being heavily sedated, no communication had been possible, but he had held a long conversation with the kitchen maid which the WPC described as insistent and persuasive in tone although she had been unable to overhear the gist of it.

'A pity he got to her,' was Mott's comment:

'but as her employer he was trustingly allowed in with a basket of fruit. It will be interesting to see if she changes her account of the fire after this. I'm sending Z in with instructions to take another detailed statement.'

Rosemary Zyczynski was met by an obstructive ward manager. There had been altogether too much excitement already for his patient. She was in too fragile a state to endure more pressure from the police. She had specifically asked not to be troubled again. Only her friend Mrs Bradshaw was to be allowed at her bedside.

'I understand,' Z granted, privately churning with resentment. 'But you realize this is a very serious case under investigation and eventually we shall need Molly's help in finding out what happened.' She treated him to an inimical glare. 'I hope we don't need to charge anyone with hindering the police in the pursuance of their duty.'

He was in no way chastened and escorted her to the door of the ward, barring her return with an extended arm. So the next move, Z decided, must be an appeal to Mrs Bradshaw.

At Barrows she found the rest of Mott's team except for Jimmy Silver who was back at base further researching Gervais Plummer's business connections and retrieving a record of his satirical cartoons published in the national press. They had set up an incident-room van on the site and were comparing witness statements on the fire.

'Plummer's brought back the daughter,' Mott told her shortly. 'She flew in overnight. Now they're rescuing what they can from the ground-floor study. The gardener and his boy are carting it all down to the pavilion by the pool. Otherwise the main house is still out of bounds. I need SOCO here to take a look, but the Boss has sent them all off to this bunker place. He's got a bee in his bonnet about it, God knows why.'

'It's that bloody can of baked beans,' Beaumont complained. 'This whole investigation is turning into a *Goon Show* episode.'

'What's the daughter like?' Z asked, but received only a shrug.

'She's a girl like any other. Go down to the pool and meet her. She'll probably set you to being useful.'

'No. I'm bound for Mrs B right now. Something specific to follow up.' And she drifted away towards the kitchen which had been reopened.

There, where everything still smelled slightly of smoke, she found the large Russian teapot in service on the scrubbed table surrounded by scattered used mugs. Mrs Bradshaw felt the china with a knuckle. 'Gone cold,' she announced. 'It'd be stewed by now anyway. Let's make fresh. I've just put a batch of fruit scones in. They'll be ready soon.'

This boded well for a conversational session. Z slid into place and rested her elbows on the table. 'I hear Mr Plummer's brought Miss Gerry home. He was visiting at the hospital first, but she didn't go in with him.'

'Wouldn't be bothered.' Her voice was dismissive. 'No love lost there between her and her mother. As for Molly, I doubt they ever passed the time of day.'

'The ward manager is turning away all visitors except you. He seems very protective.'

Mrs Bradshaw said nothing more until she had filled a smaller teapot and planted it firmly on the table. 'How's the milk going?'

Z peered into the oversized jug. 'Plenty still.'

'They let her phone me.'

Who? Z wondered.

'Molly, I mean. She's scared. Says she was always taught to tell the truth. Then she started crying, poor lamb. Soon as they've checked her over she needs to be back here. Well, we all do, but no chance because the whole top floor's gutted and we're being put up at the Black Horse. It's all right, but it isn't like home.'

And this house was? Not for long, though, because of Plummer's recent plans for upheaval.

'They wouldn't have let us in here except that the kitchen's a modern extension and the structure's been declared safe.'

'So where is the family staying?'

'There wasn't any need last night, with him

204

and Miss Gerry away and the missus in hospital. There's a vacant cottage out by the lake. They'll be going there, I suppose. It won't take me long to get it ready and stocked up.'

'That's up to you?'

'Well, I'm sort of the housekeeper as well as the cook. That's why he pays me near double. And I don't need asking twice about following him down to Cheltenham.'

'How about Mr Bowles and the others?'

'Bowles is all for going too. Says a gentleman needs a manservant of some kind. I'll miss my girls, though. They'll not want to leave the village. And Holt wants to stay on, if the next lot of people will have him. Same thing with his boy. Mr Plummer's had it drawn up that the lodge and a patch of land are to be in Holt's name for his lifetime, so he's come off rather well.'

'Mr Plummer must have had these plans in his mind for some time. I'm surprised none of it leaked out before now.'

Mrs Bradshaw lifted out two baking trays of hot scones with her padded oven gloves, eased them on to the table and waved the heat off. Enticed by the smell, Barbara appeared from the utility room to start providing cutlery, plates, butter, clotted cream and jams.

'Don't sit yourself down. I need you to go into the village,' Mrs Bradshaw told her firmly. 'You'll find the shopping list on the dresser.'

She watched while the other woman collected it, read it through and shrugged on a leather jacket from a hook by the back door. She resumed her chat the instant she and Z were alone again. It seemed that already there was a gap appearing between those who were to go and those who'd chosen not to.

'Little pitchers have big ears,' the cook quoted. 'Could be that the missus'll need to keep her on, wherever she decides to end up. And God alone knows what'll happen to the horses. I can't imagine how madam could live without her stables.'

'It must have been a terrible shock to her...' Z marvelled. 'Unless, of course, she had prior knowledge of her husband's plans. Perhaps she'd had time to make her own arrangements.'

Mrs Bradshaw turned shrewd eyes on her. There was suddenly a new distance between them. 'You know darn well he dumped it on her without warning. Your other detective was there when he sprung it. There's no way he wouldn't have passed that gem of news on, like we got it from Bowles.'

Zyczynski busied herself guiding clotted cream on to the rich crimson of raspberry jam. The scones were still hot, light and deliciously crumbly.

'What you're thinking,' Mrs Bradshaw accused, pointing the blade of a small tea knife at her, 'is that the missus went straight upstairs and set fire to the house out of revenge. Why else would she have begun it up there in the studio where he used to shut himself off?'

'Is that what you think, Mrs Bradshaw?'

The cook folded her brawny arms and her lips before opting to reply. 'It's not my business to think, miss. Police-wise, I believe the right phrase is "No comment".'

There, I've blown it, Z told herself. But she hadn't been the one to suggest the lady of the house was an arsonist. It must be a general suspicion among the servants by now.

Scenes of Crimes officers were finding their quest partly redundant. It seemed that wherever they turned in the underground complex there were the messy grey remains of fingerprinting powder. They were unaccustomed to playing second fiddle and it didn't please Brian O'Brien, the civilian scientist who was in charge. But Superintendent Yeadings had been quite specific about one place to which the MOD people apparently hadn't turned their attention – except, of course, to add their own layer of dabs in passing and so complicate matters.

He had herded the others to the lower regions while he stayed at the top of the square pit that contained the concrete flights of stairs. The maintenance team had replaced the top railings which would have been removed when the crane was run out to drop heavy equipment to the bottom of the shaft. It was the red-painted handrail that Brian concentrated on now, whisking the soft brush over its slightly worn surface to bring out all alien marks.

It had fortunately escaped repainting and the evidence brought up comprised an overlaying of smudges from decades since the place was first built. Almost impossible to lift and identify the most recent, he regretted. *Almost,* but of course they had to attempt it. He paused over one small surface scar and reached in his incident bag for the ultraviolet flashlight. Yes, he hadn't been deceived: thin blood smears showed clearly. Smears, but not spots. This had come off someone's fingers and was only in the one place. No fresh injury had dripped here.

He considered the placing. Someone had come up the stairs and reached out a hand to the railing. Suddenly tired? Even shaky? But since there was no other evidence of bleeding at this level, that must have happened below and the person leaving the smudge had become contaminated down there.

He photographed the railing and the top of the stairs from several angles, then took a swab of the old blood. This should prove to be the victim's. What they needed now was for it to be identified as the hanged girl's.

He followed up with a scrupulous examination of the area directly below the final flight of stairs and again the ultraviolet light picked up indications of injury. Some time ago efforts must have been made to clean up the floor, and to the naked eye this appeared successful. He doubted bleach had been available unless supplies were kept in the domestic offices, but there would have been unlimited water. Bucketfuls and hard scrubbing could have produced this effect. Small wonder perhaps that the survivor reaching the top of the stairs afterwards could have felt weary. Especially since the injured person had disappeared. A body physically disposed of?

So where could it have been hidden?

He followed where the others had gone ahead. In the vast, impressively hi-tech kitchen he found that the MoD searchers had been busy, leaving traces of fingerprinting spray over the openings of every cupboard and surface. The team was busy shooting the details, most noticeably at one point where a long drawer some two feet deep, and probably intended for bulky pieces of equipment, was left open.

'Bloody smears almost obliterated,' murmured Jacky Godwin as he sensed O'Brien behind him. 'Not a lot, though. If there had been considerable injury the body must have been covered by this point. There are also faint traces on the floor where it was being wrapped.'

'We're considering a fall from the top of the access stairs,' O'Brien told him. 'Two flights and a concrete floor. Far enough for the body, however caught unaware, to have tensed on the way down. There were surely serious internal injuries. It wouldn't need a serious loss of blood externally to ensure death.'

'Intentional?'

'Your guess is as good as mine. But hiding it in here certainly was.'

Yeadings called the Serious Crimes team together to give them the latest findings. 'We are left with the classic question. Did she fall or was she pushed?'

'But why hide the body away and then so much later bring it out and put it on display in such a macabre manner?' Beaumont demanded.

'Two very different actions. Two different sets of people,' Mott concluded.

'Hide and Seek,' Zyczynski agreed.

'Except that we can't be sure it was *seek*. In the bunker it could have been a totally accidental discovery. Suppose that the more recent intruders – these Urban Explorers as they call themselves on the web – opened the drawer when looking for something, and found this gruesome bundle instead.'

'Looking for a tin opener!' shouted Beaumont, stabbing at the air with one finger. 'That's the devil in the detail that we hadn't taken account of. The bloody can didn't have a ring fastener. Some idiot had overlooked that they couldn't get into it.'

'You're thinking "they", not he or she,' Yeadings fed to them. 'Have we any reason for this?'

'Three separate sets of fresh-looking dabs brought up by the MoD team,' Mott explained.

'And it needed a couple to carry the body. There's no sign of dragging.'

'One sturdy man could have done it alone.'

'All the way up the stairs? It'd take a fireman's lift or a crane.'

Yeadings watched them as they dished up and modified the theories. Like him they would be visualizing these anonymous Explorers on their laddish jaunt, exultant at gaining access unobserved. And then the ghoulish revelation on opening the drawer! Small wonder the can of beans was overlooked, but why on earth did they lumber themselves with a corpse? Did they peer at the girl's half-obscured features and believe it was someone they knew and owed some loyalty to – a rival Explorer who'd got there first?

He would need to take another look at the website claims which Silver had retrieved. Someone using the pseudonym Tankgirl had boasted a year ago of her intention to 'take the site's virginity', and this body could have been hidden there for the same time. But the body retrieved was slight, had nothing tank-like about her. So did that mean that Tankgirl had been the survivor, the one who might, or might not, have pushed her over the edge of the stairs

211

while the railing was removed by the maintenance team?

There had been no bragging claim on the site, recording their success. The death, whether accidental or intentional, had put an end to the game. Tankgirl had no intention of being associated with the place where, ages later, a wrapped body could be found.

Or was it conceivable that she had returned a year later, under the same circumstances, to remove the corpse and get it associated with some other place and quite different people? Was that the reason the hanging scene had been so blatantly spectacular? For obfuscation. In which case the same woman could have been responsible for both concealment and display.

It gets worse, he thought. More complicated. More challenging.

Seventeen

'I suppose I'd better,' Gerry said ungraciously, 'though there's no sense in it if she's in a coma.'

'Sedated, actually,' her father corrected mildly. 'More importantly, have a word with young Molly and drive the message home. Maybe take her some little gift, to remind her we're expecting something of her.'

'If she's staying on in the village she might expect Mother to give her a job. All the more motive to fib and cover up about the fire. She'll be owed a good deed in return.'

'A lot depends on what your mother admits to when she finally wakes up. We have to get there first and plant the idea that she was bravely fighting the blaze, rather than starting it. She ought to be grateful.'

'Unfortunately, there's been no way to persuade the authorities of a natural cause for the outbreak. The fire investigator's no fool. He's ruled out an accelerant, but they've found your cigarette lighter and it's pretty obvious that she used it on the film negatives.'

'I should have chucked it out when I gave up

smoking. What's going to happen with the insurance?'

'I'm covered for malicious damage, though not terrorism. Quite how they'll regard arson by a member of the family, though, remains to be seen. That's dubious.'

'Is she part-owner of the property?'

'No, everything remained in my name after I inherited. There never seemed any reason to change that. She'd have been well provided for financially if anything had happened to me.'

'So we should rejoice that she savaged the property rather than your throat with a carving knife.'

'I'll take that as a crude appreciation of my positive value in your eyes. I thank you.'

'This new place you're buying in Cheltenham, what's it like?'

'Described by the estate agent as "a gentleman's residence". Georgian, three floors; a dignified town house set back from a quiet road and behind a shady lawn and shrubbery, with a walled vegetable and fruit garden to the rear. Large, square rooms, roughly cubes; an elegant curved staircase; no Victorian elaborations; a good cellar. And, before you ask if one can fly a balloon from the property, preferably not, except the small, party kind if one feels so disposed. Definitely no stables.'

Leaning with ankles crossed and hands deep thrust in trouser pockets, Gerry stared hard at her father. 'You really have turned into quite a shit, Dad. But it took long enough. Do you feel any better now?'

He turned away to look out on the sweep of grass up to the blackened house. 'I had a lot to forgive her. From way back. Ultimately I found I couldn't. And whether it's made me any happier to be a cad, I'd say probably as much as, on waking, she'll feel about having torched what was once her home.' He sighed. 'And now can we drop the subject for all time?'

'Sure.' It was casually spoken, but she knew the memory would never be buried, least of all in his mind. They were alike in so many ways, though she had more to regret than he would ever have. If time could be turned back, it would have to be for the same long years to that fatal day in her childhood.

'There's a guest room at the new abode, I hope.'

'More than one. A suite at your personal disposal, if required.'

'A bolt-hole for the prodigal. I'm sure at some time I'll need it. Thanks.' She waved at the office clutter piled on the little Japanese tables. 'Shall we get to sorting these accounts? I can still just remember how to act as hon land steward.'

Next morning Molly Gage watched her mother fussily packing her things back into a capacious bag. There wasn't much to take home. The hospital had provided nightdresses –

gowns, they called them; embarrassing things that flapped open at the rear and showed off your spotty bottom. But in the short time she had been lying here remembering what really happened her parents had constantly popped in with little comforts. The fruit and sweet things she'd eaten, except for Gerry's gift of chocolates; the magazines were equally devoured; the stuffed rabbit, adored from when she was four, had been cuddled at night and hidden under the pillows when the handsome doctor came round.

She wasn't happy about what she'd been asked to do. And the money the master had given her didn't help. In a way it made her feel guiltier because she had to hide it from everyone instead of buying presents. She hadn't even started the lying yet, so how would she manage when it actually came to facing an inquiry? He'd said it was one of those white lies, just fibs really, that made it easier for other people. If only she could think of it as a *kindness* and not a sin.

She wished it had been someone she really liked that she was doing it for, but the missus had always been disagreeable whenever she'd had any direct contact with her. If it hadn't been for Mrs Bradshaw always coming in between them she wouldn't have wanted to stay on in service there. 'You have to understand,' the cook had explained. 'Young people bother her. It's not anything special about you.'

Mrs B was someone she'd like to tell about the worry, but she'd be ashamed. And Mum was out of the question. She'd had rules drummed into her when she was a tweeny maid in an earl's household, and people were different then. It was only in books that the gentry did awful things, like that mad Mrs Rochester locked up in the east wing.

So was the missus mad too, doing what she did? She'd looked pretty wild, standing there staring at the blaze, sort of excited but frightened at the same time really. And then when the flames roared up the front of her jodhpurs to her face, the screams!

The screams were still going round in her head every time she lay down to sleep. No matter how she'd buried her head under the bedclothes and hugged Rabbit there were those awful red patches growing on the backs of her eyelids. You never forget flames.

At the actual time it happened she'd been terrified, but then she remembered what Mr Bowles had taught them at fire drill and had got the missus all wrapped up in the carpet. By then everyone was there shouting at her. And when they'd undone the runner there was this awful burnt body. She'd looked dead, all black and screwed up like that picture in the papers of someone thousands of years old who'd been dug up from a bog somewhere abroad.

'Come along, Molly, stir yourself and stop dreaming. Anyone would think you didn't want to go home,' her mother scolded.

She must be looking miserable. She tried to put on the little smile Mrs Bradshaw had made her practise for when she'd be allowed to wait at table. Only, when she thought maybe she'd never have a chance to do that now, it made her more wretched still.

'Oh, Mum,' she whispered, 'I do feel dreadful.' She knew she was nearly on the edge of confessing what the master had asked her to tell the police. The only way to stop herself was to burst out crying.

'That won't do any good,' her mother scolded. 'You need to take care of that bad eye. They're arranging an outpatient's appointment for you over at Stoke Mandeville next week, and it's got to stay covered until then.'

Gerry and her father were still immersed in the estate accounts when Bowles approached with a visitor. Plummer looked up to recognize the superintendent, and for a moment was caught between unease and pleasure. The butler introduced him correctly and distantly as if they'd never met. Yeadings came forward holding out a hand and Plummer rose to take it.

'I thought you had complications enough of your own without being asked to drop in on me for a word,' the detective offered.

'Have as many words as you like, Superintendent, and thank you for the consideration of calling in person. May I introduce my daughter Geraldine? Gerry, Detective Super-intendent Yeadings is in charge of Serious Crimes for Thames Valley.'

Both gave little nods of acceptance. Plummer waved the other man to a free chair and after a moment's hesitation the girl walked off to-wards the swimming pool.

'My condolences on your most recent mis-fortune.'

'Thank you. My wife is being looked after in the local hospital. They're very good, but as soon as it's considered safe she'll be trans-ferred to a special burns unit in London. Molly Gage is less seriously injured, thank God.'

'I understand she's going home today. Bowles tells me the fire is extinguished so that the main part of the house is unlikely to suffer further damage.'

'Yes, it's fortunate that it started at the top. Though there'll be plenty of cleaning and re-decoration needed throughout before we let any potential buyers in to see it.'

'So let's hope the insurance people settle in good time then.'

'Yes, once the fire investigators have decided how it started. I shall be very surprised if they find any fault in the electrical wiring. I've had that renewed only recently and the sprinkler system worked perfectly.'

'Once it was turned back on, as I under-stand?'

'Yes. How it came to be switched off, I can't

imagine. Some misunderstanding with the cleaner probably. I know Bowles checks everything regularly.'

'So the cause could be human error. Unless you're considering arson?'

Plummer plucked at his upper lip. All this polite talk was unnecessary. Both were spouting options already known to each other. Now they were nearing the nitty-gritty, and this policeman wasn't one to be easily led into byways of the truth.

'They found an old cigarette lighter up there, left over from the days when my daughter used to smoke,' he volunteered. 'It was almost totally destroyed, apparently used for some purpose and ultimately responsible for setting light to a bin of discarded film. My daughter's studio hadn't been touched since she went abroad, or certainly that bin would have been emptied before now.'

'I understand that her workroom is entered from your own studio and that your outer door to the top landing is left unlocked.'

'For most of the time, that is so.'

'Does your wife smoke, Mr Plummer?'

'No. Nor to the best of my knowledge does young Molly. At present we keep the house a smoke-free zone. But, of course, rules are there to be broken. I wouldn't say the girl had sneaked off for a quiet puff, but that's not beyond the realms of possibility.'

Yeadings's keen ear for clichés told him

Plummer was emotionally slightly off balance at present. His finicky nature would normally have edited them out. Had he only just then decided to put forward that last suggestion and was unsure of whether it ought to be followed up?

'So how would she have got hold of the lighter?'

'Who knows? It could have been left anywhere in the house and she'd previously picked it up.'

He realized then that he'd half accused the girl of light-handedness. 'Or, more likely, Gerry would have given it to her when she'd no longer any need,' he corrected.

Oh crafty! Yeadings thought. But that theory hadn't obviated the need for Molly to have gone in to help herself to the lighter. On his visit there with Bowles he had noticed the lighter together with an open packet of Turkish cigarettes abandoned on Gerry's work bench. It had struck him because of the danger of smoking close to film and chemicals.

'So if your wife had wanted to fetch something from one of the two studios and imagined them locked she would have needed to fetch a key from the butler or you?'

'Bowles, I suppose, because I had just left in the car. But there was no reason to. The studios were left open.'

'Did Mrs Plummer often visit those rooms on the top floor? Or inspect the living arrangements for the staff?'

'Not to my knowledge, Superintendent. I don't spend a great deal of time here at Barrows. My work is in the City so I wasn't familiar with the daily workings of the house, except to notice that Mrs Bradshaw is a very competent housekeeper and leaves little need for overseeing.'

'Your intended move to the West Country will mean a great change for everyone here.'

'Yes. I have taken that into account. It coincides with my semi-retirement from the family business. I shall confine myself to visiting London for annual board meetings. My wife and daughter will find their own accommodation and I hope to take some of my well-trained staff with me. You are right. It is a great change for us all. For myself, I intend to become provincial, if not rustic, and devote myself to growing the largest vegetable marrow for the local horticultural show.'

'A man after my own heart,' Yeadings admitted, following the lighter turn of the conversation. 'Voltaire had the right idea in the end.'

'Except,' said Plummer wickedly, 'that I believe a sequel was written in which Candide and Co went off adventuring again. Who knows but I might do the same?'

Yeadings smiled. He was sure the man would find something to plunge his mischief-making fingers into, wherever he settled. It was the nature of the beast, like the scorpion that stung to death the frog transporting him across the river.

But Plummer didn't customarily run risks. Safely channelling any bile into his mocking cartoons, his life had been a smooth history of success until just recently. What had suddenly sent him off on this vengeful route? Had it been the same trigger that caused his daughter to leave home and take her balloon circus abroad? Something unforgivable that Fiona had done to them both?

'On the evening of the house fire,' the superintendent said slowly, as if having difficulty of recall, 'hadn't your wife just rung your daughter in Africa?'

His eyes were wandering distantly to where the girl was standing staring into the pool's turquoise water spotted with fragments of burnt fabric. Now he brought his gaze suddenly back on the other man.

Unprepared, Plummer was caught out. 'Had she?'

He looked suddenly confused. Clearly his implied ignorance was pretence. That meant it was Gerry who'd told him of the conversation, because he hadn't seen his wife to speak to since that dramatic revelation of his plans as witnessed by DI Salmon. After that Plummer had been closeted with his staff in the kitchen and then left by car, to return thirty-six hours later with his daughter in tow.

'She rang me from Morocco that night.

Gerry, I mean. Simply said she'd booked a flight home. So I offered to meet her next day.'

'By which time your wife and the kitchen maid had been injured in a house fire which made the front page in most national newspapers, coming as it did as a climax to the story already running of the hanging corpse and suspicions of black magic rites in Bells Wood. Were you ignorant of this new press interest?'

'I stayed overnight at my club in town. The night porter was still on duty when I left early and had doubtless not read the headlines when the newspapers were delivered. Otherwise I am sure he would have made some mention of it. He's quite familiar with my background and normally asks after my family.'

'And the rest of your day?'

'I spent pleasurably in the National Gallery and National Portrait Gallery, before driving to Luton to meet the plane. I had no occasion to buy a newspaper and knew nothing of the fire until I arrived home. I went straight to the hospital to see the injured, but my wife was sedated and unable to speak. There's been no opportunity since then.'

'It must have been a terrible shock for you both.'

'Both?'

'Your daughter too.'

'Ah, yes.'

'Does it seem at all likely to you with the fire coming within an hour or so of your wife's ringing your daughter in Africa that there could be some connection?'

'Cause and effect, you mean?' He spoke cautiously, as if the idea was a new one to him.

'Something of the kind.'

'We–e–e–ll, I don't know what they'd have talked about. Perhaps my wife asked for something Gerry had left in her studio which she needed to have. Or Gerry wanted some specific photograph to be sent out to her. She'd done quite a lot from high altitude which could be used in publicity. Anyway, why don't you ask her?'

He went to the door and called the girl's name. She turned from contemplating the pool and came striding back to the pavilion.

When Yeadings put the question to her she answered frankly. 'Mother was hopping mad because Dad had plans to cut free and take a place of his own. She expected me to sympathize because she wasn't included in them.'

'And did you?'

'Sympathize? No. I told her, "Not before bloody time!".'

Eighteen

The memorial hall wasn't impressive. Built to accommodate minority interests in the rural area, it had received national lottery money to revamp the kitchen and toilets. A cramped foyer allowed room for a reception table where tickets and entrance fees could be dealt with, a rack of pegs for hanging coats, and a hideous china cylinder for the deposit of umbrellas.

The lecture rooms to either side had suffered DIY decoration in magnolia scarred by dark marks where furniture had on occasion been roughly stacked against the walls. An amateur art club had been allowed to hang selected pictures, mainly subdued watercolours and garish acrylics, in the hope of making sales to help with the hall's upkeep.

The stage appeared to be in darkness, its black curtains drawn; lighting was crudely bright over the seating block of plastic stacker chairs. Jimmy Silver estimated there were between eighty and ninety set out, but he expected fewer than twenty people to turn up. He had been the eighth to arrive and was welcomed enthusiastically by a businesslike mum-type.

He guessed men wouldn't be well represented, and then not under the age of seventy.

In ones and twos the audience limped, crept or slid furtively in, hugging the rear of the seating and leaving empty seats between them. For the most part they sat in silence as if in church.

He saw Holly arrive, cautiously look around and choose a seat by the central aisle. Her eyes swept over him without displaying any sign of recognition. Z came in dressed totally in black with a large silver crucifix hanging on her chest. Bait for the diviner, he noted. He was feeling quite nervous about the role he was expected to play, quietly praying that nobody in the audience would know him or that his mother happily remained in the rudest of health.

Half the lighting was suddenly switched off and still people were coming in. There must be over three dozen by now. The stage curtains twitched and a face looked through, androgynous and set on counting the muster. It disappeared as silently as it came.

Prompt on the hour the last lights went out and the curtains swept smoothly back to reveal an empty stage. A spotlight centred on a capacious chair swathed in black velvet. From the gloom glided the medium, only pale face and lower arms visible until she entered the lit zone. She bowed to her audience and took her seat. Enthroned, Silver thought. The lady had a sense of the dramatic.

For several seconds she sat quietly, head bowed, fingers steepled in her lap. When she raised her face to the full beam of the spotlight her eye sockets appeared enormous. 'Shall we all join in gentle meditation,' she invited in an amplified whisper.

The use of a microphone alerted Silver. It opened all sorts of options for whoever was in charge of sound. Pre-recorded matter could be inserted, not to mention weird effects. This lady wasn't above employing the devices of a charlatan.

The sound system emitted a single unprofessional boom and then settled to a pattern of five notes repetitively played on a nose flute with a low background throbbing like a heartbeat. The medium raised one white arm and the wide black sleeve fell back, almost obscuring her face.

'Listen,' she whispered, 'to the pattern of your life. Your own life. Nobody's but your own; because you are unique. You exist in all time. You can reach out into the eternal darkness and find light. You can speak and be heard. Only ask. I am with you on your quest. Let us encounter the truth together. In all humility.'

There was total silence from the floor. The music became more insistent, almost urgent. Not yet, Silver told himself. Let her come to him. He was quite sure by now that she would.

Someone spoke from the back of the room; a woman's voice broken by emotion. 'I had to come. I must tell you. It was just how you said. She wasn't gone for ever. They've found her. She's going to be all right. How can I thank you enough? You gave me the courage to hang on!'

A murmur ran through the gathering, barely breathed, like a breeze passing over a field of standing corn. Silver could not believe that the intervention was other than staged. Start with a success story. Stimulate faith.

The amplified whisper came again. 'Joy. Yes there is joy among us tonight; but sorrow too, and anger at injustice. Someone has been robbed. Not of money, but of just desserts. A soul is crying out for a terrible wrong to be righted.'

There was silence, then a stir as chair legs scraped against the wooden floor. 'It's so unfair. Father never meant it to be like this.'

The man's voice came choked by fury. 'He even wrote it in his will. *Amicably,* he said. We were meant to settle it all amicably.'

The clairvoyant spoke. 'Someone has failed to hear his voice in the written word. But you have heard, and you can put this right.'

'I mean to. I'm only the youngest, but he loved me the best. I know he did. He wouldn't have wanted me to be left out. The other three are to have a share, only they say not me because I never did a hand's turn on the farm. I couldn't. I was too busy working for my scholarship. That was the way he wanted it. For me to be clever, go to university, become a professional. But I'm his son just the same as them. It's my home, for God's sake. They can't turn me out.'

'Gotcha!' Silver said under his breath. This was a real teaser. Let's see how Maud Button will handle this.

She said nothing, appearing to be almost asleep, then her whole body jerked, her head fell back and her mouth gaped open.

'Am–i–ca–ble,' breathed a new, deeper whisper. There seemed some constriction in the man's throat as if he had difficulty in speaking. Then it came clearer, stronger. 'Act always ... in friendship ... as true brothers.'

The whole room became electric, listeners straining forward in their chairs.

'You too. You especially ... must act from brotherly love,' the deeper voice continued. 'Offer what you have.'

'How can I? I'm only a student; I'm skint, in debt for thousands and shall be for years yet.' He was becoming truculent, unpersuaded by the ghostly voice.

'What you have is of more value than money. They have problems you do not know of. Offer them your knowledge, your acquired wisdom. With your heart. Things will be well again. Now go home; tell them what I say.'

The medium lay motionless, but a chair scraped again on the boarded floor and a young man pushed his way to the end of his row, going home, as he was instructed.

More cheering news, Silver noted cynically, satisfied that this time she had clearly committed herself to deception. The sound manager had probably activated some device to deepen the voice from a microphone hidden in her dark clothes. It didn't matter that what she'd said was actually common-sense advice. It was still fraud. Now what he needed was an apparition, a stream of ectoplasm at least.

Maud Button sat up and spoke in her normal voice. 'I'm feeling an influence. It's coming from someone in this room, an unbeliever who wants to speak to me but is prevented. Again it is a young man. He is torn two ways. He has instructions and something inside him forbids him to carry them out. Now I am getting the letter M. It is concerned with M. Could it be his mother? She does not want him to speak a lie.'

She stopped and appeared to be listening. Then she said, 'Who are you? Why do you wish me harm?'

At that moment Silver was not the only one hesitant over lying. Molly Gage faced up to DS Beaumont and a girl not so much older than herself. Molly and Holly, she thought: a bit alike, but she could never do the job this one did.

'What exactly woke you? What did you see when you opened your eyes, Molly?'

'Smoke,' she said cautiously. 'It was choking me. I'd left my door open. It's a bedroom I share with Barbara, and I wanted to know in advance if anyone came upstairs looking for me. I only had my nightie on, you see.'

She had said almost as much before to one of the other detectives. If she kept adding details that were true it could put off the moment when she had to decide whether to do as the master had asked – had actually *paid* – her to do.

'I'd gone up to lie down because I didn't feel very well. Mrs Bradshaw told me I should, because she didn't want anyone working in the kitchen if there was anything wrong with them. She's awfully careful about germs; makes us keep washing our hands all the time. We have to put a blue plaster on our fingers if we show the slightest little spot of blood. And she's ever such a good cook. Not just baking, but roasts and all that. Four or five courses when there's guests invited.'

'I'm sure she's marvellous,' Beaumont allowed, 'but what I need to know is what actually happened up on the top floor when the fire broke out. Did you see it start?'

'No. I told you. I was asleep and the smoke came in from the landing. I started choking and it woke me up. I knew what to do because Mr Bowles holds fire drills regular like, but I was a bit dopey for a moment. You have to alarm everyone and get them out of the house, then wait for the fire engine to get there.'

'Is that what you did?'

She kept him waiting for the answer. 'The smoke alarms were going off, but for some reason the sprinklers hadn't started. I could just make out someone through the smoke, but I didn't know at first who it was. And then she made that sort of screechy noise and suddenly the flames from the master's studio went rushing up her legs and her clothes all took fire.'

'What was your mistress doing?'

'The missus. We call her that.'

'Well, what was she doing? Had she anything in her hands?'

'No.' Molly wasn't sure she'd said the right thing there, took a deep breath and plunged into her first lie. 'Yes, I mean. I couldn't see exactly what it was but she was trying to beat out the flames with it.'

'Would it have been the piece of carpet you later used to wrap her in?' suggested the girl detective helpfully, earning a scowl from her partner.

'Yes, that's what it was. She was fighting the flames back, ever so brave she was. Only they were so fierce and there was a dreadful smell that made me want to be sick. She must have felt ill too. And then I pushed her down to the floor and took the matting and flung it on and rolled her in it till the flames went out. By then there was a whole crowd of us and the men took over. I just saw the missus once when they shifted her into a blanket, and then they sent us away. She looked awful, sort of black all over.'

'You're sure she was trying to beat the flames out?' the detective pursued accusingly.

In for a penny, in for a pound, Molly told herself. 'Absolutely positive,' she said with conviction, and her face flushed more ruddily.

'Useless,' Beaumont muttered to Holly afterwards, and gave her up as a dead loss.

In the memorial hall Silver wished he could crawl out on his belly unobserved, but he was saved from answering by a timely intervention. He recognized Z's voice sounding curiously hesitant and unsure.

'Are you certain that it's a young man, and not a young woman you're getting these vibes from? Because I think it could be me. My name's Marion. That's an M, you see. And it is about my mother. We're terribly at cross purposes at present and I don't know what to do.'

The woman on the stage turned in her direction. 'Would you raise your hand so that I can see where you are?'

In the gloom Silver saw Z rise to her feet. Apart from the large crucifix catching some reflected light, only her skin showed pale. She raised her right hand as though she were taking an oath.

'There is something I want with all my heart to do. I know it is right for me, but she forbids me. I fear that if I have my way it will mean a terrible breach between us.'

The medium too left her chair and came to stand at the edge of the stage. She stretched out an arm. 'I feel for you. You stand at the parting of the ways, about to make the great decision of your life. You do well to ask for my help. There are things we need to talk about, intimately, because I understand. You wish to join a community in which she will find no place. And, without you, she is alone.'

'Yes, oh yes. My father died three years ago and my brother had emigrated to Canada as soon as he left school. But I have a life too, a vocation to serve.'

'And you have been called. That is a rare and wonderful thing which must not be denied.'

'What am I to do? Must I wait until she's less adamant. Or worse, until she dies?' Her voice was caught in a sob. 'That is the last thing I want for her.'

God, she can act, Silver marvelled. She sounded little more than a teenager. Even he felt moved by the dilemma, almost convinced that Rosemary Zyczynski was admitting a secret longing in her life. She was so credible, so devoutly convincing, a respectable middle-class twenty-year-old deprived of the freedom to choose a cherished and saintly ambition.

'Have patience,' the medium said. 'Release will not be long coming. I cannot see clearly how, but we should work together and I know a message will come. Perhaps your father...'

'Oh, poor Dad, if he had only lived a few years longer. He understood, you see. He had once wanted to take holy orders, but was prevented by being called up for the Falklands War. And then, afterwards, he married my mother. So everything changed.'

'Fate has brought you to me in time. We shall find a solution together, my dear. I will ask you to wait behind after the meeting is concluded.'

Z clasped her hands about her crucifix, bowed her head and resumed her seat modestly.

Maud Button moved centre-stage, turned her back on her audience and stood erect, both arms outflung. A respectful sigh ran through her watchers. She had performed wonders tonight and there was more still to come.

'There is someone here who wishes to tell me a secret,' she said, spinning to face them again. 'Come forward, and do not be afraid to speak it...'

The team met up later to evaluate what they'd discovered. 'So,' Yeadings confronted them, 'what did you make of the lady?'

'Eight out of ten for the stagey presentation,' Z said.

'Silver, what response did you get?'

Shamefaced, he had to confess. 'She listened, but I'm not sure she accepted my story. Earlier on she'd been expecting me to be reluctant, even hostile to her. And that was uncanny because she'd hit the nail right on the head. Maybe she really can pick up some vibes.

'I wasn't sure just then that I could do all that bereavement stuff about my mother. It seemed too much like tempting fate, and she'd have hated me making a mock of it all. But then Z intervened and took over. She'd set up a brilliant story about wanting to join a religious community and her mother was piling on the personal blackmail, standing in her way. She was absolutely convincing, had the audience gawking for more.'

Yeadings nodded, waiting for the rest.

'She was dressed all in black with a whacking great crucifix round her neck, acting the called-by-God part superbly. She sounded like a lost kid.'

'I can see it,' Yeadings responded. 'With what result?'

'Teacher asked me to stay behind after school,' Z said mischievously. 'I have a private session with her set up for next week. She intends contacting my dead father. I guess it will be expensive, so I hope I can claim off expenses.'

'No doubt we can disguise it as something more acceptable to the auditors. Well done, anyway.'

'And DC Silver put on a good performance straight after. He stuck with the storyline you suggested.'

'I couldn't chicken out of it after what she'd

done,' Silver mumbled.

'Good. Regard it as your first experience of undercover policing. A debut in deviousness. There's no knowing how far you'll go, now we've wrested you from your computer. But rest assured, we'll return you now to your comfort zone.'

He looked over his half-moon reading glasses at the real apprentice. 'And Holly, how about you?'

'I just sat through it all and looked impressed. One of the ladies from Needlecraft recognized me. She came up as I was leaving and said she hoped I would find an interest and comfort in following a course with the wonderful clairvoyant. So I said yes, and mentioned it had really opened my eyes.' She grinned. 'Which it did. I'd say she's an out-and-out fraud.'

Nineteen

While Yeadings sounded out Maud Button's claims at the meeting for Contact and Comfort for the Bereaved, DCI Mott had promised himself an evening at home with his family. They ate late, after Astrid had fallen asleep over her bottle and been taken upstairs to her cot.

Paula had chosen red mullet at the fishmonger's that morning and served it delicately seasoned alongside petits pois, cherry tomatoes and asparagus in Hollandaise sauce. Foraging in the freezer had produced a pineapple cheesecake which was still a little on the chilled side.

'There's some wine left,' Paula said as they finished, offering him the bottle, but Angus was already leaving the table.

'Best not. I need my head clear.' He stopped himself in time from suggesting she finish it, because he wasn't happy about her drinking alcohol so soon after Astrid's birth. It meant she'd given up breast feeding completely and all the books he'd read had recommended it as the best, the perfect way, for babies to build natural immunity.

'I'll take it into the lounge with me then, since obviously you've brought more work back. A pity, because I'd picked up a couple of old videos you'd have enjoyed and thought we could have a cosy evening together.'

'Sorry, love. Work's stacking up at the nick. We've three current cases to prepare for CPS, as well as this stupid business out at Barrows which the press keep stoking up for lack of real news.'

He ran a hand through his mop of blond hair. 'And now the Boss is chasing a sideline with this self-styled forensic psychic. He's put three of the team on watching her perform tonight at some spooky meeting.'

'I thought he even drew the line at profilers. Does he take clairvoyance seriously?' She stood at the open door, bottle of Montrachet in one hand, apparently prepared to leave the dessert dishes in place.

He ignored the question. 'How about filling the dishwasher? I'll need the whole table to spread my papers.' He heard the testiness in his own voice. But dammit, that was part of her job. He tried to do his share of the chores while they'd no one to help in the house, but police work had to come first.

She muttered something about it having been a hell of a day anyway. Some people thought caring for babies was simple, but the smaller they were the bigger the messes and the louder the screams. He should try being tied to it day in and day out. Sometimes she almost understood those mothers who gave the little horrors a good shake and ended in police court charged with abuse.

All the while she was deftly clearing used dishes, glasses and cutlery on to a tray for whisking away. He noticed that she had left the remnants of the wine behind, but she came back a final time to collect it while he was stacking the table mats.

'I'll say goodnight then, and turn in early,' she threatened. 'Try not to wake me when you come up.'

Now he was in the doghouse just for having work to catch up with. And behind it was the continual irritant for her that she wasn't yet able to pick up her own career again.

He opened his laptop, logged on and began to spread the workload from his briefcase, paper that computers were supposed to have obviated. Instead, they had clearly created a whole new hunger for it.

He glanced at his wrist, noted it was nine twenty-three p.m. Silver, Z and the new girl on the team would be in thrall (or otherwise) to the ridiculous Maud Button, inflating overtime costs. He sometimes wished the Boss would leave organizing stake-outs entirely to him as SIO, and not insert his own outlandish whims. But, admittedly, on the odd occasion when he did, the intrusion would often come up a winner. This time, however, Yeadings seemed to have joined the weirdos who were grabbing centre stage at Barrows.

He turned now to the spurious abduction of a schoolgirl by her ransom-seeking older man friend met on the Internet. It wasn't certain she'd stick to her admission that they were to have eloped on the proceeds.

After he'd spent a solid hour on building a strong prosecution line for CPS to present, the phone in the hall rang. Straightening his stiffened back, which reminded him he'd missed out too often on water polo practice, he went to answer it. The call was from Control at the local nick: a query whether he'd accept a call put through from a Miss Jo Golding.

The name meant nothing to him. 'Who the devil's she? What does she want?'

Apparently she'd been hoping to contact Jimmy Silver, but he wasn't at home and he'd switched off his mobile.

Jo. He remembered now. That was the girl young Silver was being ribbed about in the canteen. For God's sake, didn't the stupid moo know better than to go chasing her boyfriend through his senior officers?

'He's out on a job,' he told the sergeant shortly. 'And I don't want to know.'

'She says it's in connection with the Barrows hanging case. Something you might find useful. And she's sorry it's after hours, like.'

It wasn't likely she'd have anything worthwhile to tell him, but since Control had passed it on he'd better be seen to show some interest. 'Put her through then.'

She had a pleasant voice, sounded educated, even intelligent. Lucky Silver, in that case. Not that he'd any interest in censoring or counselling lower ranks' love lives. Leave that to the old 'uns who gloomily warned of inevitable break-up in police couplings.

Jo apologized for bothering him. She'd hoped to pass the item to DC Silver but he wasn't available at present. It happened that she'd seen a photograph in the late edition of the *Evening Standard* with a half column on the unexpected return from abroad of Geraldine Plummer, due to the disastrous events at her Thames Valley home.

Jo's point was that she then realized she'd met her. Gerry had been their pilot for the hot-air balloon flight she and Silver took a week or more back. And she'd heard since that Gerry actually owned the outfit. That's why she'd have gone out to Africa. She'd said at the time that she was planning to chase the winter tourists to Morocco, the season in Europe being over now.

'Does that help at all?' she ended hopefully.

'It's information we hadn't actually recorded,' he said cautiously. 'Thank you, Miss Golding.'

'Jo,' she told him. 'Everyone calls me that.'

On a sudden whim, he felt she needed encouraging. 'I look forward to meeting you sometime. Tell Jimmy that, will you?'

'Thank you, Chief Inspector.'

'Angus,' he corrected her. Then he pulled himself up. Had she manoeuvred me into that? he asked himself. Bright girl.

As he replaced the receiver Paula appeared on the staircase, carrying down a grizzling baby. 'Was that work again?' she demanded. 'I thought they knew not to use the landline. It woke Astrid and she's not best pleased.'

Angus stretched and held out his arms. 'She'll need changing. Give her to me for a minute while you get her a rusk to suck at.'

When Astrid was sorted he rocked her in his arms. She was warm and smelled of baby soap. She gazed up with those startling blue eyes and stopped crying. One of her little fists came up, opened, and the tiny fingers snatched at his chin.

'I'm all bruffly,' he apologized. 'I didn't shave before dinner.'

She didn't seem to mind and smiled at him. He was sure she could, although everyone said she was far too young.

When Paula returned from the kitchen she carried a tray with two mugs of coffee as well as the rusk.

To hell with work, Angus decided. This mattered more.

It was late when Yeadings released the trio

244

from their debriefing. Jimmy Silver hoped to creep into the house without rousing his parents, but as he carried up a mug of hot tomato soup to drink in bed, he saw a light come on under their bedroom door. No inquisition, he begged silently, as his mother emerged in her dressing-gown.

'Police work,' he said curtly and immediately regretted the tone.

'Your young lady rang earlier.'

'Jo. You know her name, Mother. What did she want?'

'She wouldn't say. She sounds nice; asked after Dad's arthritis.'

He remembered then that his mobile was still turned off. 'I'm tired, Mum, gotta snatch some sleep. You too. There was no need to stay awake waiting for me. Get back to bed now. I'll return Jo's call tomorrow.'

In his room he shrugged off his clothes and looked at his phone for messages. Jo had rung three times without saying why. It was too late to bother her with ringing back.

He flung open the bed, ready to sink in, caught sight of his discarded clothes on the floor, went back to pick them up and hang them on hangers as he'd long been taught to do.

Life would be a lot easier if he had a place of his own. But that would be more expensive than staying with his parents and he had reasons now to be saving for later, in case Jo came round to thinking the way he hoped.

Buoyed up by his final success with Maud Button, and the Boss's hint of further undercover opportunities, he rolled over and quickly fell into rosy, dream-filled sleep.

'She dropped off quite a while back,' Angus told Paula. 'You don't look much brighter yourself.'

He would have told her ten minutes ago except that he was enjoying the warm cuddling of the now milky-scented baby. He'd fed her the bottle Paula brought in, burped the little bundle and suffered a stream of curds down the back of his decent shirt. But all pleasures must have an end.

'Bed,' Paula yawned. 'I'm absolutely whacked.'

When all three were sorted into their accustomed places she didn't seem so weary, sliding an arm over her husband's shoulder and pulling him close.

To hell with the impossible work load, he told himself, life can be pretty good.

In the ITU at High Wycombe Hospital a nurse bent over the still form of Fiona Plummer. She had caught the faint twitch of a finger in the hand with the cannula insertion. As she watched, the eyelids flickered in the small gap between bandages. The patient tried to draw a deeper breath, and choked. There was toxic smoke still in the lungs, and coughing was likely to bring her round while overexerting her heart.

'Alice,' the nurse said, 'can you hear me?'

It was awkward because she'd never nursed a titled woman before. Maybe she shouldn't have used her first name like that before she'd asked permission.

Fiona groaned, failed to recognize that she'd been spoken to and was conscious only of growing discomfort. There were pins and needles all down her left side; she couldn't move her arms and seemed to have some hard obstruction in her mouth. And then pain started creeping up her legs, her abdomen, increasing until it reached her burnt face. She tried to lift one hand to brush off whatever was covering it but it failed to budge. Someone was leaning over her insisting on talking. She wished she'd go away. She'd had bad falls before. It was what you expected if you hunted.

Why didn't the fool woman go and chase after the bloody horse and leave her to come round properly?

Jimmy Silver rang Jo at seven a.m. She was carrying a mug of tea to her father's room and hoped the ringing would continue until her hands were free. She was unlucky because Dad was complaining of a headache and she had to unearth his pills from a locked drawer in the study.

Jimmy waited another ten minutes and tried again, luridly imagining her naked in the shower. 'You rang me last night,' he said, adding proudly, 'I was on a spot of undercover and had to switch my mobile off.'

It surprised her. She didn't think Jimmy was into heroics, and she hoped it hadn't been anything dangerous.

'Just devious,' he told her. 'I'm not used to telling lies, but in the end I think I managed to sound convincing. Was there something special you wanted to tell me?'

'I contacted DCI Mott at home instead. I hope you don't mind. He was very nice: said he'd like to meet me sometime.'

'How did you get his number?' Jimmy sounded panicky.

'Through Control. They asked his permission to put me through, and he was quite willing.'

'But what did you say to him?'

'I told him we knew Gerry Plummer.'

Silver was caught wrong-footed. 'Do we?'

'She was our balloon pilot. So he might want you to be the one who follows her up. What's the chance of that?'

'I dunno.' He considered his position. Her intrusion could have been embarrassing, but it had done no harm. Someone would need to question Gerry Plummer about her mother's phone conversation on the night of the fire. It could have sparked off Mrs Plummer to set the place alight.

'They do seem an eccentric family.'

'We get to meet all sorts.'

When he entered the CID office that morning he found a Post-it note on his screen. He was to make it ASAP to the Boss. Apprehensively, he made his way upstairs to find Angus Mott already installed with a cappuccino.

'We're considering Mrs Plummer's behaviour,' Yeadings told him. 'And further feed-in wouldn't come amiss. Was there any rational motive behind her action, and if so, what was it?'

Silver hadn't given much thought to this, his own experiences of last evening having preoccupied him to the exclusion of all else. If anything, he'd assumed she was overcome by fury at her husband's sudden decision to up sticks and walk out on her. But now, in view of what Jo had told him, there could be an alternative reason.

He needed to watch what he said. Having already given him a minor undercover job, the Boss was even extending his role, inviting his opinion.

'She used her daughter's lighter, didn't she? So she started the fire in that inner room. Following the phone call, maybe she was more furious with her than with her husband. Gerry was the first one to have walked out on her anyway.'

'Is that all she'd done?'

'The hot-air balloon circus. Plummer must have bought it for her – or given her the money to take it over. Jealousy, perhaps. Her own needs overlooked.'

'But natural enough. A father's gift to a favoured child, his one surviving child.'

'This studio was the only remaining thing of Gerry's she could wreak her spite on.'

Yeadings nodded. 'It was where she used to develop and store her photographs; another interest her mother was excluded from. A part of the house her husband and daughter appear to have made their shared place of privacy,' he followed up.

Silver was conscious of the other two watching, waiting for him to take it a stage further. They'd been feeding him to this point.

He launched himself on a fresh notion. 'She wanted to destroy some of the photographs. There could have been something too revealing among them that mustn't be seen. Something involving her and which her husband wouldn't forgive?'

He waited for the Boss's reaction. Was that interpretation too wildly far-fetched?

And then he saw how he could be of use. Gerry's stuff was all destroyed, but there could be substitutes, at least for any shots of the estate recently taken from a considerable height. Both he and Jo had been snapping away with their digital cameras for most of the flight, and they had covered the whole of the Barrows domain and surrounding countryside.

Since then he had transferred his own shots to his laptop and could easily print off copies for reference. Jo would certainly have done much the same at home. He must warn her before ever she deleted any as being less than artistically perfect.

He took a step towards the superintendent's paper-strewn desk. 'You can have my pics,' he said eagerly. 'And Jo's. We took them from Gerry's balloon. They just might reveal something at ground level that her mother didn't want anyone to see.'

Yeadings and Mott exchanged meaningful glances. 'We thought you might have done that,' the Boss said serenely. 'I wouldn't have taken a flight like that myself without keeping some record of it.'

Twenty

Zyczynski awoke to the threat of an aural thermometer. She brushed the offer aside, reaching instead for the cup of tea ready on her bedside cabinet.

'Wrong order,' Max said crisply. 'Temperature first, hot drink next.'

She sat up groggily. 'What on earth...?'

'Not *what*, but *why*. You've been muttering and mumbling half the night.'

'About what?'

'Can't you remember?'

She frowned, obediently offering her ear for the thermometer. She had a jumbled impression of having just been with the team. Yeadings had assembled them but instead of a briefing they seemed to have gone on a coach ride somewhere abroad. Mott and Salmon were wearing paper hats like at a kids' party. And no one but herself had noticed that there was no driver. In his seat sat a large green frog, its throat pulsating as it croaked in rhythm with the engine's diesel throbbing. The coach had been driving itself faster and faster, and while everyone chattered, shouting each other down, she couldn't find her voice to warn them. She had to but she couldn't.

The outcome had been lost somehow. Perhaps, as so often in dreams, there was no conclusion, because then she was into the next sequence, running towards a stretch of water. At one moment it was the Atlantic with surf breaking under her balcony in Madeira, and then transformed into a lake with a surly, unmoving surface that promised infinite depths. And with every heartbeat she was getting perilously nearer, with no power of stopping. In one hand she'd been waving a small red flag.

That was when Max had leaned across the bed to stop her madly shouting.

'Thirty-eight point seven,' he said in the real world. 'I'll ring Angus that you're not coming in today.'

At least he'd not said 'I told you so,' about returning too soon to work. Last night she had felt a tad feverish but blamed fatigue. She was sure she'd be normal by morning.

'I was dreaming,' she admitted. 'I think you just saved me from a watery grave.'

'Your clairvoyant lady would probably interpret that as an omen. Water's supposed to signify insecurity. Was the day sunny or dark?'

She frowned to remember. Already the images were fading. 'It started brilliant, and then instantly it was overcast. But I don't accept all that foreknowledge nonsense. Dreams are shreds of undigested memory from the subconscious. They give a jumbled hint at where you stand emotionally. It all takes some untangling, but can even help in resolving a dilemma.'

'Or warn that your poor driven brain is having a tough time with the job in hand. Now, drink your tea before it goes cold. I'm making crêpes for breakfast. Tell me what filling you want.'

He rang Mott from his own flat across the landing. 'Rosemary's running a temp. Not very high but she's feverish, babbling all sorts of rubbish about dreams of water. It could be an infection starting up. I'm getting the doc in.'

When he returned with a tray of breakfast she had given up protesting and was asleep again, flat on her back with her mouth open.

Mott repeated Max's message verbatim to Yeadings, who took it seriously. 'We've too many casualties in the Barrows case and a sad lack of progress,' he grunted.

Before their morning briefing was through there came further alarming news. Molly from Barrows kitchen had spent no more than five hours at home before being rushed back into hospital vomiting blood.

'Never heard of that as a result of smoke inhalation,' Beaumont voiced for them all as they dismissed. 'You'd almost believe there was a hex on everyone at that place. Small wonder Plummer wants to pull out.'

Yeadings agreed silently. It was time, he decided, to catch up with that gentleman. Here was an excuse to abandon desk and deal with personalities. But first he'd get a few things sorted in black and white.

He took a page of unlined copy paper and wrote Gervais Plummer's name at the centre. From that point he began to draw lines radiating to everyone connected with him, until the sketch looked like a sunburst. The only names missing from the case's entire *dramatis personae* were those of Maud Button and the year-old corpse supposedly retrieved from the bunker.

She would undoubtedly have entered the site as an Urban Explorer. This reminded him to sift among his notes for a memo from young Silver who'd been asked to get an identity for her. The acronyms in Silver's jotted notes left with DCI Mott meant nothing to Yeadings, still a reluctant student of IT. He rang down to the CID office and requested that Silver join him.

'Sounds like a coffee date,' Beaumont informed him enviously. 'The Boss would otherwise have said, "Send young Silver up ASAP."'

He appeared at Yeadings's open door, however, with an anxious frown and his laptop under one arm, to find Beaumont's prophecy correct. The machine on the window sill was burbling and two *Crimewatch* mugs were standing ready with spoons in them.

'I need a little illumination,' the Boss said. 'What are ISP and IP?'

He listened while the young DC explained. It had been a good move sending him on that police IT crime course. Over the last ten years the division had expanded to keep up with the increase in computer deception, particularly with the entrapment of young children by paedophiles posing as friendly contemporaries.

ISP, Silver explained, stood for Internet Service Provider. 'You can regard the Internet just like your telephone line – except that you type down it rather than talk. So the ISP is the company that physically connects your house to the Web, and charges you line rental for the pleasure. Similarly, your IP or Internet Protocol address tells everyone where to find you. And, usefully for us, just like a phone number it reveals the town the caller is located near.'

The ISP had been approached for a precise address. This had been granted on pressing police authority and revealed an Internet café in the student area of Nottingham. The registered name for the year-old entry was no longer available and had been erased from their archives by special request.

'So that's a dead end?' Yeadings demanded. 'What about rights of public scrutiny?'

'Data Protection Act,' Silver told him. 'There are all these criss-crossing laws nowadays cancelling each other out. Luckily, there are always ways of getting round deletions. I was going to request a trip to Nottingham, sir, to see what I could do about it.'

Escape from the desk, Yeadings thought. Does he too sometimes feel trapped? He saw the DC's eyes on his desk-pad sketch and turned it to be read more easily.

'It helps to analyse connections. Next, I run lines between the peripheral names, where appropriate, and see where the groupings lead me.'

He sighed. 'In this case, to fetch more paper. And don't start talking spreadsheets. That's a language I haven't caught up with.'

Silver looked mildly embarrassed.

'Well, come out with it then,' the Boss countermanded. 'Don't stand on one leg.'

'I was only going to ask – could I photocopy that diagram page, sir? To work from?'

'If you let me have it back right away.' He felt encouraged by the way the lad had picked up on his old-fashioned pen and ink method. And the notion of working in parallel with his media skills could benefit them both.

He hoped young Silver wasn't expecting too much from being made an acting DS, because once Z was fully back in harness it must cease. Already his two sergeants, competing for a deserved inspectorship, were having a long wait.

In a hotly argued deal to keep Mott out of transfer to uniform on his promotion after Bosnia, the ACC (Personnel) had foisted Salmon on to the team. Now he stood in everyone's way like a bed-blocker in a crowded hospital ward.

This reminded him he should check on young Molly Gage. After Silver left he rang through to DCI Mott to ask if there was a progress report.

'Just about to call you, sir,' Angus said. 'A further complication in the Barrows case. We now have a possible murder attempt. Path Lab reports finding powdered glass in Molly Gage's vomit. She's bleeding quite badly from the stomach and throat. They've yet to analyse what she'd been given to eat but there was a quantity of chocolate present. Nobody else at her home has the same trouble.'

Why Molly? Yeadings asked himself. What did she know, or had seen, that was a threat to someone? It surely had a connection with the house fire, which implied Plummer's wife was involved; but she was definitely out of the action at present. That left Plummer as a suspect. He'd spent some time visiting the girl. Immediately after that she had wanted visitors kept away and Gerry Plummer had been barred by the ward manager.

On being discharged, Molly had amplified her previous statement, claiming that the missus had been fighting the fire and been 'ever so brave'. For some reason, it seemed, her employer had supplied her with a new version meant to eliminate any suspicion of arson from his wife. She might have started the fire by burning certain photographs in the studio waste bin, but there had been no intention of causing greater damage. Pure accident in that case.

His reason to provide such cover might have been a late feeling of compassion for the wretched woman or the more mundane one of guarding against the small writing in his house insurance policy.

Molly had followed instructions. So why should he go further to silence her when she'd done as demanded? He would surely protect her against being persuaded to withdraw the later statement.

And, from the purely practical view, how had anyone outside her apparently loving family had access to poison her? Unless, on the belt and braces principle, he had taken something edible with him to make doubly sure.

But Plummer was no fool. He would know suspicion could fall on him. Using powdered glass had nothing subtle about it and would be instantly recognizable. Also, the girl might have ingested it too soon, before she'd given her new version to the police.

Yeadings rang down to DCI Mott. 'Angus, contact the woman PC on duty at the hospital. I want to know whether Plummer was carrying a package when he visited Molly Gage.'

'That's covered, Boss. He'd nothing with him unless in his pockets. And whatever contained the glass would have a certain bulk, unlike a lethal tablet.'

'And were there other Greeks bearing gifts?'

'Just her mother, with various bundles, but I think we can rule her out. Gerry Plummer was turned away. Mrs Bradshaw visited.'

'A cook would have every chance to put the glass in some home-baked confectionery, and she's almost certain to have taken the girl something edible. Molly might have picked up an embarrassing secret about her that she'd want to keep hidden; but I honestly can't see her in a murderous light.'

Mott agreed. 'Are we expected to write this one off as another accident? I just hope she pulls through and the case doesn't turn into a full murder hunt after all. CPS agree that our original body can't be proved in court as a deliberate attack.'

'But don't push it into the background. Other cases may be more serious, but this one's had prime publicity. The press are going to give us some stick if we don't make a positive move soon. This latest development may keep the excitement up, but they're going to want some action on it.'

'Tell me something I don't know,' Mott muttered, after he'd laid down the phone.

The house down by the lake had once been a keeper's cottage and provided for a large Victorian family. There were five bedrooms, two reception rooms, a nursery under the eaves and reasonable-sized domestic offices. Since Plummer had given Barrows staff a week's paid leave, he and Gerry elected to look after themselves in a spirit of holiday camping. They were sharing the simple cooking and Gerry made herself responsible for keeping things roughly tidy while her father drove off to Aylesbury with a long shopping list. They had installed minimal personal possessions and found the sketchy furniture left in the building adequate for their needs. Emergency services were still carrying out tests on the main house and Gervais had booked builders and decorators for a fortnight's time.

When Silver, after a follow-up visit to the Nottingham Internet café, visited them there, he brought a selection of aerial photographs he and Jo had taken on the balloon flight. Gerry was almost embarrassingly grateful. It surprised him, revealing a softer side of the woman that he hadn't come across.

'We haven't lost all the family records,' Plummer said. 'Before ever you took up photography I used to snap everything with my old film cameras, especially when you children were young. I got the photos developed and printed in town; never had a dark room of my own. The albums will be in one of the office cupboards.'

He turned to Silver. 'That's on the ground floor. No harm if I cross the tape again to fetch them, is there?'

'I'll come with you.' The young DC was keen to get a sight of the house interior.

All three walked up together through the blackened wood. A forestry gang were at work sawing and removing the debris. Two huge flatbed trucks were already half-filled with charred logs. Work stopped as they passed. It was like the sudden hush in a village street as a funeral went by.

There was plenty for the three of them to carry back, all the thick leather albums labelled on the spine with comprehensive dates.

'I'm not sure I'm ready for all this nostalgia,' the girl said as they piled them on a bench under the kitchen window. 'I'll make tea.'

'The universal panacea,' Plummer murmured, 'even for regrets.'

Regret wasn't the overwhelming emotion when Mrs Silver brought out their family snapshots. Jimmy always tried to disguise his boredom as they were passed around and drooled over. There were some really shameful ones of him with a knitted woolly hat askew over one eye, or offering the contents of a potty. His parents had looked quite young in them, barely recognizable. 'Time changes us all,' he found himself saying, and caught a stricken glance between the other two.

'I can't believe we've done this,' Gerry said as she poured tea. 'Are you thinking of carting them all down to Cheltenham? I thought you intended breaking with the past. What we should do is have a mighty bonfire of the vanities. Except that there's been more than enough set alight round here lately.'

But after they'd cleared the scrubbed wooden table in the kitchen, Plummer set the albums out in chronological order. He opened the first on formal photographs of a wedding. The bride had been beautiful, tiny and dark-eyed. In one photo the camera had caught her gazing up at her husband in open adoration. Plummer turned pages quickly until the subject was a child in an elaborate christening robe.

'Is that you?' Silver asked Gerry.

'My big brother,' she said in a strange voice.

Little could be seen of the body, but the face looked pinched.

'Half-brother,' Plummer corrected her. 'I married twice.'

Then Silver remembered the family background notes Yeadings had insisted they all read. This was Penny's child and she'd died after a difficult birth. The little boy survived, to suffer from cerebral palsy.

This was the son who'd later drowned in the lake after a summer afternoon picnic. He'd been seven or eight years old. And his name was Freddy.

Suddenly there was a skittering sound as Gerry spun on her heel, hands raised to cover her devastated face, and rushed from the room, knocking a chair off balance.

'I'm sure you've heard the story,' Plummer said in an over-controlled voice. 'In some ways we've not been a fortunate family.'

Twenty-One

Jo's father, the MP, had been selected as a delegate to a commercial mission to China. She rang Jimmy Silver in a state of barely controlled excitement. 'He needs me with him because of his arthritis,' she said, 'and he's determined to trudge at least a part of the Great Wall.'

'That's great,' he told her. 'But...'

'I know what's coming next. It's "take care".'

'Well, yes.'

'Now I wonder why? Is it dangers of foreign travel, international terrorism or fear that he'll illegally include me in his expenses?'

'I don't want anything awful to happen to you. I just wish I could come along too.'

'To protect me? That's nice, Jimmy, but it's not a jamboree, and it's somewhere I've always been curious about, so I'm breaking into my piggy bank for the journey of a lifetime.'

'How long will you be away?'

'Eight days. We fly out on Tuesday. There's a lot to plan, but maybe we can meet up before then. Say, come over for supper this evening?

Dad'll be here then and you can meet him.'

So much happening so fast. He felt uncertain. But if Mott would clear him to leave early he could get his decent suit to the cleaner's for the express service. 'What time?' he heard himself asking.

'Anytime after six. It'll give us a chance to talk first. Dad'll be held up at the House until nearly eight. We'll be fixing the dinner.'

Of course he'd do as she asked. He felt shaken, invited for a meal, getting a chance to see inside the Pimlico apartment where he'd only watched the lighted windows from street parking. Meeting her father! He'd so often wondered what the man was like and had never dared ask. Some Members of Parliament got their names in the newspapers for this and that, but not Harold Golding. Not even a smudgy press photograph in a group shot of the party. Now he was going on a fact-finding mission to China. That meant he was considered responsible. It also implied he was shrewd. This left Jimmy scared.

DS Beaumont was just leaving the nick for a morning in court when the duty sergeant on reception caught up with him. A tearful woman had asked for whoever was in charge of investigating the recent fire at Barrows. At this stage it was mainly the fire service; but he supposed CID would agree to see her. She'd refused to divulge what it was that had upset her. The name was Gage.

That would be the kitchen maid's mother, Beaumont guessed. And the girl, Molly was back in hospital suspected of having been poisoned with powdered glass. This promised more excitement than the mundane GBH case he was due to give evidence to as arresting officer, but he'd no time to pick up on it. His case was top of the court list that morning. Uniform had already allocated a constable to call on her, but she'd beaten him to it.

'Inform DCI Mott. Stick the lady in interview room two and get her some tea,' he shouted as he left the building.

When Angus joined her she was sitting bolt upright, refusing all refreshments. 'You need to see this,' she said, opening a capacious plastic carrier bag advertising the local health store and producing an unwrapped and opened box of dark chocolates.

Fingerprints, Angus thought, groaning inwardly. She must be the only person left who didn't read crime or watch TV.

'I found it under her bed,' she babbled, 'when I was changing the sheets. Me foot knocked it and when I pulled it out I thought that's what she'd been eating that the rest of us hadn't. She musta hidden it away because I'd been on to her about putting on weight.'

He asked the expected questions about when and how it had been delivered, but Mrs Gage was adamant that Molly must have received it in hospital and smuggled it home unopened. 'One of her visitors brought it in. They must of.'

'Who do you think?' he asked.

'Someone who knew what a weakness she had for chocolate, especially the dark kind,' she said darkly. 'That Mrs Bradshaw was always giving her little treats, and didn't care how fast she grew out of her clothes.'

'Do you suspect there may be glass in the chocolates?'

'Well, what else? There wasn't none in anything I gave her to eat at home. I'm not saying Mrs Bradshaw knew there was anything wrong with them. No, more like it'd be someone slipshod in some factory, having an accident and not owning up. Only, I know you people have a way of looking inside them and finding out anything that's wrong. But it's a terrible mistake to make and they ought to be sued for it.'

He looked at her sharply. She'd jumped from blaming a visitor from Barrows to accusing the manufacturer of endangering the public. Her reported tearfulness had quickly passed to self-righteous protest and now she was verging on the litigious.

'How is Molly now?' he thought to ask.

Reminded of the risk to her daughter, she sat back and seemed to crumple. 'She's really bad, but they say she's stable. She'll be all right.

Her throat's packed with ice.'

On the outside, he hoped. 'Thank you for bringing in the chocolates. I'll have them examined. I'm very sorry for you. It's a worrying time. Go home now and get some rest, Mrs Gage. She'll be very well looked after where she is.'

He saw her to the exit, having slipped the lock on the interview room door to prevent anyone entering and touching the evidence.

He'd get it wrapped and sent across to forensics for fingerprinting and chemical analysis. For the present he must work on the assumption that what the girl's mother suspected was correct. He returned to his office and committed the interview to computer, adding the names of known visitors who could have delivered the chocolates and the manufacturer's name.

Uniform had already left a note listing hospital staff, with addresses, of all who had been in contact with Molly when she was treated for her burns. Reports on interviews with them were due at any time.

Gervais Plummer was studying the prints from Silver's digital shots on the kitchen table in the cottage. Some of them were irrelevant and he set them aside, keeping any which showed the bounds of his estate. These he examined carefully under magnification, but could find nothing amiss. Any aerial shots taken now would have shown a very different story; but with Gerry's balloon circus away in Africa he would need to hire a Cessna from Denham airfield to get an up-to-date appreciation of present damage.

He collected the pics and stood a glass paperweight on them. Next he examined areas farther afield, identifying familiar roads, farms, villages and towns. He identified three shots where Halton RAF station and its living quarters sprawled beyond Wendover, then traced the route back to Barrows. Midway between he picked out the old bunker site at Beacons. Despite its internal roads showing lack of upkeep the security appeared formidable. On close sight the wartime RAF station could be taken for a prisoner-of-war camp, and there was evidence that the guardhouse was retained in use, also a small Portakabin with a tended garden behind. A more solid building that could be taken for a dwelling had a larger square structure as an extension which he guessed must cover the vital underground floors and provide secure access.

He remembered that it had possessed vast radar dishes and been manned by the RAF back in the fifties, at the height of the Cold War. Information released since then under the thirty-year rule revealed that it had housed the Kelvin Hughes Projector, an iconic interception plotting table of the period. A continuous strip of photographic film passed across the

front of a cathode ray tube which was displaying the sweep radar trace. The film then ran
through a processing plant which developed,
fixed, and dried it before finally a large lamp
shone the image on to the underside of a large
translucent plotting table. Standing above this,
plotting staff with Chinagraph pencils and
senior controllers directed fighter aircraft to
defend UK airspace from the invaders.

Recognized as a valuable wartime asset, the
system had the disadvantage that action lagged
a minute behind real time, just about workable
in the days of wartime propeller-driven aircraft, but woefully slow for the ensuing jet age.

Although such information was now publicly
released, he would never have known of this
project but for archives retrieved from his
father's involvement in secret supply of com-
ponents from his electronics and photographic
company. He had grown up with a special pride
in the connection and regarded the installation
almost as part of the family estate.

Now he gathered from recent police interest
in the locality that curiosity about Cold War
bunkers had given rise to an adventure culture
among the young who fancied themselves as
'explorers' when penetrating similar areas still
under government control.

It appeared that the Beacons bunker was
being seriously considered as a scene of either
fatal accident or crime which could account for
injuries to the dead girl found hanging in Bells

Wood from the Wishing Tree.

It was well known that from time to time a maintenance crew moved into the old installation, and although no sign of activity appeared on the aerial photos there were two commercial vans parked close to the bunker entrance. It could be worth while calling in at the Eagle's Head and casually enquiring whether strangers had been drinking there of late.

Impatient for results, DCI Mott dropped the chocolate box in at the lab in person.

The chief, Norman Ransom, looked dubious about his demand for chemical analysis and DNA for handlers.

'You're running up expenses on a possible non-crime death, aren't you? And there's a helluva wait for DNA results at present. God knows when we'll get results back. The box of chocs could have been handled by half a dozen different people.

'Tell you what I'll do – just give you any blood groups if they come up. If you've any for comparison, you may decide which is worth following up with the full break down.'

Mott grimaced. 'Guess I'll have to settle for that. Can you have the group matching done today?'

'I'll send it round before six.'

Angus returned to find Silver hesitating at the door of his office. 'Something new?' he asked hopefully.

'No. Just a request to knock off early.'

'No. We're all under pressure.'

'I know. Sorry.'

He looked chastened, and Mott reflected that in the DC's place Beaumont would have invented some excuse to slope off without permission and later claim it was a vital chase after information.

'Is there some special reason?'

Silver drew a deep breath. 'Jo Golding – you know she was helpful about having met Gerry Plummer? Well, she's off to China with her father in the next few days and wants to see me first.' He halted, and his face flushed with embarrassment. 'Tonight could be my only chance to meet him before they go.'

'They live in London, that right?'

'Pimlico. He's an MP.'

'I don't care if he's a dustman or a pest-control officer. But it happens that you could look in on the burns unit Mrs Plummer's just been transferred to. She's conscious now, but refuses to talk to the Met detective who questioned her. It's more likely she'll feel happier with a local man she's seen working on the earlier incidents at Barrows.

'You need to work with a DS Featherstone-haugh who's on that job. He'll join you at the hospital. You know what vital details we need. I'll inform him you're on your way. Send whatever you can obtain to the incident room instantly.'

273

'Right, guv.'

'Well, get on with it then.'

Mott turned his back. 'And good luck with the father,' he called over his shoulder.

It couldn't have turned out better. At Baker Street Jimmy dropped into the florist's near the station to buy out-of-season roses for Jo. He knew there was some underlying superstition about yellow, and he felt red was pushing it a bit, so a dozen long-stemmed pink ones seemed the safest choice.

Featherstonehaugh raised a supercilious eyebrow at the florist's wrapped bundle when they met. He was a long-limbed man in his middle thirties with a hooked nose and deeply recessed grooves from nostrils to the down-turned corners of his mouth.

He offered no excuse for not getting a statement from the badly injured woman and clearly expected no more success from the comparative amateur sent up from the shires.

At the door to the high dependency unit a nurse informed Silver that flowers were forbidden on two counts: due to fear of infection and inhalation difficulties for severe fire victims.

She would have swept off with them, but he managed in time to explain their real purpose and she softened. 'I'll put them somewhere safe.'

Featherstonehaugh sniggered.

To cut out the early evening sunlight, curtains

were drawn on one side of the bed Mrs Plummer lay in. A small area of her face was free of gauze bandages but a nose mask and transparent tubes made her unrecognizable. Both arms lay outside the bedcovers, heavily protected.

'Hello,' Silver approached her, feeling foolish. With his head so full of the coming meeting at Pimlico, he'd given little thought to tackling the official interview. 'I'm from Thames Valley Police,' he offered. 'Acting DS Jimmy Silver, come to see how you're getting on.'

The red-rimmed eyes turned on him, blinked once and appeared to be offering silent converse. She looked smaller here. He realized he'd barely ever seen her not on a horse. The arrogance had disappeared. She could be feeling frightened. Jimmy horrifically imagined his mother there under the sterile wrappings. They were of much the same age.

'You thought at first you'd had a bad fall from your horse,' he sympathized. 'But you know now what happened. It was a terrible experience.'

He was dimly conscious of Featherstonehaugh turning away, rolling his eyes in exasperation. Maybe this approach sounded pathetically unprofessional, but it seemed to be having some effect. The woman's eyes followed him as he reached for a chair to sit on.

'Everyone sends their good wishes,' he lied.

'The fire damage isn't as bad as it looked at first.'

It appeared that nobody from home had been in touch. His was the initial personal comfort on offer. Hadn't Plummer or his daughter followed her up with a visit? She may have been a touch slow in displaying family affection, but such callous indifference considering the circumstances made him angry.

She moved one of the bandaged hands towards her face. He thought she was trying to free her mouth from the mask. Leaning over, he lifted it off. She mumbled something that sounded like 'ud'.

'Take your time, Mrs Plummer.' There was a tumbler of water on the bedside cabinet, with a straw in it. He lifted it in one hand, passing the other under her neck. She gave a little moan of pain but strained to move higher and reach the drink.

A nurse came forward and came between them. 'Leave it, please. I'll see to this.'

Silver gave way, waiting until the patient was again recumbent. She fixed him with her eyes, pleading. 'Maud,' she managed to get out. 'I – need – Maud.'

There was only one person he knew with that old-fashioned name. 'Do you mean Mrs Button?'

Her eyes blinked again in confirmation.

'Am I to ask her to come and see you?'

'Ye–es.' As her eyes closed, he replaced the

mask over her nose and mouth. That was all she was likely to give at present. He wasn't prepared to press her further.

'Who is Mrs Button?' Featherstonehaugh demanded as they stood again on the steps of the hospital.

'She calls herself a forensic psychic. If anyone can get the truth out of her, that will be Mrs Button. But whether she'll pass it on or consider herself bound by professional discretion, your guess is as good as mine.'

The Met CID man shrugged and wished him joy of it, before continuing jauntily down the street alone, leaving Silver to retrieve his car and phone a detailed report back to DCI Mott.

Superintendent Yeadings knew the instant he saw her that he'd made the right decision in coming in person. She barely looked the same woman. Her normally well fleshed face sagged in pouches. Her eyes were haunted. She looked on the verge of panic when she saw him.

And then he knew more, an intimation of the whole story: the fact that she was there at the centre. That if she had taken a different decision at one point then none of this would have happened.

And then the knowledge vanished, left him amazed because he couldn't even see the outline of what had happened or why he could have assumed that. Yet he knew that flash of intuition had been right. In the briefest instant something had sparked between the two of them. And she too had known just then that he had grasped the essential about her.

He could accept now that she truly possessed psychic power, and so strongly that some of it had leaked across to him. But since it was withdrawn he stood there bewildered and didn't know what to say.

'Yes?' she asked, fearful of some climactic disaster.

'She has sent for you,' he told her.

She had known already. He didn't need to speak a name.

Seated beside her in the rear of the police car, his last doubt cleared. He had done the right thing to come himself. He was the one she had first approached.

Perhaps even then she had known it must end this way, in some kind of intimate passing of knowledge.

But end how? She still hadn't shared that much understanding with him.

Twenty-Two

Norman Ransom was as good as his word. The call from the lab came through at five fifty-seven p.m. as Mott was preparing to clear his desk for going home. He sounded wry.

'One of your smudges was nearly off limits. It was the only one which turned up, on the sharp edge of a corrugated foil wrapping.'

'And?'

'The foil was sharp and I found a microscopic trace of blood. So I'd the pleasure of matching it with one already on record.'

He paused for dramatic effect. 'You aren't going to believe this.'

'Surprise me then. I need a gift from the gods right now.'

'Same rare blood group as your dead girl's: AB negative. How's that for coincidence? But it's still a chance in a hundred. Do you want me to follow through for a full DNA check?'

He'd good reason to doubt a link. How could a girl dead over a year ago suddenly turn up to give Molly Gage chocolates dosed with powdered glass only a couple of days ago?

Mott jabbed down the end of his ballpoint

pen on his notebook and started reversing it rhythmically between thumb and forefinger while he frowned over the decision.

'Ye–es. This is such a screwy case there's just a chance we may have a family connection here. I'm sending you two more specimens for group checking. The cook was known to give Molly little gifts. The other visitor might have done so undercover, knowing Molly was kept on restricted calories by her mother.'

Norman hummed doubtfully. 'There's still the same six weeks' delay on DNA results. Is the expense really worth it?'

'I could have the case cracked by the time they come through,' Mott said, wildly optimistic. 'Forensic confirmation is vital in court.'

He rang off and sat pondering the new possibility. If Mrs Bradshaw was related to the dead girl, her age could have made her mother or aunt. But in that case she would surely have been prostrated by that hanging in Bells Wood. She was one of the few to have seen it.

If Geraldine Plummer had shared the same rare blood group, she could have been sister or cousin to the dead girl. He liked that more, because recent events at Barrows had suddenly brought her back from Morocco, breaking into her profitable plans with the balloon flights. When Gerry dropped in to check on the kitchen maid's progress it would be natural for her to bring some little present. She'd have had a childhood habit of frequenting the kitchen and probably still did so, picking up recently that young Molly had a secret weakness for chocolates.

But assuming that hers was the single print on a doctored chocolate, had Geraldine Plummer actually intended to kill the kitchen maid? What reason would she have had to do so? And with the same rare blood group as the dead girl left hanging in the wood, would DNA eventually prove familial – the unknown girl killed in the bunker possibly an unsuspected illegitimate sister? Geraldine would still have been living at Barrows at the time she fell to her death. They could even have met up.

But surely that was stretching the imagination too far, even supposing that Gervais Plummer had been freely exercising *droits de seigneur* in the neighbourhood and an illegitimate daughter had existed in the past.

One supposition he could dismiss out of hand, however, was that a reputable chocolate manufacturer could have produced a single product with a lethal content and no great press scandal have been aroused about contaminated food in general.

Go home, he told himself. You're straying into a world of wild fantasy.

Yeadings waited for the woman to precede him, but she was hanging back by the notice about visitors using the chemical cleanser for their hands.

281

'Mrs Button,' he invited, holding the swing door open.

She looked through him, into the small ward with its four beds and electronic equipment connected to monitors on the nurses' station. With a strangled cry she ran forward and threw herself at the injured woman's bed. 'Alice! Oh, *Alice*!'

Yes, of course. Yeadings saw it now. Their friendship went way back to those years before Lady Alice had chosen to be simply Fiona, Mrs Plummer. He should have asked himself why she had dropped her title, changed her first name. There had to have been a reason.

And clearly this was no mere friendship, but much, much more. They'd been lovers, were still moved by something of the old passion.

He walked away from the doorway, leaving them together. Fiona's pathetically bandaged arms striving to hold the other woman close as she knelt alongside the bed. He was aware of the unit nurse aghast, faced by something outside even her experience.

He found himself a chair in the corridor and tried to sort in his mind what this could signify. Just when had this intimacy been severed and why? It had clearly been no casual thing. Had Fiona's marriage to Plummer been the cause of the rupture? But that didn't explain her dropping the title and changing her forename. There would have been nothing socially unacceptable about 'Gervais and Lady Alice

Plummer' in their introductions.

The wedding would have been some thirty years back and certainly covered by the local press. How had she been described then? He would need to look through the *Observer*'s files. But the couple could have married abroad somewhere, meriting only a marginal note on their return. Was it possible that she had been obliged to cover up some scandal at a time when a title gave celebrity status guaranteeing front page headlines? And what would it have cost the wealthy Gervais Plummer to ensure that a lesbian relationship was kept under wraps?

But then why should he want to keep secret the past of the woman who was to be his second wife? Why go ahead and marry her at all?

Only, surely, because they had already been married by the time she discovered her real and only enduring love. Yes, she was already his wife, stepmother to Freddy and mother of Geraldine. Faced by the truth, her husband would have done almost anything to break the two women apart.

That was what had caused the rupture between the couple. Why they'd given the impression of being no couple at all.

Between them they had cobbled up a conventional arrangement to make their partnership appear respectable. Money was the bargaining tool. Maud Button, the third side of the triangle, had been persuaded – undoubtedly well paid – to withdraw. This scene he had just observed might well be the first reunion between the two women since they had parted some twenty to thirty years ago.

Such a sad story conjured up by a single, abandoned embrace. But intuitively he knew he was right. And there was a lot more to be discovered, now that the partial truth was revealed.

Mott tried ringing the Boss but his mobile was turned off. He left a message and decided that the day's work wasn't yet over. He couldn't settle at home until he'd sorted the question of the chocolates.

Mrs Bradshaw was being put up at the local pub and could easily be followed up. He drove there now and found that she and Bowles had been given a shared sitting room upstairs. The privacy it afforded was limited, raucous sounds from the bar seeping through the floorboards as a tightly contested game of darts took place below against a team from the Robin Good-fellow.

Bowles, who had given up on trying to read a thick paperback, was engaged in a game of draughts with Mrs Bradshaw.

'Shall I leave?' he offered when Mott asked for the cook.

'You stay right there,' she ordered him. 'We don't have no secrets between us, Mr Bowles and me. Now, young man, how can I help you?'

She seemed shocked by his question. 'Me? Give young Molly anything so fattening? Not on your life! Her mum would have me guts for garters,' she told him. 'No; she'd've got them chocolates from someone else.'

'Miss Gerry,' Bowles offered. 'That's who. She got them as a present from a friend, to celebrate her coming home. She found they were all dark chocolate, and she only likes the milk ones. So she planned to pass them on.'

'So they were a gift to Miss Plummer in the first case?'

Mrs Bradshaw removed the reading glasses she'd worn for the draughts game and now scrutinized the DCI. 'But they were poisoned! You're telling us it was really Miss Gerry someone wanted to harm? What a terrible thing. I had been hoping against hope that it was some awful mistake at the chocolate factory.'

Mott turned to the butler. 'So who gave them to Miss Plummer?'

'Nobody that I know of. They were left on the front-hall table, gift-wrapped with her name on and a note inside. This was before the house took fire. I took them to Miss Gerry and she undid them there and then. She was disappointed they were the wrong sort.'

'You said there was a note enclosed. Did you see it? Where would it have ended up?'

285

'She read it out aloud. Waved it about and said, "Silly donkey; they've forgotten to say who it's from. Just a scrawl. Glad to hear you're back. See you soon." Then she left the box in the morning room, but I guess she thought of Molly later and decided to take it along when she visited.' He turned worried eyes on Mott. 'She was a high-spirited, wild young thing at one time, but she'd never have wished harm on anyone.'

Next stop the cottage, Mott told himself.

When he knocked there Plummer came to the door in his shirtsleeves. 'She's gone for a walk,' he said. 'Can I help you instead? I really don't want her worried any more.'

'It's just one small question to tie something up,' the DCI said reassuringly. 'Do you know which direction she's likely to have gone?'

Plummer hesitated. 'She'll most likely be over by the lake.' It sounded like an admission.

Mott followed a worn gravel path downhill. The evening light was fading and he was anxious for her safety. By now whoever had sent the chocolates would know the attempt to poison her had failed and might look for an alternative way to strike.

At first he failed to pick out the unmoving figure on the grass beside the little jetty, but then, when her head turned as she picked up his steps on the gravel, he felt a shot of relief. 'Gerry?' he called. 'Miss Plummer?' And then as he came close he saw her face was wet with tears.

Squatting alongside, he laid a hand on her shoulder and she turned to him, leaning her face against his chest. For a few seconds she was racked with sobs, then after a short silence she drew away, shaking her head.

'I loved him so much,' she said brokenly. 'There was only ever him and me.'

Him? he said to himself. Who did she mean? If it was her father, why wasn't he out here providing the comfort she craved? Or could it be the man she was once rumoured to have had an unacceptable relationship with?

No; he couldn't see anyone so positive and determined as Gerry Plummer giving up an enduring passion because of parental disapproval. The man she wept over was dead.

The scent of her hair was disturbing. He recognized sandalwood from some personal memory of years ago. His mother had used a French toilet soap perfumed with it.

'Gerry,' he said tenderly. 'Who? Who did you love so much?'

She mumbled incoherently, and then freed her face from his embrace enough to repeat the word clearly.

He still wondered if he'd got it wrong. It made no sense.

The high dependency ward nurse had insisted her patient needed rest and quiet. Her friend could come back in the morning after the doctors' rounds.

Yeadings steered Maud Button to the relatives' room which was fortunately empty. 'I must find somewhere close to stay,' she pleaded. 'I can't leave Alice alone up here.'

He suggested a quiet hotel only a few streets away and she gratefully accepted a lift there. While she booked in, he sent the police driver to an overnight chemist to buy toiletries.

'I interrupted your evening meal,' he reminded her. 'You need something inside you. I'll ask for a table in a corner downstairs. I need to talk with you.'

He knew she would have preferred room service in decent privacy, but he counted on the normality of the conventional dining room to help her hold her feelings together. She refused the full menu, so he ordered omelettes for them both with single malt as a bracer.

He left it to her to start explaining. 'We go back a very long way,' she said, resting her knife and fork on the side of her plate. 'I was a widow. I answered an advertisement for a nanny-governess. There was a little boy of seven, rather younger than my daughter. The girl Geraldine was only five. I took care of them all, although the two girls went to school and the boy had a visiting tutor because of his condition. It was an unusual requirement because, although both the Plummer children were naturally bright, the older one had these severe health problems.'

'Cerebral palsy,' Yeadings put in, nodding.

'So I needed to be both teacher and nurse. It was demanding, but I took it because it was residential and would allow Cara to stay with me. We had lost our home when my husband died leaving some rather large debts.'

Her fork played with a few shreds of salad on her plate before she gave up again. 'Gervais was my employer, but I saw little of him. Indeed, that was true for us all. This was his second marriage and I think he had looked for a mother for Freddy rather than having any personal needs of his own. He had been devoted to Penny and devastated when she died in childbirth.

'We were all lonely,' she said wonderingly, 'or it could never have happened. I had to fill a place for everyone, because Alice – that was her name then – had little feeling for children. We became a bonded family, one with two mothers, the way it's become quite accepted nowadays. But then, of course, it was different.

'When we first realized what was happening, we were quite ashamed, but the need was so great. Can you understand? I believe you do. I don't think the children ever knew what Alice and I meant to each other. We tried to be discreet, but there was one summer evening...' She broke off.

'Because of the heat we decided to sleep in tents in Bells Wood. It was to be an adventure.

Bowles brought our supper down in a hamper and stayed on until he was satisfied the camp-fire was properly doused. So it was really late when we crawled into our tents. The children were together in one, while Alice and I shared another.

'We thought they would be tired out and quickly asleep, but they were over-excited from playing cowboys and Indians. Cara suggested a midnight raid on our tent and the children broke in, ululating.

'I don't know what they saw, or understood, but nothing was quite the same between grown-ups and children again. I struggled to maintain my authority, but we had lost something important we had enjoyed before. Cara was perhaps the only one who had picked up anything about sex. We didn't discuss things like that with children in those days and I sometimes caught her looking at me strangely, sniggering and then turning away.

'Whispers started among the staff and eventually Gervais couldn't close his eyes to it any longer. He said I must look for another position. I had two months to find something.' She sighed. 'And then, two or three weeks later, there was that terrible accident by the lake, Freddy falling in and drowning. I was suspected of negligence. It was generally accepted to explain my departure. I took Cara with me to a position in Harrogate. We changed our names when I married an elderly patient

I was caring for. Some twenty years after we'd left I came back to Thames Valley, when I was established in my new career as a clairvoyant. I had changed in my appearance too. Nobody recognized me.'

'Until Alice, today.'

She smiled mistily through tears. 'I could never deceive Alice.'

Twenty-Three

'Right,' muttered Beaumont, scowling at the rain streaming down the windows of the CID office, 'it'll be outdoor order of the day for the lot of us.' He'd spoken under his breath, but the Boss had picked up on it.

'I've actually something more in your line, I think. We shall be mainly entertaining ladies today. For vital information.' He nodded at the wall where Salmon had attached photographs, some from the albums Plummer had rescued from the house; others were old local newspaper cuttings.

'Miss Geraldine Plummer; Mrs Maud Button; and hopefully at some later date when she has recovered from her injuries, Mrs Fiona (or Lady Alice) Plummer.

'By now you've all come across each of them while investigating incidents at Barrows, the family home of Gervais Plummer. I leave you with DCI Mott in the sure and certain hope, as the funeral service puts it, that he will now conduct the final rites on the series of incidents there.'

And on that he walked out on them, leaving

behind the lingering smile of a Cheshire cat.

Angus surveyed their startled faces. 'Some of us work into the night,' he said smugly. 'Now this is how you'll be working together,' and he attached the schedule sheet alongside the photographs.

Beaumont pressed forward. As expected, he was again teamed with the Limpet, Holly. As far as he was concerned, he was saddled with an untried amateur again. But provided that she got the message to hold her tongue throughout, he could make career progress on this. Their interviewee, due at ten thirty, was to be Miss Geraldine Plummer.

Mott addressed them formally. 'That leaves you adequate time to become familiar with notes I made yesterday evening after an un-recorded and unwitnessed informal conversation. You will follow strictly correct procedure in taping a questioning session, covering only the subject matter already obtained. Bear in mind that although it may contain nothing giving rise to any charge being brought, anything you record may be required at a later date in court.'

'Blimey O'Reilly!' Beaumont exploded. He shot a warning glance at the Limpet to prevent any comment, seized the pages of computer printout from Angus and hustled the girl from the room.

'Explain,' she demanded outside in the corridor, and stuck out her chin.

'Canteen,' he ordered shortly. 'You're buying.'

Seated as far as possible from the enticing scent of onions frying, he filled her in on DCI Mott's academic background.

'When he goes off all toffee-nosed like that, take warning. Before he went off on the Bosnian stunt he'd done an external degree at King's College, London. Same place and same time as his wife did it full-time. They both qualified LLB. He continued in the humble Bill while she became a minor celebrity in London chambers as a defence barrister. When they married and the baby made its appearance she only temporarily gave up her career. Now there's always the possibility of them meeting in court locally, with bared teeth.'

'So everything has to be super-duper fault-free.'

'How right you are, Limpet. How right, it seems, you always are. And that's what we'll need to be over this stuff. So let's get into it. I see he's run off two copies.'

Silver wasn't best pleased to find he was to partner DI Salmon for the interviews. He was shattered to discover that the subject of their questioning was the self-titled forensic psychic, Maud Button.

'But I've met her undercover,' he complained. 'Now she's going to know that my story was a heap of garbage.'

'More embarrassing for her than for you,' Mott assured him grimly. 'And she may be grateful to find herself opposite a familiar face.'

Good cop, bad cop, Silver thought. Is that what I'm meant to pick up from that – go easy on the lady, because Old Fishface won't?

His eyes skimmed over the sheets of notes in his hand. Amendments in the margins and crossings out were in the Boss's unmistakable hand. So he was the one who'd been working into the night on this lady's information. Was he coming round to believe in this clairvoyant lark? Maybe he was already halfway convinced, because he always showed respect for intuition.

Beside him, Salmon snorted, enraged. He was a couple of pages ahead in his reading. 'Half an hour,' he commanded. 'Interview room one. And be sure you're up on the details. If there's anything you don't understand, consult a dictionary.'

'Patronizing berk!' Silver muttered under his breath as Salmon slammed out.

Angus rejoined Yeadings in his office. Someone had cleared away all the debris of their earlier snack. Coffee beans pouring out their aroma from the grinder promised a needed refill.

'We're to tackle the last bit together?' Angus checked.

'Both confessions? Yes, probably tomorrow. But I can't yet see exactly where they'll lead us.'

Jimmy Silver had put hard work into becoming liberal-minded, accepting modern standards prevalent among some of his colleagues. Nevertheless, remnants of his elderly parents' prejudices hung on in the more spider-haunted reaches of his brain. Gay men he almost understood, but – *women*? He couldn't see how technically it would work.

He told himself to imagine Plummer's wife younger, perhaps rather attractive, less horse-obsessed, taking on the ready-made family. Not easy, especially as the little lad had such a serious health condition; and then finding, despite giving birth to a daughter, that she didn't count for much in her husband's life. He was still in love with Penny, and you can't compete with the dead.

The other woman had come to help her out. She was young too, a disappointed widow left in poor circumstances. She also had a daughter, ten years old. Freddy then was seven and Gerry only five. Maud had seemed heaven-sent, a strong-minded woman with the confidence that Alice lacked...

Fiona; or was it Alice – that perplexed him. Which was he to think of her as?

'Why do we need to bother the poor woman? There's nothing actionable in any of this and it all happened so many years ago,' he protested as they waited for their victim to appear.

Salmon showed his long, irregular teeth like a basking shark sensing the presence of blood. 'You never know what may come out of it,' he threatened.

Maud Button was embarrassed to find herself confronting two men across the table. She thought she might have been given at least one kindly female face.

Last night the superintendent had been different and the emotional circumstances overpowering. It had brought such relief to talk. Now, in harsh daylight, she felt incapable of opening up.

The older detective had cold, fish-grey eyes and was severely inquisitorial. The younger hardly counted.

And then, as she looked at him, she seemed to visualize him elsewhere, in a darkened hall, struggling to express himself over some family tragedy.

'You were actually a policeman?' she accused him. 'A spy sent to trap me?'

Silver shivered despite the overheated little room. He wasn't sure he had the right to be here probing into the unfortunate woman's early life. Since then she had done well for herself, was attempting in an odd way to pay a debt back to society. Whether in fact she was genuine or a fraud, she meant well and was causing no damage in her new career.

Salmon's harsh voice broke in, introducing them both by rank and name; stated date and time, and drew attention to the presence of recording equipment. He explained how she would receive a signed tape at the end of the interview identical with the one that could be used as police evidence in court.

She closed her eyes as the words flowed over her, knowing that this man detested and despised her. He represented what she had always found fearful and alien in men. This was the hell on earth she had to go through. What she had already spoken of with living emotion was now to be cut open and exposed post-mortem.

Beaumont smiled at the girl opposite and received no answering warmth.

'Look,' Gerry said once he'd done all the official introductory rigmarole, 'I'd simply like to make a statement, read it through, correct it if necessary and sign it. Then can I go?'

'That's quite acceptable,' he said cautiously, with a warning glance at the Limpet in case she quibbled. 'But first will you look at this photograph and tell me who these people are?'

In the picture a tartan rug was spread on short grass with the remnants of a picnic. There were two women in their late twenties or early thirties wearing summer dresses and three children. The oldest, an overweight and sulky-looking girl stood awkwardly with one bent arm holding the opposite elbow behind her back. At her feet a younger boy sat cross-legged, his arms wrapped round bony knees. A plump smaller girl stood uncertainly beside one of the seated women.

Geraldine leaned forward for a better view. Her voice was subdued. 'This is from my father's album. The little one's me. The others are Mummy, Nanny and her daughter, and my brother Freddy, nearly eight.'

'Thank you. Do carry on.'

'It all happened a very long time ago. I was only five, Freddy two years older and Cara was ten. Mummy and Nanny were the only adults with us. It was a very hot, oppressive day and we had taken a picnic down to the lake. You can see there was no fencing then. A small rowing boat was tied up at the end of the jetty, but there were too many of us to go out in it and no boatman to do the rowing. We were all bored and getting short-tempered.'

She halted, frowning, and when she spoke again the detachment had gone. She seemed to be reaching back for detail.

'Yes, I must have been five because I'd started school after Easter and I found it em-barrassing still having a Nanny. Mummy said I was to share her with Freddy because he was so special. Even then I knew he suffered from cerebral palsy. It was due to being deprived of oxygen during a protracted birthing. His mother, my father's first wife, had died of severe haemorrhaging at the same time.

'I only partly understood this, but I accepted that his body was different from other children's. He made strange sudden movements and I'd overheard people refer to him as a spastic. Whatever it was, I knew it couldn't be changed, although I longed for him to be able to run and play freely like me. He was such a lovely big brother and would hug me when everyone else said I was wild and did wicked things. He was always there when others weren't, because he didn't go to school. He had a retired schoolmaster come in daily to tutor him.'

Her voice had taken on a new sing-song tone as though she were back there in a lost wonderland, living it for the first time. 'That hot, sticky afternoon I remember I was in trouble for taking off my knickers to be cool. Nanny said I was rude and must wear them on my head like a hat after that until we were ready to go home.

'I remember eating tea, sitting on the prickly grass because the others had crowded me off the blanket, being the littlest. There were sandwiches with some kind of meat, perhaps chicken, and I hid the streaky bits under the hamper. There was fruit too but they'd gone warm in the sunshine and I was nearly sick over my banana.

'We'd played enough and afterwards all I wanted was to lie down on the jetty and watch the cool water lapping under the slits in its boards. I think I must have fallen asleep when it happened. I was aware of someone bigger than me stepping over my body as I lay, and distantly voices were raised in some little squabble. I don't know who it was or why. And then I heard Freddy give a funny little noise, something between a cough and a gasp. Almost at once there was a loud splash.

'I sat up and Mummy pushed me aside as she ran to the end of the jetty. I never saw the others. She started shouting Freddy's name and waving her arms about. I think she had a stick in one hand. Then I knew someone had fallen in the water. But I never actually saw anything happen.

'Later, policemen and other strangers came to the house asking questions, but no one spoke to me about it. I was sent to sit in the kitchen. It was as though everyone was pretending to me that nothing had ever happened. Only Freddy wasn't there any more. Never was going to be.

'I know the grown-ups spoke about it between themselves because when they saw me coming they'd shut up and pretend to be busy over something important. Life was supposed to go on just the same, but it couldn't because there was this terrible gap where my lovely big brother had been. I would cry and cry and cry in the night and there was no one to come stumbling in and hold me close.' She seemed suddenly to become aware of where she was and that she had revealed all that was expected of her. 'That was the beginning of it all, but at the time I never understood. Do you think I could have a glass of water?'

In another interview room along the corridor Maud Button completed her longer story in fewer words. First came a calmer edition of the confession she had poured out to Yeadings the previous evening. She directed her eyes down to the Formica-topped table, avoiding the man's riveting gaze, and spoke coldly of the intimate relationship as though it had happened to someone she was hardly concerned with.

And then, on cue from Salmon, she was invited to give her own version of the drowning of her little charge Freddy Plummer. She made no attempt to accept or escape blame for not having taken greater precautions. Two adults should have been able to keep an eye on three children. They weren't toddlers or nincompoops. Family picnics had often before been set out near the lake without disaster of any kind.

'You say *family* picnics, Mrs Button. Is that how you saw yourself and your daughter – as part of a single, unnatural family with no father, but two mothers?'

Oh, give the poor woman a break, Silver groaned inside. This persistent probing was unhealthy. The man must have rotten sexual experience. And hadn't he heard of political correctness?

'Mrs Button,' he broke in, 'did you actually see Freddy fall in the water?'

She looked directly at him. 'No, I didn't. I was talking to Al...' She stopped, horrified at what she had admitted: such a normal, natural, everyday action, but the abominable man opposite was going to put an unpleasant interpretation on it. He would see her love for her dear friend as obsessive, crowding out every other consideration in life.

'I fail to understand,' she said, struggling for cool detachment, 'why you are bringing up this unhappy accident from so long ago.'

'Because, madam, there is cause and effect. We believe what actually happened at that moment has had terrible repercussions.'

And then, for the first time, even as she raged against his them-and-us police culture, she saw that perhaps he was right. It had been the beginning of everything going wrong, right up to today.

Twenty-Four

'We have yet another witness statement about the death of Freddy Plummer,' Yeadings announced. 'It has been dictated to DC Duncan of the Metropolitan Police Force, dated and signed by the child's stepmother. It has been witnessed by the high dependency ward manager where Mrs Plummer is now being nursed while considered of sound mind if not of sound body. I will ask DCI Mott to read it out to you all.'

Angus took the single page from him and faced the rest of the augmented team. "'The children's nanny and I were the only adults down by the lake. Her ten-year-old daughter was with us that day because it was a school holiday and she was keeping an eye on the little ones. Freddy was seven, nearly eight, and my daughter Geraldine was five. After tea the children had been playing some game – hide-and-seek or something similar. They were tired and getting rather fractious.

"'I started putting things together to start back to the house. Nanny had gone back into the trees for a call of nature. Her daughter was

304

arguing with Freddy who'd picked up a fallen branch and was swishing it about like a sword. I called to them all to come and pick up their belongings. Nanny came back and we were talking together when I heard a child scream. I think it was Gerry. Freddy had disappeared.

"'I ran along the jetty and saw him struggling in the water. The girls were dangerously close to the edge, trying to reach out for him, but his wild floundering was taking him farther away. I pushed them behind me and reached out for him with the broken branch but he couldn't get hold of it. I started pulling off my clothes, ready to wade in. Then I remembered it was deep at this end, being the edge of an old quarry. I had always been scared of water and could barely swim. The girls were clutching at my legs and wouldn't let me go. I tried to shake them off and then when I looked again Freddy had disappeared completely. I was appalled.'"

'That is all,' Mott concluded. 'The two earlier witnesses are still here helping us with our enquiries. Neither has been arrested nor charged with any offence. We shall be continuing to follow up and correlate their statements. Meanwhile, you are all dismissed to normal duties, apart from those required to direct the subsequent interviews.'

There was no disguising that something very special was about to happen. Expectation crackled like static electricity in the air. Superintendent Yeadings nodded at Silver to go ahead of him into the observation gallery. He considered the youngster had won himself a stand at the cup final. They looked through to where the girl sat alone in the windowless room, facing the mock mirror. She must have known what it was, he thought. These days everyone is schooled by TV crime fiction. But she made no attempt to move to the seat opposite.

When Mott and Salmon came in, she stood up, like a disciplined schoolgirl facing her teachers, and when Mott indicated she should sit again she shook her head. Her face was emotionless, her voice robotic as she identified herself.

'This is about the woman found hanging in Bells Wood,' she said. 'I want to confess. Her name was Adele Carrington. And I killed her. It was over a year ago, and I only know what happened to her then. Not later.' She paused, her gaze roaming the small room as though she hadn't noticed it before. Then she made a visible effort to return her concentration to what she had to tell them.

'I met her on the Internet. She called herself Tankgirl.'

'But—' Silver protested, and was silenced by the superintendent's raised finger.

'She blogged an item on the Urban Explorers' forum. It's an association of lively minded people who want to do something different, measure themselves against others, challenge authority. I was feeling wretched at the time after an unhappy love affair. I'd defied my parents who'd warned me against the man I was living with. And then he was the one to walk out on me. I was humiliated, felt so in the wrong. I wanted something to fight back against, to punish anyone smug enough to think they were always in the right. This project of undercover defiance of officially restricted targets appealed to me. It allowed me a small rebellion with unaccustomed physical exertion, and nobody was to get hurt by the risks taken. There'd be security men and guard dogs and barbed wire and electronic surveillance to get past – far better than all that dungeons and dragons virtual reality on screen. The Explorers boast that they take only photographs and leave only their footprints.'

She gave a small, bitter smile. 'It wasn't quite like that with us.'

She seemed to have stopped talking. Mott broke the silence with a question.

'So you got in touch with Tankgirl and decided to meet. Was she as you expected?'

'Not a bit. The photo she'd posted on the forum hadn't shown her face; but the back view of a female in dungarees and heavy boots crawling through an underground ceramic pipe looked as though she'd weigh three or four times as much as the girl I met. She'd used another woman's photo to preserve anonymity, in case her antics ever stirred up trouble. She thought the deception was amusing, but that's when I first had misgivings.

'However, she had experience, all the right equipment and was very knowledgeable about this bunker quite close to my own home. I agreed to go along on a twosome jaunt.'

'Where did she obtain her information from?' snapped Salmon, interrupting the flow.

Geraldine looked down on him as he sat opposite, and he was mortified that they'd allowed her to continue standing. 'In 1970, under the Freedom of Information Act a whole lot of previously secret government information was made public including a new edition of the War Book. It contained details of Burlington, the government's secret central bunker under the Cotswolds near Corsham in Wiltshire including a national news service. There were at least a dozen others all round the country intended to be manned as regional hubs of power during extreme crisis. The BBC had an individual one as well in Worcestershire. Ours at Beacons was one of those nearest to London.'

'And how did she intend to make this covert entry?'

'She had information that on a certain weekend in late September an air-exchange filter tower would be left open. I don't know who told her. Some government source, I suppose. Maybe he or she was also an Urban Explorer; but Tankgirl insisted that the Beacons installation had never been logged as entered. She spoke of "taking its virginity". I rather fancied that. Achieving rape, you see. Revenge by the despised and rejected female of the species.

'Anyway, her information was accurate and we got in. It wasn't all that difficult and I found the place interesting. We took photographs of each other in possession. You won't find any among Daddy's album collection because afterwards I burned them all in a garden bonfire. We Plummers seem to go in for torching things.'

'You've claimed you killed Tankgirl. How did that happen?'

'Ask rather *"why* did it happen?"'. It was because of how she taunted me. She waited until we had done the whole tour of all levels and were on our way back to the surface. She turned to me as we were about to go up the main stairway in a sort of square pit, and she had a new, sneering expression on her face. She said, "You've no idea at all, have you?"

'And I hadn't, because she had changed so much. Twice my age when we'd known each other as children, I would've remembered her as very tall, but I'd outgrown her since then. She had lost all her surplus fat, having suffered an eating disorder, and her mousey hair was now long and dyed a quite fierce rust colour.

'Adele Carrington had once been Cara Martin, only child of Nanny Martin. You know her now as Mrs Maud Button. Both have been using their later married names and Cara had replaced her first forename with her second.'

'But why should you mind so much that she had stolen a march on you?' Mott asked quietly.

'It wasn't that – not just the deceit and scoring a point over me. It was what she said about when we were children. She started mocking our comfortable home life and the way we were a complete family. And she spoke disrespectfully of dear Freddy, calling him a – a disgusting little mutant. All the time she was climbing up the stairs behind me, lugging her backpack with her gear. I reached the top and started to move away, trying to control my anger. I didn't want her to see I had tears in my eyes. It would only have made her more triumphant.

'She wouldn't stop, wanted to hurt me as much as she could. She taunted, "He was a revolting little monster, couldn't even walk straight. And everyone making such a fuss over him. I'm not sorry I hit him. He was right on the edge. Someone like him should have been drowned at birth. In the end it was better for everyone!"

'It was unbelievable, what she was admitting. Something snapped inside me. I turned on her as she stepped on to the top level...'

Geraldine's voice died away. 'I still don't know if I would have thrown myself at her, but she must have seen the anger in my eyes. She

310

recoiled, caught her boot heel on the top step and disappeared backwards, her arms wildly flailing. The guard rail had been removed for the maintenance men to deploy the big crane. There was nothing to save her. She screamed and I heard her body strike the concrete floor far below. Then nothing. When I went down she was already dead, although there was so little blood it didn't seem possible. I never touched her, but she disappeared and she was dead. I'd killed her.'

Nobody spoke. Eventually Mott looked up from studying his folded hands. 'You say you are responsible for her death. But who arranged the gruesome funeral display a year later?'

Gerry's face was ugly with scorn. 'Her crazy mother, of course. The woman's a sadistic weirdie.'

Behind the observation mirror, Silver found he had broken into a sweat. When he furtively went to dry his forehead the tissue fluttered in his nervous fingers. He had never expected to be so moved by this unimaginable girl. He kept his face turned away from Yeadings.

'All of which leaves a great deal unexplained, don't you think?' the superintendent asked him mildly.

Silver was reminded of a school oral examiner gently suggesting a line to follow. 'The bits between,' he agreed. 'Where the body was hidden for a year and how it surfaced again.

311

How Maud Button – if it was her – would have got to know where to find it. What help she had. It's a whole new case opening.'

'A new can of worms, as you might say. Or perhaps of beans. Yes. Go away and think about it.'

In the interview room Geraldine Plummer at last sat down. She felt drained. Her head sank on her chest, forehead resting on both hands. 'Are you going to charge me now?'

Mott looked up from sorting his notes and sliding them into an envelope file. 'With what?' he asked. 'Concealment of a body?'

Salmon, his lips a single straight line blanched of any red, regarded the woman severely. 'Perhaps not murder, but certainly we could try for manslaughter.' It didn't worry him to be speculating in front of her.

'Your father's here,' Yeadings said, putting his head round the door. 'He's been waiting over two hours. I think you need to take him somewhere for a late lunch.'

'That went rather well,' he told the other two when the girl had been shown out by a uniform. 'Now for the tricky bit. Beaumont's going for this one, with me sitting in.'

Maud Button was clearly disturbed. 'What has that girl told you?' she demanded as soon as she was seated and the two detectives took the chairs opposite. 'I must warn you I've telephoned my solicitor and he should be here by now.'

'He is,' Yeadings assured her. 'Just having a wash and brush up. He's been involved in a slight street accident and it's rather shaken him up.'

Barely comforting, Beaumont registered with some pleasure.

'Of course, you've known Geraldine since she was a very small girl,' said Yeadings comfortably, looking round for somewhere to hang his discarded jacket and settling for the back of his stacker chair. 'What kind of child was she?'

Taken aback, Mrs Button regarded him with suspicion. 'Nothing remarkable, I suppose. Parents all like to hope they have bred someone rather special. She was intelligent, healthy. Unlike the older brother of course. He was a problem.'

He seated himself and rested his elbows on the table. 'My wife and I have a daughter with Down's syndrome. I suppose you would say the same of her.'

Behind him the door opened and Oliver Goodman entered, but not in time to cover her discomfiture. 'Couldn't your father come?' she demanded.

It was not a promising start. A vein showed at Beaumont's left temple as he watched the solicitor seat himself opposite: the one-time college friend of Angus Mott's wife. Personalities could get tangled over this, he foresaw.

313

What would the clairvoyant be making of it?

'We've concluded our interrogation of Miss Plummer,' Yeadings said for general consumption. 'Her father's been here for over two hours as well. It's good to have everyone so co-operative. Just a few details then, to be cleared up.'

'What did she tell you?' the woman repeated, her eyes strained. 'And why him?'

'Because we want everyone's story confirmed in your own words. Detective Sergeant Beaumont will be asking the questions. The interview is being recorded, as already explained to you.'

'Right,' Beaumont began in a crisp, business-like voice. 'So who told you they'd found your daughter's body?'

They had set it up too well. Mrs Button gave a high, peacock-like cry and slid forward over the table. Oliver Goodman bleated objections, and they spent twenty minutes reviving the woman before they could continue. By then she had no resistance, refused tea, silenced the solicitor's warnings and came clean.

Gervais Plummer had come to see her as soon as his head gardener had reported it hidden in a little hollow beside the ice house. Actually Fiona's horse Tony had nosed it out, going there to lap water after a hard ride. He had been trying to keep his wife's name out of it.

Asked how they came to recognize the young

314

woman after so long a gap during which her appearance must have changed, she never hesitated. 'Because Geraldine had told them.'

'Told them what?'

'How she'd killed her a year or more before.' Maud frowned at his slowness to pick up the thread. 'Why else had Gervais given her all that money to buy into the balloon circus and get away from home? All the time I was waiting for my daughter to turn up after we'd had our disagreement, she had been lying cold and murdered inside that awful bunker, with nobody else knowing, She could have lain there rotting until World War Three with no recognition and no proper funeral.

'But once she was found – on their own estate – she had to be acknowledged and they sent for me.'

'But not one of you thought of informing the authorities even although you believed she had been murdered? Why weren't you crying out for justice, Mrs Button?'

'How could I? It was because of what she'd done all those years ago – Cara, my daughter. They all knew by then how she'd attacked Freddy and pushed him in the lake. We lied, Alice and I. We both saw what happened. But Geraldine didn't, or she was too young then to understand.

'It was only when Cara mocked her with the truth, there in the bunker, that she made up her mind to do to Cara what had happened to her

315

brother. But it wasn't water my daughter fell on. It was concrete. An eye for an eye, the Bible says. It was what you would call case closed. We all had too much to admit to, and we weren't going to court publicity. It was a final pact of silence.'

'You gained publicity enough in the end. Who engineered all that hocus-pocus display of the body?'

There was no need for an answer. 'She had become so beautiful,' the woman said brokenly, 'even while she rotted inside. She deserved honourable acknowledgement, holy rites.' She looked up with a new, mad light in her eyes. 'I took off her stinking clothes and washed the body, tenderly, with love and prayers to all the gods humanity has ever known. And I wrapped her in a white sheet and crucified her, but upside down for extra magic. When I threw the rope over a branch and set her in position, one of her ankles came free and she hung like the Hanged Man, which meant she also had the Tarot's blessing. A martyr. So I left her there all alone, on the Wishing Tree, with her long red hair hanging down to touch the grass...' She fell silent, eyes closed, her face rapturous. 'And all the country heard about her, mourned her as a saint.'

'Guess what!' Jimmy Silver, ignoring all protocol, rushed into Yeadings's office where the others sat stunned in the aftermath of Maud

Button's revelations.

He was waving a printout but his enthusiasm melted as their silence reached him.

'What you asked me to do, sir. I've got it. I was going again through the photos Jo and I took that day we went up in Gerry's balloon. It was something that kept recurring, and once in a farm lane only a mile or so from the hole that was made in the bunker's outer wire defences. We moved so slowly, you see, and it was travelling at normal road speed. Then I remembered where I'd first seen it.'

'Seen what, kiddo?' Beaumont demanded in a tone expressing utter boredom.

'The newly sprayed green Ford Transit van. It had drawn up beside my MG in the pub yard before we went on board. So I enhanced the photos, to come up with a licence plate. And in the pub I'd actually seen the men who travelled to the bunker in it. It belongs to a fireman working out of Acton Station. So now we know at least one of the Urban Explorers who brought the body out of the bunker! We can find the others through him.'

'The final detail falling in place,' Yeadings said, looking round them with satisfaction. 'Good work, team.'